CU00919794

A SINGLE ACT OF KINDNESS

SAMANTHA TONGE

Boldwood

First published in Great Britain in 2024 by Boldwood Books Ltd.

Copyright © Samantha Tonge, 2024

Cover Design by Lizzie Gardiner

Cover Illustration: Shutterstock

A CIP catalogue record for this book is available from the British Library.

Paperback ISBN 978-1-83518-991-7

Large Print ISBN 978-1-83518-987-0

Hardback ISBN 978-1-83518-986-3

Ebook ISBN 978-1-83518-984-9

Kindle ISBN 978-1-83518-985-6

Audio CD ISBN 978-1-83518-992-4

MP3 CD ISBN 978-1-83518-989-4

Digital audio download ISBN 978-1-83518-983-2

Boldwood Books Ltd
23 Bowerdean Street
London SW6 3TN
www.boldwoodbooks.com

For Jenny, who works for Wigan libraries. Thank you so much for your act of kindness.

Tilda Wright was the kind of woman who found joy in the things other people barely noticed. She hurried down Station Road and passed a graffiti-covered takeout restaurant, a brash betting shop and dingy launderette. Itching to stop and make them over, Tilda became their cheerleader and imagined how she'd transform them, dreaming big, able to see past the surface ugliness. Loosening the top of her shirt, in the mild, evening air, she continued towards an even more unsightly building, its crude design softened by colourful hanging baskets out the front. Half render, half red brick, the oddly placed, detached house stood with a porch that was a mere ledge of wood, with moss-covered roof tiles and peeling window frames. As for the fumes from passing traffic... Yet it was home and inside it sparkled. After all, Tilda did own a cleaning business.

Crouchden had proved affordable for a first-time buyer, due to it being one of the more rundown areas of Manchester, with the occasional rough sleeper, like the man who'd turned up last month, out of nowhere, the man she always felt drawn to look at, Tilda didn't know why. Upgrading the shoddy exterior of the property was her current project, having spent months doing up the inside. The small side yard used to be a square of cracked paving slabs, invaded by weeds, but she'd turfed it over and had a path laid down the middle, ending at a modest patio. Fencing had gone up along the side near the road and Tilda had treated herself to mature climbing jasmine plants, already tall enough to hide the wooden panels. This summer she'd work on filling the borders at the bottom, near the rickety old shed that would need replacing eventually. Tilda loved her tiny garden, a private, natural breathing space at odds with the busy, grimy street. It looked out of place – like Tilda felt she often did. So as she walked along the road, Tilda didn't mind having to avoid litter or over-flowing wheelie bins. Soon she'd reach her private oasis.

As dusk approached, she neared a streetlamp that would light up, any minute. Underneath, on the pavement, that man was camped, once again, in the sticky heat, a short distance up the road from her home. He sneezed loudly and blew his nose, as if it were winter and not an espe-cially balmy last week of May. She could veer around him too, pretend he didn't exist, like so many people did. However, that would take her back to boarding school and the students who'd acted as if she were invisible – unless they were terrorising her in the dorm. Tilda noted the hopeful lopsided smile he shot at pedestrians, amidst an air of embarrassment. Each time she'd walked past, the last couple of weeks, an inner conflict had commenced. She hadn't got change, only carrying bank cards these days, but should she meet his eye regardless? What if he was unstable?

Yet he often read discarded newspapers, calmly sitting cross-legged, a pen his hand, doing crosswords, thick hair jauntily sliding forwards as he looked down. Also, he'd stacked his sleeping bag and rucksack in a neat pile by his side. She'd nodded at him a couple of times. Once, she'd handed him a chocolate bar she didn't fancy. It had been going cheap, an impulse buy. Tilda wasn't used to acting spontaneously. His top and jeans were ruffled but not grubby and, despite the dark rings under his eyes and a straggly beard, he didn't appear as downtrodden as the rough sleepers in Manchester city centre.

For the first time, Tilda considered he might not be homeless at all, but a grifter not prepared to work hard like she'd had to. She pursed her lips. No one had given anything to Tilda for free, she'd scrubbed floors and cleaned toilets to build a shiny, new, safe life. She readjusted her sunglasses. The evening sun wasn't bright now, but they made her feel protected from any interaction. However, a pair of almond-shaped green eyes fixed on her from his lap, the cat's small pointy face almost smirking in the knowledge that house-proud Tilda wouldn't like her flirting with dubious strangers.

Tilda stopped. 'Dettol?' She took off her sunglasses and shoved them loosely in her trouser pocket.

'She's yours?' asked the man, and he wiped his nose with a ragged tissue. 'Nice name.' His mouth twitched. He stroked the cat's brown and grey striped back. 'You're a beautiful girl, aren't you?'

Dettol arched her back and purred. Tilda's eyebrows knotted together as she bent down and nudged the cat off. But Dettol stepped back onto the man's legs, purring even more loudly as if to annoy her. The previous owner of her house had left the cat behind. Tilda hadn't wanted to take the pet in but at first the cat wouldn't leave and then Tilda had reflected that she could prove useful, scaring off vermin. With no idea what to call a pet, Tilda had named her after a favourite cleaning brand and taken her to the vet for a de-flea treatment. Most importantly she'd outlined a list of house rules – no dead birds in the house, no sleeping on the beds, and no pretending to care for Tilda. Too many people had done that in the past. The cat didn't need to fake love to be fed and sheltered. Dettol seemed to understand and had never shown her affection.

'Thanks to your Dettol, I've been given a heap of coins today. I'll have enough for a B & B in no time.'

Tilda inspected him again and her eyes narrowed. Local parents skipped meals to feed their kids, others took on two jobs to pay the rent. Imagine earning a living from leaching off the income of others doing their utmost to cope with the cost-of-living crisis. He may have been on the pavement in daylight, but his spotless nails told another story about the life he led after dark.

'Sure you will,' she said and made to leave.

He tilted his head. 'What?'

Tilda hesitated and then waved her hand across his body. 'It's as if you go home every night and scrub up.'

The twinkle left his eye. 'Ah. Right. I can only be genuinely homeless if I look the part? I don't fit the mould if I go to the public toilets every morning to wash off the grime, if the woman in the launderette takes pity and cleans my clothes now and again, if an occasional lucky gambler from the bookies chucks me a tenner.'

Tilda could have sworn Dettol shot her a disapproving look.

'I've not been on the streets long, guess I'm not that weather-beaten. I sofa surfed when I first lost my job, then crashed in a hostel for homeless men.' He picked up a small stone and gripped it tightly. 'Never again. My phone was almost stolen and I got roughed up. The second night I slept holding a pen, it was the only thing I had to defend myself. In the end it was safer to camp out on the street by myself.'

Crap, now Tilda felt obliged to listen. But why should she? She didn't owe anyone anything. That's how she liked it and... wait. He slept holding a pen to protect himself? She met his gaze and for a moment saw teenage Tilda, at boarding school, reflected back. She pushed the memories away.

'What line of work were you in?' she asked politely, keen to get back for a refreshing shower, to wash away the perspiration from her last cleaning job. Her favourite Netflix series had released a third season today. She drummed her fingers against her thigh.

'Nightclub management. So, I know about cleaning products. I assume you're a fan, what with Dettol?'

'I own a cleaning business,' she said stiffly.

'Wowclean's another great make, isn't it? Nothing like it for getting sick out of carpet.'

Oh. He did know his stuff. Wowclean was a niche brand, and Tilda had to order it off the internet.

'Thanks for the chocolate, by the way.'

'It's okay. I don't like the white stuff.'

His lips twitched again. What was so funny? She was only being honest. Tilda didn't let people laugh at her. Not any more. She bent down and picked up Dettol who protested loudly and squirmed like a toddler having a tantrum, leaving the man staring as she walked the short distance to her house. A sneeze shot down the street. She hoped Dettol wasn't carrying any of his germs – unless he had early hay fever. She walked along her garden path, put down the cat who pawed at the side door that led to the utility room, as Tilda rarely let herself in through the front. It'd once been the dining room but Tilda had bought a small table for the kitchen and instead converted the dining area into a functional laundry and storage space. Fickle as ever, Dettol didn't try to run back to the man, it was dinnertime. Tilda opened the door and gasped.

Water everywhere?

No, no, no, this wasn't happening! That lino flooring was brand new; this was the last room in the house she'd done up. What about germs if the water caused mould and...? Tilda took a deep breath. She'd left the washing machine on, as she always did. What had gone wrong? Heart thumping loudly in her chest, she stood stock still.

'These fell out of your pocket,' said a voice behind her.

She swung around to face the man, sleeping bag and rucksack clutched under one arm, squinting in the day's last rays of sun. He handed over her sunglasses. She looked up and stepped back.

'What's the matter?' he asked.

'Nothing.'

He gazed directly at her.

'It's just... you don't look that tall, sitting on the street.'

His gaze moved over her head and he let out a low whistle. 'That happened at the club, shortly before I left. Huge flood. Caused such a mess.' He threw down his possessions and dropped his screwed-up anorak on top. For the first time she noticed how thin he was, his rock band T-shirt looking too baggy. 'Let me help.'

'No need,' said Tilda abruptly. She put up her palms. 'I'll manage. Thank you.' No one went in her house. She had no family to speak of. Kept herself to herself and, after eighteen months of living here, she still didn't know the names of the neighbours, nor did she want to. Tilda didn't know this man either. He could be lying about his past and recently out of jail, a burglar... or worse. And it would be dark soon.

He bit his lip, the colour drained from his face, the smile he'd mustered slipped away. 'I wouldn't let me in either,' he said. 'It's good that you're cautious. You never can be sure. I got taken for a fool, at work last summer. A guy staggered in, as I was about to lock up for the night. Said he'd been mugged. Looked pretty shaken. I went around the side of the bar to make him a strong coffee. By the time I'd come back he'd emptied the till and scarpered.'

She looked back at the sodden floor. Annoyed with herself, practical Tilda accepted that she couldn't fix it. She put up shelves, could change a tyre, wire a plug, determined never to have to rely on anyone else, but she'd never had a broken washing machine before. She was busy enough with work. Calling out a plumber would be yet another thing to add to her to-do list.

'You could take a quick look,' Tilda said, with difficulty. Whilst she fetched clean towels from the nearby laundry basket and carefully placed them down to mop up the mess, the man brightened up and went inside. He turned off the water and wiped his perspiring forehead with his arm, before pulling out the washing machine. He examined the back of it whilst Tilda eyed the storage cupboards that contained plenty of cleaning products to spray in his eyes if he'd faked his good intentions.

'Punctured drain hose,' he said eventually and pointed to a small hole in it. 'A bit of waterproof flex tape should fix it.'

'Oh. Right. Thanks.' She stood up straight, cue awkward silence. She supposed he wanted money in return. What if he expected to come right into the house? She left the utility room, closing the door behind her, and came back seconds later with the only cash she had in, put aside for the window cleaner.

Oh. The man was already outside. Dettol sat by his feet.

As he stuffed the creased anorak under his arm, the man frowned. His nose was running and he wiped it. 'I don't need paying. Homelessness steals your possessions, your dignity, but it doesn't take away your good-will, as long as you keep it hidden from those who see it as a weakness.' He picked up his rucksack. 'It's reward enough to be useful, doesn't happen often these days.'

Tilda eyed him curiously and a flicker of something warm and unfamiliar tickled the inside of her stomach. She pushed it away. People didn't do something for nothing... And his jeans hung so loosely. Tilda thrust the note into his hands. 'Saves me the trouble of getting you takeout pizza from up the street – as a thank you,' she said gruffly.

He hesitated. 'Okay. Cheers.' The man met her gaze. 'I'm called Milo, by the way.'

When you got a close look, Milo's eyes, brown as umber, deep and intense, didn't match the surface banter.

'My name's Tilda,' she blurted out.

'Wondered if it might be Cillit Bang. Disappointed.'

Dettol rolled over and covered her face with her paws, as if in fits of laughter.

Milo scratched his beard and looked at the money again. 'I'll treat myself to a razor. This beard's damn hot and itchy in this heat.' He turned to go.

'Hold on,' she muttered and disappeared again. She came back with a pink razor. Tilda always doubled up on toiletries, keeping a spare of everything. It made sense. She never ran out. Milo took the razor and, for a second, his chin trembled. Or did it? No. Tilda must have been seeing things. Either way, she didn't do emotion. He opened his mouth to speak but Tilda muttered goodbye and closed the door. It would take more than a flood to make him more than a stranger.

2

Tilda woke up at seven the next morning. She checked WhatsApp for the latest message to do with her secret project. Reading, she gave a small smile, as handsome Yves had called her '*mon petit chou-fleur*', though Tilda remained baffled as to why the French considered *my little cauliflower* to be a term of endearment. Then she sat cross-legged on the floor and did ten minutes of meditation. Humming 'La Vie en Rose', she took a cold shower in the name of good health, brushed her hair, and then changed into black trousers and white shirt. Tilda applied her favourite scent, she'd worn it for years, made from jasmine flowers – her gran's favourite. At seven thirty precisely she walked into the lounge with its neutral tones, with the squared-off pile of magazines and DVDs regimentally lined up in a glass cabinet. The electrical fire was compact and discreet, and Tilda put it on in the evenings, in the winter, to save switching on the central heating for the whole house. She drew the curtains and peered out the front window, onto the street that was far more cluttered. It was one week on from the washing machine flood, the first Friday of June, and wispy white clouds parted like theatre curtains, signalling the start of another busy day and, according to forecasters, an even warmer month. Tilda stared at the pavement and despite the early morning sun rays, a shiver ran down her spine as she imagined having to sleep on it.

Indignant meowing floated in from the utility room. Dettol's plastic litter tray had survived the flood, but she'd had to put down old towels for her to sleep on, until the cat bed dried out. Tilda always called the cat in at night, due to drivers' vision being worse in the dark. Veterinary bills weren't cheap. She let Dettol into the kitchen and tipped cat food into a bowl. Twenty to eight and it was time for Tilda's breakfast, the same every day, cereal flakes with fruit, five walnut halves, a small handful of raisins and two tablespoons of probiotic yogurt on top.

At eight o'clock sharp, after brushing her teeth and flossing, and rinsing out with mouthwash, Tilda settled down at the kitchen table with her laptop, making a note to order a mini cooling tower. She'd set up Wright Cleaners three years ago after a... traumatic incident. She used PayPal for payment processing, and job websites and ads on Facebook for finding cleaners. Research had led her to a popular online platform that managed the client bookings and individual cleaners' schedules. It also allowed Tilda to line up jobs so that staff could claim them without having to consult her first. She met each new cleaner in person first, as she did every client. Currently one of her best employees, Iris, was off with a summer flu bug that was going around. Tilda had agreed to cover her shift every weekday, starting late afternoon, until she came back. Admin took up most of her time these days, so she embraced an excuse to be hands-on again, even though it left her time-pressed. She'd set up her business with modest goals, focusing on residential jobs around Stockport, but over time had accepted commercial clients as well, many of them from Manchester city centre.

Now and then she considered taking on an office assistant, but that would mean working alongside the same person, day in, day out, online at the very least; it would mean getting close.

A hard no to that.

A sharp rapping at the front door made her jump and an image of Milo, sitting amongst litter, came to mind. He was still hanging around their street. It was harder not to make conversation now that he'd helped her, though Tilda had said the minimum to him since. They'd talked about a downpour of rain, a welcome break from the unseasonably hot rays. The local ice cream van had a half-price June promotion on, so she'd bought one for Milo, hesitant at first, as she didn't want to come across as patronising, as if she were treating a child. However, his face had lit up, even though the ice cream was melting by the time he got it. Milo was always polite, good-humoured, despite his circumstances not turning around, despite his sneezing getting worse. But amiable as he was, she wouldn't invite Milo inside. Perhaps he thought her an easy touch, what with the money she'd given him, and had spent this week putting on an extra friendly act, trying to fool her into offering him a more cash. Tilda flexed her hands and went into the hallway. She could deal with a chancer. By the sixth form, ten years ago now, she'd developed a sharp tongue and swift punch. She'd had to. The girls who'd made her life a misery for so many terms finally kept clear.

Tilda pulled open the door, morning sunrays stroking her face. Oh. The postman handed over two envelopes, one pink, one yellow. Ah, yes, of course. She recognised both sets of handwriting. Tilda walked back into the kitchen. She dropped the unopened envelopes into the bin, rolled up her shirt sleeves and continued with her day, answering calls from employees over scheduling, illness or emergencies, from pleased clients as well, or those angry because a cleaner had done a bad job or hadn't turned up. Not that that happened often – Tilda carried out thorough interviews and checked references in detail. She was very protective of her staff. It was important to look after those you were responsible for. If someone had looked out for teenage Tilda, her high school years might have been so much happier. Other tasks included unscheduled drop-ins on jobs to oversee quality. Sometimes this involved going out in the evening. During the day Tilda would check running social media ads, creating new ones and following up on hot leads, as not as many people could afford cleaners these days. Keeping her staff busy was most important, otherwise they'd seek out another company to work for. Her website had a blog as well, she updated it regularly with cleaning hacks, and she contacted clients now and again, encouraging them to leave reviews.

Tilda liked to keep occupied, especially today. It muffled the voice in her head saying she should open those cards in the bin, even though she knew the lies they'd contain.

Lunch was a sandwich, cut into four triangles, with a packet of low-fat crisps, a sliced apple, and glass of ice water. At five she had a snack, before heading out to cover Iris's shift that she'd start at six, one of her company's navy work tunics in her bag. She'd rung Iris after lunch, concerned about the woman with such a hearty laugh and knack for emailing Tilda humorous reports if a client ever acted up. She'd even googled how to treat flu before calling.

'Hello Iris, how are you doing?'

'I'm not so good, Tilda. Sorry, it might be a few days before I return to work.'

'Don't you worry about that, just look after yourself. Stay hydrated and a zinc supplement might strengthen your immune system. Maybe watch one of those afternoon romance movies you rave about.'

Dettol trotted out of the door too and onto the lawn, dropping to roll on her back and stretch. Tilda was convinced Dettol thought she'd turfed over the old paving slabs just for her.

It was easier to get to the job by train, especially in the rush hour. She'd normally drive to residential jobs, taking her own products, but this particular client was commercial and had everything she needed on site. Thank goodness the building had aircon as well. Tilda considered crossing the road to avoid Milo. She didn't want to get talking again. The only regular people in her life or home these days were those she met in books and TV series. She'd tried to remedy this in the past, but it had proved difficult.

Yet, compelled to see that lopsided smile again, she walked towards him. At boarding school, Tilda had eventually learnt that facing your fears often turned out to be less scary in the long run. She'd also learnt what it felt like to be on the outside, looking in. As she passed, Tilda glanced sideways. Her jaw dropped.

Cue that smile. 'Took a while to shave off that beard. I'd almost forgotten what a handsome guy I was. Next, I need to sort out my hair, it doesn't half curl up in this hot weather.' Milo spoke in a muffled voice, full of cold, and he gave a big sneeze.

A police car, siren on, drove past and snapped Tilda out of studying him. 'Got to go,' she muttered and headed off. As she walked away, Tilda looked over her shoulder a couple of times.

It was a two-person job in the large office in Stockport, and Jazz, in her twenties too, worked alongside her. Yet despite the focus required to do a good job, Tilda couldn't get Milo, and how the lack of beard had transformed his appearance, out of her head. His words came to mind. *Handsome guy*? Some might say so, with the square chin and boyish dimples. Tilda scrubbed the toilet bowl even harder. Good looks didn't always reflect a good heart. When she walked back past, several hours later, Milo was talking to an elderly man who handed him a takeout cold drink. Milo sucked the straw sticking out of the blue slushie. Clearly he was as capable as Tilda when it came to looking out for himself during the roughest of times.

After a late dinner – fish and chips on Fridays – Tilda washed up straightaway. Then she escaped into her current read, sitting in the lounge that was cool in the evenings, wearing a T-shirt and shorts. Finishing a book never saddened Tilda as she'd enjoyed writing as a child and, still these days, would continue a novel's story in her head. Over the years she'd mentally written many sequels for the likes of Pratchett and Gaiman. Tilda loved visiting Waterstones in Manchester Arndale, with its very own café. She didn't work much at weekends which wasn't so hard, residential jobs dropped off on those days. After Dad died, her mum's career, and that of Tilda's brother, had been the focus, and therefore Saturdays and Sundays were no different to weekdays: work, work, work. At least that's what she remembered up to the age of eleven, before being sent away. Tilda always swore that when she grew up, she'd leave the weekends free for family time – even if that family only contained one person – like it had been whilst Dad was alive, until she was nine. Oh, Mum always worked more than she should, but Dad took the whole weekend out, despite her criticising him and saying he'd never progress at the bank. He'd take Tilda and her little brother, Logan, swimming, to the park or cinema, laughing loudly at comedies and pouring far too many sprinkles on their ice creams. Like Tilda, her dad found huge pleasure in the little things – or perhaps she was the one like him... an unusually shaped cloud, an especially crumbly biscuit. Mum would only take time out for something important like seeing Logan play football in the latest school match. What Tilda did, as her daughter, never seemed to be considered as significant.

After several chapters, she went to call in Dettol. It was a special day for Tilda and she couldn't wait for the treat she'd bought herself to eat in front of the TV later, watching what she wanted, in peace. The culmination of her secret project, in a few weeks, of which Yves had become a part, originally might have meant an end to enjoyable evenings, like these, on her own. Not now.

Funny things, secrets, they only existed if you kept them hidden from people. But Tilda had no one in her life to hide her project from, so perhaps it couldn't be called secret at all.

An urge swept over Tilda to sit in a bar and wallow, over a glass of wine and bowl of peanuts. She gave a big sigh then shook herself, took out her phone and sent Yves a photo she'd taken of her fish dinner. Despite his glamorous life in Paris, as a fashion designer, supervising shoots, working in glitzy studios, he loved exchanging photos of what they both ate each evening. Yves enjoyed English food as well and would shop at an M&S food store near him, in the French capital. It was a habit Tilda had become fond of. She'd never exchanged fun messages with anyone else. The only photos her only long-term boyfriend, Shane, had ever sent, weren't ones you could open in public. He used to say she was old before her time and that all his previous girlfriends had loved them. He said a lot of things towards the end and Tilda frowned as she recalled his reaction when she'd taken on a woman with autism, Connie.

'Takes one to know one,' Shane had said. 'What with your routines, your awkwardness.' He'd pushed Tilda's shoulder and smirked. 'Don't worry. Only joking.'

He really didn't know her at all, thinking she'd view being called neurodiverse as an insult. Tilda hadn't bothered explaining that life had shaped her, not a brain wiring. As she got to know Connie, who was one of her best employees now, bit by bit, Tilda learnt of the challenges that woman had experienced from birth, unlike Tilda's whose life had been easy until she'd lost the dad she'd cherished.

Dettol wasn't at the side door. Tilda called and checked the front of the house, the cat's name making a passing group of beery youths laugh.

Unable to settle in front of the television again, she headed back to the utility room thirty minutes later. A frantic scrabbling at the side door greeted her. She turned the key and opened it. No wonder the cat was keen to get in. The air, moist now, released hesitant drops of water as if the sky was deciding whether or not to shower.

Despite this, meowing loudly, Dettol walked away.

'Come back here, you silly animal,' said Tilda, and she held out her palm. The raindrops fell consistently now, faster, bigger.

Dettol came back and stared Tilda in the face, then she padded away again to the gate by the pavement. It was as if she wanted Tilda to follow, despite the poor weather. Well, stuff that. Tilda closed the door and returned to the lounge. Her phone buzzed. Tonight, Yves had eaten out and had sent her a very professional-looking photograph of a bowl of mussels. She texted back a wow face and settled down once again. Expressing feelings through emojis was far easier than doing so in real life. Tilda had become used to stuffing her feelings away anyway, deep down, out of sight. After several minutes of fidgeting, she switched off the television and tossed down the remote control. That cat was far more trouble than she was worth. Tilda pulled on a light jacket and slipped into trainers. Grabbing the keys, she went outside and locked up. She put up her hood, missing the melodic early evening birdsong that had accompanied more cheerful weather, since spring had passed the baton to summer. Dettol meowed again loudly and went onto the street. Another cat might have got into difficulties. Honestly, who did she think Tilda was, the local Samaritan? Muttering under her breath, Tilda followed and... Dettol turned right. Really? They were going back to Milo? This was ridiculous. As rain pelted down now, Tilda walked more quickly, hoping to pick up Dettol before they reached him. But Dettol built up speed, as if sensing the ambush. Out of breath, Tilda stopped by Milo. She went to speak, but something wasn't right. He was leaning to one side and... was that blood on his face? Tilda took a sharp intake of breath. She bent down and shook him gently. His clothes were already sodden.

'Just take the money,' he mumbled, barely coherent, without opening his eyes, putting an arm across his head as if to protect it.

His words, his actions, winded Tilda, as if she'd been the one to receive a punch. She touched his face, it was cold. She straightened up. Dettol snuggled down onto his chest. 'It's Tilda. I'm ringing the police,' she said, 'I'll tell them to bring an ambulance.'

Milo's head moved. 'No,' he said, in a rough tone. 'I'm fine. Leave me alone. Rough sleeping is a criminal offence... if I'm arrested, get a record, it'll be even harder to get another job.'

'But...'

'Just fuck off!' he exclaimed.

Tilda's eyebrows shot up. Rudeness she could deal with, unreasonable customers had proved that was her forte. She went to dial 999, but caught his eye again. Milo shook his head and pulled his rucksack towards him and hugged it. In that second, she got it. Being in control of his own life was all he had left. There was only one thing to do, if he agreed. Tilda couldn't believe she was considering this, but he hugged his rucksack even tighter, like she'd once hugged her pillow in the dorm, at high school, a throwback to toddler days when a cuddly toy solved so much.

'Then you'll have to come to mine and let me clean you up. That's what I do, after all.'

Milo wiped his nose with his hand, blood staining it. 'But you don't know me. It's not right.'

A flicker of warmth, again, in her stomach. 'Is that a yes? I haven't got all night.' She bent down and slipped her arm through his. Milo flinched as he got to his feet and leant on Tilda, limping to her house. Hardly able to see, due to the downpour, they went into Tilda's garden and into the utility room. She took off her dripping jacket and hung it on one of the hooks in a row by the door. Tilda stopped before opening the kitchen door. Hesitated. He was so... imposing, despite his lanky frame, with those long legs, and shoulders broader than the male protagonist's in her favourite TV show. Yet somehow, on the street, next to his sleeping bag and coin cup, he'd looked so very, very small.

'I'd bend down, the next door's shorter,' she muttered, tearing her gaze away from the dark curly brown hair, straggly like the beard had been, matted with blood.

'What's wrong?' he mumbled. 'Bet you're thinking six-foot-three me should have been able to defend myself?' he said in an embarrassed tone, already more like himself. 'Sure. I get it. Even though there were two of them. Wish I'd got a few punches in.'

'No, it's not that.'

'Then you're worried about catching this damn bug?' he said and coughed. 'Don't blame you, I've got a blinding headache. But I promise to cover my face when I sneeze and cough.'

She lifted her chin. 'It's... nothing.'

Milo looked down at himself then returned her gaze, shock emanating from his face. He closed his eyes for a moment as he rubbed his hand over them. 'You're frightened. You really believe I'd hurt you?' His voice came out in jerks. 'Tilda, I would *never*...' He moved back.

Yes, she was wary. But also wasn't. Tilda had learnt at boarding school that physical strength wasn't always the tool people used to cause the most hurt. She pulled the door open. Dettol darted ahead, into the kitchen.

'I'll stay in here if you prefer,' said Milo, holding back, in the utility room. He staggered and rested against a work top. Tilda shook her head and led him into the kitchen by his elbow. She put on the kettle and Milo collapsed into a chair at the table. He put his head in his hands.

'We'll wash your face first,' she said, in a measured tone, 'and—'

Tilda froze as Milo started crying.

3

Sobbing. In front of her. No one had ever done that, no one had ever been close enough, since her childhood. Not even her ex, Shane. Their relationship had lasted for just under one year and it had ended last July, when she'd worked out his real motive for dating her. They hadn't talked about emotions and that's how Tilda had liked it, and Shane never voluntarily opened up about anything deeper than his sales job, Manchester United and chicken nuggets.

Should she get Milo to talk? Or say nothing? Boarding school had drilled into her that displays of emotion were unacceptable, self-indulgent. Teachers told the girls their parents wouldn't want them crying. When she'd first arrived, it had been like a bereavement, leaving Logan, even Mum, and the house still smiling with memories of Dad; leaving the garden she'd loved playing in and the bedroom she'd had all to herself. Boarding school had made Tilda feel like a captive given a seven-year prison term.

But she'd got on with it, gritted her teeth, knowing she'd never let herself down. Tilda could always rely on Tilda.

She picked up the kitchen roll holder and sat down at the table. Milo tore off two squares of the quilted paper, blew his nose loudly and coughed into the tissue.

'Sorry,' he said. 'It all got too much.'

Don't say anything. He's not a friend. 'What did?' she asked.

'Life.' His voice wavered. 'Me. How did it come to this? On top of everything else, I've never had a cold so bad.' He rummaged in his rucksack. 'Yep. It's gone.' His voice hitched. 'My bag of money. I almost had enough for a B & B for tonight. I dreamt of finding one where they needed a handyman or someone to help out. If I could pay for one night, get cleaned up, then tell them about my credentials working in the club...' He pressed his palms into his eyes, wiping away more tears. 'Then I'd have had a permanent address then and could start making out job applications for management positions.' Tilda took her hands off the table and put them in her lap, clasping them tightly together. 'It's okay. I'm not expecting to stay here. With this hot weather, I'm the lucky one, camping outside.' He gave a wry smile. 'Almost.'

Her eyebrows raised. People didn't usually read her that well and she never understood why not. Surely Tilda *was* a book you could judge by the cover. She didn't laugh at people's jokes if they weren't funny, she didn't flirt or smile at strangers, her novel's jacket wasn't bright and breezy and hiding the more sombre air underneath. Yet people were still taken aback by her abrupt manner. 'Uptight,' Shane had called her, at the end. Her book jacket used to be brighter, when she was little, like those uplifting women's fiction ones you see – all pastels and beaches. Dad used to make Tilda feel oh so loved, and somehow brought out a softer side to Mum. But then she sent Tilda away, and that young girl's world became a darker place, where laughing at the other pupils' jokes and doing her best to be one of the in-crowd had only made her an object of fun. They formed cliques, used swear words in a cool way, talked about things they'd done with boys that Tilda didn't understand. Despite her efforts, in the beginning, to bend to an ideal, to shape her personality, Tilda didn't fit in. But it didn't matter in the end, because she worked out that the most important thing was fitting in with your own conscience.

She fetched a flannel and a couple of towels, one for him to dry his hair. She filled a bowl with warm, soapy water. She washed Milo's face, approaching it like a client's valuable ornament or picture frame that needed a good clean. How satisfying to remove the blood on his cheeks, on the strong nose. She patted his eye and forehead dry and his top lip that wasn't quite straight.

Not that cleaning clients' possessions ever made her stomach fizz or made her hyper-aware of every breath she gave.

Tilda dabbed on antiseptic and applied plasters, leaning back when he sneezed and coughed, although he kept to his word and used the kitchen roll.

'Cuts anywhere else?' she asked.

'My arms and chest hurt.' His voice was monotone.

'We'd better take a look then,' she said briskly and motioned for him to stand up like she had. Tilda was nothing if not thorough.

For a second his eyes went shiny again. He stood up and she cleaned his hands first, the scar on the right-hand one, old and deep, hard to ignore. Tilda inspected his arms first. Only bruising.

Only. That wasn't the right word, it diminished the damage. Ugly purple marks had already formed on swollen mounds of skin. Milo pulled up his T-shirt, wincing. Tilda clenched her jaw, determined not to show a reaction, but rage against the people who'd done this lit up her insides. They must have kicked him with steel toe-capped boots, or hit out with a sharp instrument. She washed his chest more gently than she knew she could, her fingers brushing the skin, the brown hairs.

For some reason, disappointment surged through her when the job was over. The last man she'd touched in such an intimate way, was Shane, although she'd never needed to be gentle with him. If only he'd been gentler with her feelings, instead of proving, yet again, that Tilda wasn't a person anyone could love. That was simply another cold, hard fact of her past, her life, and she accepted that. Tilda didn't do parties, especially pity ones.

'Sorry about the smell.' His cheeks went red. 'Deodorant is expensive.'

'You've got worse things to worry about,' she said over her shoulder as she went into the utility room to fetch the mini hand sanitiser from her summer jacket's pocket. She came back and squirted some into her palm, put the bottle on the kitchen table and rubbed her hands. Milo stared at the floor. Well, she didn't want to catch impetigo, ringworm, scabies or any other of the diseases a rough sleeper might carry. Yet his face took her back to youth and how, after the year seven holiday, the other girls had laughed at her in PE. Underarm hairs had appeared and her mum had been too busy with her brother to advise her what to do that fortnight she'd been home after summer camp. She gave him a tentative smile. 'I'm just being careful, I really don't want to catch that nasty cold bug of yours. I run my own business with no one to stand in if I'm ill.'

Milo's face relaxed.

She caught sight of Dettol finishing up her daily quota of cat biscuits. 'Right. How about something to eat?' Did she really say that? Tilda peered out of the window to the left, above the kitchen sink. It was still raining. 'There's a bowl of leftover beef stew from yesterday, in the fridge. I'll heat that up.'

'*Homecooked* food?' he said, as if she'd offered him gold leaf caviar. Ten minutes later he wolfed down the stew, dipping in pieces of bread. The rain continued to pelt outside, the rhythmic noise was comforting. Milo gave a big sigh when the lot had gone. 'That's the best meal I've had for a very long time,' he said and gave a thumbs up.

'You don't need to do that,' she said. 'Don't act as if it's something special, when it's not.'

Shane had once used to say her cooking was five-star, and that her raven black hair and pale skin was a sexy combination, that it was so cool how she wasn't bothered about clothes or make-up, that her serious, sensible attitude was refreshing. That's what had hurt her most when they'd split, discovering that all the time they'd been dating, he'd only pretended to find her worthy of his attention, when he'd secretly had another agenda. At least Dettol was honest about not liking her and in fact, that was also the one positive thing she could say about her dorm mates at school, who'd called her a weirdo for her book choices and liking stories about characters who had horns or wings.

Milo's brow furrowed. 'But it *was* delicious. Reminded me of...' His voice petered out before he straightened up. 'Those orange cubes were swede, right? I could taste the thyme, and unless I'm mistaken, a hint of barbecue sauce?'

Tilda put two green teas down on the table and almost smiled again. He'd guessed her secret ingredient. She went to the fridge, paused and then pulled out a mini chocolate cake, covered in icing and smarties, a rare treat she'd bought for herself that evening. She cut it in two exact halves and handed Milo a slice on a plate.

'Are we celebrating something?' he asked, eyeing the tea warily.

Dettol interrupted with a demanding meow. She shook the rear end of her body as if about to leap. Milo pushed his chair back and patted his knees.

'Don't worry,' said Tilda, 'she doesn't like sitting on laps.'

Dettol jumped up and butted her head against Milo's stomach.

'You are gorgeous, yes you are,' he said and he tickled behind her ears.

Tilda had never seen Dettol behave in such an undignified manner. They ate in silence as Dettol curled up and settled on his lap – ridiculously unhygienic, Tilda should have lifted her onto the floor. She left to use the bathroom and when she came back, Milo stood by the bin, the two envelopes in his hand.

'I went to throw my kitchen roll away when these caught my attention. You must have got rid of them accidentally.'

She snatched the envelopes away. 'I'd prefer it if you didn't go through my private things.'

'Sorry, I didn't. I... I was trying to help tidy up.'

Tilda threw them back in with the rubbish. She jerked her head to the window. The rain only spat now. And his clothes had dried out a bit. 'The weather's improved.'

'Right. Of course. I'll get going. Thanks... thanks for everything.' He went to Dettol who was now asleep on his chair. Milo bent down and scratched behind her ears, before kissing her on the head. Kissing an animal? Hadn't he heard of E. coli and parasites? Tilda hurried into the utility room and opened the side door.

'Thanks again, Tilda. Best stew ever,' said Milo and he limped towards the gate where he sneezed loudly before carrying on. She closed the door behind him and went back into the kitchen, about to pick up her phone and go on WhatsApp. Dettol gave her a look dirtier than her worst client's bathroom. Tilda went to the bin and retrieved the two cards. She placed them on the table. Slowly she tore each one in half and then threw them away again. Gestures, like these cards, meant nothing if there was no sincerity behind them.

They didn't.

A realisation punched her in the stomach and for a second, she could hardly breathe.

There was no way *she* was going to be like one of the fakers who'd sent them.

Not even changing out of her slippers, Tilda unlocked the side door and ran into the street, cursing as she went straight through a puddle.

'Milo!' she hollered. *Don't make the offer, you won't be able to take it back.* 'You can stay on the sofa. For one night only.'

The huddled figure turned. Relief, gratitude, spread across his face. He hobbled back.

'You're sure about this?' he asked when back in the kitchen. Tilda was squeezing water out of her slippers. 'Letting me kip here far outweighs me fixing a hole in your draining hose.'

'I've got a lock on my bedroom door,' she said in a measured tone. A throwback to boarding school. It was the only way she could sleep soundly, although Tilda suspected she wouldn't get a minute's sleep with a house guest. Her beloved gran used to swear by a glass of sherry before bed. For a split second, Tilda wished she had in a bottle of that old-fashioned tipple.

'Right. Yeah. Of course. Good. I mean...' He exhaled deeply. 'Thanks so much for this.'

'I'll get the lounge ready. If you want, take a shower early tomorrow morning, before you leave,' she said pointedly and went for the door.

'Cheers. I appreciate it so much. And Tilda?'

She turned around.

'The cake was delicious. Happy Birthday.'

4

Tilda woke up at seven the next morning. She checked WhatsApp for the latest message from Yves, who'd inadvertently become the focus of her secret project.

> Chère Tilda, ma belle, just an early morning hello from me. I so look forward to your replies, chuffed that such a busy businesswoman finds time to answer back. I know the work it takes to be your own boss. You and Dettol have a great day! Bon, I must hurry, my needle awaits. Let us chat for longer, later. Hope your washing machine is working okay. Yves xxxxx

Five kisses? Tilda ran her fingertip over them. No one had ever sent her that many. It felt like an achievement and an urge swept over her to buy a bottle of champagne and toast the moment. She re-read his words, noting, as always, how good his English was, like using the more colloquial word 'chuffed'.

Twenty... six days, that was it, from now, and her project would come to an end, all her efforts would come to fruition.

Or maybe they wouldn't.

He often mentioned Dettol, having told Tilda previously about a childhood cat who used to sleep in the bathroom sink. A sweet personality hid behind the other glamorous texts about his celebrity clients and catwalk friends, like him checking in about the flood in her utility room. He was an unusual mix. Tilda typed back.

Hi Yves, good luck with your needlework. I can't imagine sewing together a whole garment, darning a hole is enough for me. Sorry you have to work on a Saturday, instead of enjoying yourself in Paris. Perhaps you can get out for lunch in the Eiffel Tower, like you often say you do. It's amazing that you saw President Macron there once, and that he spoke to you. Yes, thanks, the washing machine is working fine now. A day of domestic chores here. Speak soon. Tilda.

'Speak soon' was the closest Tilda got to expressing any affection. She didn't do kisses, not in messages, never had, wasn't used to it. Frivolity had never been part of her adult life. She used to believe Shane had liked that about her, until he made it clear that hers was a soul way too conservative for his. She read her message to Yves, wondering if a fashion designer, in Paris, would find it boring. And yet, he kept messaging. Perhaps she should have talked about helping out a rough sleeper, to up the drama factor. However, she felt a sense of loyalty to Milo, the troubled man from the street who she hardly knew. Silly really.

Tilda sat cross-legged on the floor and did ten minutes of meditation. She took a cold shower, brushed her hair, and then changed into grey trousers and a plain beige T-shirt. She applied her favourite scent, reminiscing about her gran and the hours she'd spend reading to Tilda and Logan. At seven thirty precisely, she arrived in the kitchen, even though it was the weekend. Indignant meowing floated in from the utility room. She let Dettol into the kitchen and tipped cat food into a bowl. Twenty to eight and it was time for Tilda's breakfast, cereal flakes with fruit, five walnut halves, a small handful of raisins and two tablespoons of probiotic yogurt on top.

Except today it would be breakfast for two and, reluctantly, she delayed eating. Tilda opened the kitchen blinds. The window looked out onto the bargain hardware store next door. Overnight the rain had cleared. She normally did her weekly supermarket shop on a Saturday afternoon, after catching up with laundry. If she brought it forward, said she was going out this morning, it would be easier to get rid of Milo, he'd have to leave too. She had hoped he'd take the hint and get up first thing and shower. Face pinched, she went to knock on the lounge door but hesitated.

Why had she let him stay overnight? Yes, she'd been locked in her bedroom but he could have taken drugs, lost it and kicked the door in.

Yet, deep down, she'd sensed that he wouldn't.

He might have already snuck out, having stolen her TV and iPad she'd left in there. Tilda should have cleared her valuables out of the lounge. She rapped her knuckles on the door before entering. Okay. He was still here. She grimaced, glad for her supply of air fresheners. Underneath his sleeping bag, he still lay on the sofa, feet hanging off the end. Tilda opened the window and traffic noise poured inside.

'The bathroom is free,' she said, in a sharp voice. 'There's a large black towel in there, use that. Up the stairs, turn left, it's the small room at the end. Leave your towel on the base of the shower when you've finished. If you don't mind hurrying, though? I'm heading out to the shops soon.'

Nothing.

She bent over Milo and shook his shoulder. He didn't move a millimetre. For a second, she feared the worst and a painful emotion washed over Tilda... It had to be indifference, yet indifference didn't hurt, it didn't leave a mark, not on the person feeling it – only on the intended target. She exhaled with relief when Milo grunted because calling the police would be awkward, that was it, that's why she'd been concerned, explaining what a dead homeless man was doing in her house. Dettol ran in, before Tilda could shoo her away, and jumped on top of him, climbing along his body to his face. She meowed and licked his ear. Tilda's eyes narrowed. Did Milo shift? Right, so he was pretending to be asleep.

Much more vigorously she shook his shoulder. Milo roared and sat bolt upright. She gasped and backed away to the other side of the room. Dettol fell to the carpet.

'Get off!' he croaked. 'I haven't got any more cash.' He sat dazed, taking in his surroundings. His chest rattled and he gave a loud cough. His throat sounded full of phlegm. He rubbed his eyes. 'Tilda? It's you? Of course. Sorry...' His voice wavered and she stepped forwards again. Milo surveyed the room and placed his hands on the sofa, either side of his shaking body. He went to push himself up but panted. 'I... I'm going to be sick,' he said and gagged.

Tilda raced into the kitchen and returned with a bowl. Yet he might have been exaggerating his symptoms. She pressed her hand against his puce forehead. He was burning up. Adam, one of her cleaners, had also messaged her late last night, saying he'd come down with flu and wouldn't be able to do his weekend shifts. It was most unlike him to be ill. In his early thirties, Adam had spoken – during his interview – of how he ran marathons. But he'd said one of the other cleaners had already agreed to cover for him. Clearly Milo had caught the same bug as Iris and Adam.

Milo clung onto the bowl. 'Sorry, sorry,' he kept saying, the words coming out disjointed. He dragged his legs around, onto the floor and stood up unsteadily. 'I can't face a shower. I... I'll sit in the bathroom, if that's okay... in case I'm sick, then... I'll have a quick wash and... I'll get out of your hair...' Breathing noisily, he fell back onto the sofa again. He rubbed his head and groaned.

Somehow, despite his height, despite his unsure feet, she helped Milo upstairs into the bathroom and he collapsed onto the floor by the toilet, gagging again. She fetched him a glass of water, and escaped onto the landing, stopping by the spare room opposite. She opened its door and stepped inside, its pristine carpet and military-standard-made bed calming her down. Tilda never had guests but always kept the small single bed that the previous owners had left behind made up. With rising living costs, she told herself it would come in useful in case she ever needed to take on a lodger.

Yet she hadn't even let Shane move in that time his landlord wanted to sell up. Living on her own was something she'd worked hard to achieve. The privacy. The safety. The zero judgement. The freedom to create the exact home environment she wanted. It was only since breaking up with him that Tilda had reconsidered her life choices. If she was totally honest, tucked away in the corner of her heart was a dream of finding her *tribe*, that's what social media liked to call it – someone or some people with whom she could share her space, without feeling imprisoned, without needing to set rules or boundaries, without being... scared. The last time she'd felt that cosy sense of belonging was when she was tiny. With their parents often wrapped up with work, especially during the week, Tilda and her brother always ate together, played together – he was only two years younger. They'd had sleepovers, making silly ghost faces at each other using torches. In his company, she'd lived a carefree life. Things began to change in the last year or two that she had lived at home, after Dad's death and when Logan's talent came to the fore, but they were still close. Their mum enrolled him for football development programmes, in preparation for him going to a local football academy. She could hardly talk about anything else, as if planning for Logan's future would make her forget the one she'd dreamt of having with her husband.

Tilda became invisible to her mother even before she was sent away to board, but Logan still saw her, or she'd believed he did, yet she heard nothing from him after she left.

Tilda missed that happy-go-lucky companionship.

Retching from the bathroom brought Tilda back to the present. She sat on the spare bed and rested her chin on her hands. Three years ago, at the point of that traumatic event, in Market Street in town, that one she didn't like to think about – that had changed everything – Tilda had hit rock bottom. She'd needed help to climb out of the abyss.

Was this the universe asking for payback? Yes, that must be it, tit for tat, because it couldn't be that she genuinely wanted to help this stranger, not Tilda who hadn't a single friend in the world. Friendship had always felt like too much of a commitment, too suffocating, after being forced to live year in, year out, twenty-four-seven, with people who weren't family. Yet she'd developed a genuine... affection for her employees. Oh, they wouldn't realise, Tilda kept things strictly professional, apart from the birthday cards she sent and the Christmas chocolates. Boundaries – boundaries kept you safe.

By the time Tilda had eaten breakfast and washed up, the retching upstairs had stopped. She tapped on the bathroom door. Milo sat on the edge of the white bath, drinking water. She took his arm and pulled him

up, as well as she could. He leant on her shoulder and she led him into
the spare room. Tilda pointed to the bed and he gave a double take.

'A couple of nights, until the worst of your flu passes. Do you have any
more clothes in your rucksack downstairs? I'll wash them, you can change
into them later.'

'You don't have to do this.' He wavered unsteadily on his feet.

'Is that so?' she said crisply. 'I doubt you'd make it as far as my gate
and it's going to be another belting hot day. That won't help your fever,
with no respite outside.'

He shook his head. 'No... Believe me. I don't deserve any of this.' His
words caught in his throat. He made to leave. 'I'm bad news.'

'It's a good thing I can look after myself then, isn't it?' she said and
folded her arms, hoping what they said about animal instincts was right
and that Dettol wasn't the exception in having a penchant for terrible
humans.

Milo mumbled that he wanted to see the hostel manager, to give his
room to someone else, he didn't want to stay there, didn't deserve it
anyway. A high fever could cause delusions, Tilda hoped that's as far as
his went. Back in the kitchen, Tilda opened his rucksack. She pulled out a
T-shirt, khaki trousers, used socks and underwear. A jumper got caught
and she gave it a yank. Something metal and square flew across the
kitchen table. A plastic card too – a driving license that showed Milo was
thirty, a couple of years older than her. She picked up the metal square.
Oh. It was a photo in a frame. It had seen better days, but then he was
living on the streets. It was of a little girl who, apart from her red hair, was
the spit of him. Milo had a daughter. She looked about eight. She stuffed
the card and frame back into the rucksack, next to an open, worn toiletry
bag, and put his laundry into the washing machine.

She sat at the kitchen table. Her own laundry wash was now messed
up, her comfortable weekend routine blown apart. The rest of Milo's
clothes, everything he owned, had to be in storage somewhere. Crouchden's Saturday market opened at nine. She could pick up some bits for
him, cheap. Tilda couldn't face him moving around her spotless home in
grubby clothes.

She went into the lounge and unplugged the TV, grabbed her iPad, put them both in her bedroom; her laptop too, along with her whole DVD collection, a first edition novel, a painting from the hallway, and a collection of vintage teacups. When she came out of her bedroom the last time, having stored everything in there, handbag over her shoulder in preparation for a trip to the market, Dettol was scratching furiously outside the spare room. Forehead perspiring, Tilda shushed her away but she sat and those almond-shaped eyes stared up defiantly. Tilda held her gaze and, to her annoyance, was the one to blink first. She pursed her lips and opened the door. Dettol darted in, jumped up on the bed, breaking house rules. The cat lay down next to Milo's chest, curving her body against his, studying him, along with Tilda, as his rattling chest moved up and down. Tilda went over to the window and opened it slightly, letting in a faint breeze, then she pulled the curtains.

About to leave, a pen caught her eye. Milo was holding it tightly in his hand. The frown disappeared from her face. Tilda approached the bed and gently prised it from his fingers. She placed it on the bedside table next to him, fighting the urge to reach out her hand and gently brush the long fringe away from his face.

5

Before leaving the house, for the market, Tilda had already put zinc supplements, for Milo, on her shopping list. Shane's health had always been robust apart from the time he caught Covid. He'd been chirpy enough on the phone but insisted they didn't see each other for ten days. When they'd finally met up he positively glowed, with tanned skin and a chilled expression. He said it went to show how ill he'd been last time she saw him and Tilda had nodded, not wanting to believe he'd gone on holiday without her.

Being at boarding school had robbed her of those moments where, as she got older, she'd maybe have looked after Logan, even her mum, if they'd been poorly, or a pet if they'd owned one. Whilst her brother stayed at home amongst his friends and belongings, their mum had said it was too stressful to look after two children at once, and juggle work. Tilda's holidays were mostly spent at her gran's, a woman who'd rarely suffered with more than a cold – until the end when she caught pneumonia. The majority of pupils seemed to love living away from home with their contemporaries, no doubt pleased to swerve such responsibilities. All they had to do, as a boarder, Tilda included, was look after themselves. Apart from that one time she found her music teacher, Miss Taylor, at the school gates, sitting in her car, engine switched off. She looked as if she'd been crying. Tilda had been in year ten and was finally finding her confidence, standing up to the bullies, giving more eye contact and conversation to teachers. Gently she'd knocked on the window and Miss Taylor gave a start and wound it down. She wasn't like the other teachers. She observed the little things, like red eyes after a bad night, like daydreaming not always being due to laziness but serving as a much-needed escape.

'Sorry to disturb you, miss... Is everything okay?'

Miss Taylor had dabbed her eyes. 'Nothing I can't handle, Matilda, thank you.' She paused. 'Man trouble.'

'I'm never dating,' said Tilda, still shy with the opposite sex she didn't get to meet often.

Her teacher actually stopped crying and smiled. Job done. Young Tilda embraced a rare sense of achievement as she didn't do well at studies, perhaps a little on purpose. Why bother? Any success, in her mum's eyes, would never match that of her son, the up-and-coming football star.

'You might change your mind, over the next couple of years,' said Miss Taylor. 'But promise me something, when you meet a young man... Don't sing his song, because when you split up, you'll have lost your voice. Harmonies are the way to go, blending together individual pitches, different tones, to form something rather beautiful where each part retains its own character.'

It was the sort of thing Tilda's late gran would have said, she'd passed away the year before. 'Is that what you've done, miss? Lost your voice?'

'Yes. Love can do that. Steal your independence. Like how he's a gym fanatic and all these months I've given up chocolate, gone along with his low sugar regime.' She shook her head. 'Don't ever forget, Tilda, you have to put yourself first. You go into a relationship on your own – come out of it that way too. You are the only constant you can rely on. Don't ever bend or hide yourself for the sake of a boy.'

After Shane, Tilda realised that she'd lost her voice with him, daring to dream she'd met 'The One' that movies and novels talked about, acting as if it was worth it to be less Tilda and more the type of woman who'd truly suit him. So she'd eaten chicken nuggets even though she hated the texture and watched Man United play, counting down to the final whistle.

Never again.

She'd bought her music teacher a box of chocolates and given them to her the day after their conversation. Years later, the day after she found out the truth about Shane, and the true reason he'd pursued her after that first day they'd chatted, she'd bought the same brand of chocolates for herself and eaten them in front of the telly, watching the shows she loved, in the blanket hoodie he'd called unsexy.

When Tilda got back from the market, glad for an iced drink, her home was quiet. The house hadn't been trashed or emptied. Dettol appeared in the kitchen. Biscuits before boys, Tilda had to give her credit. After feeding Dettol, Tilda went upstairs with the cheap pyjamas she'd picked up at the market. She refilled Milo's glass and nudged him. Eyes opened. Grunting, he pushed himself up. She handed him the glass and two paracetamol and a zinc tablet.

'Knock them back,' she said and then pointed to the pyjamas at end of the bed. 'I'd change into those, they'll be far more comfortable. I'll wait outside and when you're done, I'll pick up the stuff you're wearing now.'

'I don't understand,' he muttered. 'Why are you doing this?'

No idea.

'The sooner you're better, the sooner I get my home back,' she said instead, and folded her arms.

* * *

Tilda postponed her weekly shop until the next day, sacrificing her usual early Sunday swim at the local pool. Milo had slept all yesterday, couldn't face food last night, so after leaving him a cup of tea, she spent the rest of the evening giving the lounge a deep clean – after sending a photo of the fajitas she'd made to Yves. She'd asked him to send her a photo of the latest design he was working on, but Yves said he couldn't risk sending anything via the internet in case the photo somehow got into the wrong hands and his idea was stolen. Tilda checked in on Milo before she left this morning. The room as suffocating as a sauna, she opened his window wider, breathing in the watermelon smell of cut grass, mixed in with traffic fumes. The council gardeners must have set to work early in the nearby park. He was snoring and if she was quick, wouldn't even notice she'd gone out. Tilda bought soup, a deodorant for him too, razors, and a toothbrush to replace the one in his toiletry bag with frayed bristles. She stopped the car outside her house, in its parking spot. It was the one time of the week she went in through the front. As she opened the door the sound of running water and coughing came from the kitchen. She left the bags in the hallway, locked up and hurried in there.

Milo stood, in the long-legged pyjamas, still a good few inches too short on him.

'Just filling up my glass,' he said, in a scratchy voice. 'Talk about a humid night. I reckon this June is almost as warm as last year's July.'

'You could have done that upstairs,' she said and eyed him suspiciously.

'I was always taught not to drink bathroom water,' he said and looked sheepish.

Her face softened. 'How are you, now?' Her employee, Iris, had got over the flu, but now developed bronchitis, her husband had texted earlier. Tilda had bought her a Get Well Soon card.

'Still got a blinding headache but, overall, heading in the right direction. No idea how I'd have coped on the street. Thanks again, I—'

She reached for the paracetamol bottle by the kettle. 'Take some more of these.' She reached into one of the bags and pulled out the toiletries. 'Keep these in your room... I mean, the spare room,' she added swiftly.

'You bought these for me?'

She handed him the toothbrush. 'Well, I don't think Dettol cares much about mouth hygiene. Right. I'll get some soup on.'

'I don't know what to say...' Another coughing fit ensued.

'Probably best that you don't say anything,' she said briskly, although she liked the way he talked. He gave full eye contact as if her listening mattered.

He hesitated, went to his rucksack, collapsed into one of the seats.

'You don't have to hide things,' he said, in a flat tone.

Tilda stiffened. 'What do you mean?'

'The TV in the lounge – I went in to get my phone, it had fallen on the floor and was under the sofa. Wasn't there a painting in the hallway? I'm not going to steal anything Tilda. In fact...'

Crap. Awkward. But then why should she feel bad? 'Milo. Go to bed. You look dreadful.'

'Dettol told me you were a real smooth talker,' he said and almost smiled. She almost smiled back. He ran a hand over the deodorant. 'I... want to pay you back.' He unzipped the rucksack's inside pocket. 'I was saving this, to pawn, put the money towards a stay at a B & B. But everything you've done for me... you deserve it.' He handed over a ring.

Tilda put down the soup can and sat opposite Milo. She picked up the ring. Opal perhaps. It was white with iridescent hues of purple, gold and mint.

'It's shaped exactly like a dragon's egg,' she exclaimed. 'Beautiful.'

Milo perked up. 'That's what I thought.'

He did?

'A guy gave it to me a few days ago. He was walking past, slouching, slowly as if he was... anxious about his destination. He was mumbling to himself. Shaking his head. Then he paced to and fro and dropped the ring into my cup. Said that, "She would never say yes."'

'An engagement ring,' said Tilda, still dazzled by the shape and colour.

'He chickened out, for whatever reason. I reached out to hand it back in case he changed his mind, but he shook his head and hurried off.'

'It's truly stunning,' she said. But it wasn't hers to keep. Milo needed all the money he could get. Yet it would make good leverage for him to leave. 'I'll keep it safe for you,' she said and slipped it into her jeans pocket. 'I'll give it back when you're better.' She pointed upstairs. 'Go on. Another day and you might be fine. I'll bring up the soup.'

He tilted his head. 'What made you compare it to a dragon's egg? I don't think most people would have said that.'

Tilda thought again about her music teacher, about Shane, about singing your own song unashamedly. 'I love dragons. Always have. I've got a vintage set of tea cups with dragons for handles.' She turned to the glass cabinet above the sink. 'I mean...'

Milo nodded. 'The set is hidden from me. It's okay. I get it. You were saying?'

'I was obsessed with the movie *Eragon* when I was ten, *How to Train Your Dragon* in my teens, have always loved *Dragonheart*...'

'What about Falkor, The Luck Dragon, in *The NeverEnding Story*?' he asked.

'Yes!'

'Have you read all the *Eragon* books? Utterly brilliant.'

'Wait... so you're a dragon fan, too?' she asked.

'Yep. A fantasy buff – despite the ribbing I've always got from my mates, although they almost got it when *Game of Thrones* briefly took over the world. Netflix just keeps giving. *Shadow and Bone*, *The Umbrella Academy*...'

'What about *Sweet Tooth*?'

'Love it. Any book by Neil Gaiman, too, or Stephen King...'

'Pratchett, Tolkien...' she added.

'That painting of yours caught my attention – a lovely garden at first sight, but it had fairies in it, right?' Suddenly exhausted, Milo sat in silence until the coughing came back.

As he walked out of the room, to head upstairs to bed, Tilda took out the ring and studied it once more. In Chinese culture dragons symbolised good luck, were seen as friendly, as positive in the East, as wise creatures – unlike in the West where they represented evil and destruction. She held up the gem in the sunlight coming through the window and tried to work out which of the two beliefs applied to Milo.

6

After a sticky night, Tilda woke up at seven on Wednesday morning. Before doing anything else, she checked WhatsApp for the latest message.

> Sorry chère Tilda for sending this dinner photo so late. I had to work all hours on altering a jacket for my imminent show. I need to get every detail right, I'm hoping this new collection takes my reputation further. Hence the baked beans on toast for dinner. Good night. Yves xxxxx

She sat more upright. In the early hours he'd sent another message.

> Tilda, ma mie, I cannot sleep. What a shock I had yesterday. I didn't want to worry you about it, but you have such a kind heart, are such a good listener. My sister, Beatrice, rang. She's in trouble again and owes two thousand euros to a cartel that will harm her if she doesn't pay by July. I've put everything into my new show that, for certain, will triumph, but right at this moment, in Beatrice's hour of need, my cash flow is non-existent. It's all tied up in the business. We have no parents, no other siblings, I am the only hope she has of raising the money. Eh bien, but this is my problem. Sorry for indulging myself but

it is good to talk. To get it... off my chest, as the English say. Give little Dettol a hug from her friend, Yves. That stray cat sneaked in again last night. I'm sure he has adopted me. I... I don't know why. I'm not always a good person. Yves xxxxx

He'd sent a photo of the ginger cat that sat on a windowsill. Tilda narrowed her eyes, looking at the street outside in the background, noting how French lampposts looked exactly like English ones. He'd called her *ma mie* and Tilda looked up the translation. *Mie* was the soft, fluffy part of a loaf of bread. Funny that. Nice. Most people would probably have compared Tilda to the hard crust.

She sat cross-legged on the floor and did ten minutes of meditation. Thoughts about Yves' sister kept intruding. He'd talked before of Beatrice's drug problems. The words of the latest message ran through her head. Yves was such a mixture of glamour and simplicity, of confidence and low self-esteem. His good heart shone from the screen. Success as a fashion designer could have made him act arrogantly, but instead Yves always spoke as if he was an ordinary Joe Bloggs from up the street. No doubt, his neighbour's cat was a sound judge of character, like Dettol, who had never warmed to Shane. Her ears would go flat on the rare occasion he tried to stroke her back.

Tilda took a cold shower, brushed her hair, and then changed into brown trousers and a slate grey blouse. She applied her favourite scent. At seven thirty precisely she arrived in the kitchen. Indignant meowing floated in from the utility room. She let Dettol into the kitchen and tipped cat food into a bowl. Twenty to eight and it was time for Tilda's breakfast, cereal flakes with fruit, five walnut halves, a small handful of raisins and two tablespoons of...

Ah. She'd better check on the invalid's appetite first. Dettol disappeared out of the kitchen, tail erect, as if leading the way. Yesterday and the day before Milo had mainly had to stay in bed, although he could now stomach more food and had eaten toast with more soup at the kitchen table last night. He'd made a joke but with dark rings under his eyes, and a sore throat that still made his words come out raspy. Tilda said he could stay one more night, even though she couldn't wait to get her home back

to herself. Tilda knocked on the spare room door and went in. Dettol
jumped on the bed. She tensed up, waiting for him to react, to assume he
was in a hostel or on the street and being attacked. Instead, his hand
reached for Dettol's head. Milo yawned, eyes still closed.

'How's my favourite girl?' he whispered.

Dettol purred her response, like Eartha Kitt rolling her Rs.

Embarrassed for both of them, Tilda cleared her throat.

'Oh, I didn't realise we weren't alone.' He shuffled up and brushed his
hair out of his eyes and yawned again.

'How are you today?'

'My throat's stopped hurting and I hardly coughed last night.'

She moved forwards and pressed her hand against his forehead. 'Your
temperature has gone.'

He took a tissue from the box next to his bed and blew his nose. 'I'll
take that shower now, if that's all right?'

'Of course. I'll leave clean clothes in here for you... What would you
like for breakfast? Before you leave.' She shot him a pointed look. 'Cereal?
Toast? Tea or orange juice?'

Dettol walked up his chest and butted Milo's chin. He buried his face
in the fur for a second. Finally, he emerged. 'I'm so grateful for anything,'
he said, in a full voice. 'Whatever's easiest. You've been a superstar. Thank
you, thank you.'

'Flattery will get you nowhere,' she said sharply.

Milo cocked his head.

'Breakfast will be on the table in twenty minutes – and then I need to
get on with work.' She left as quickly as she could and stood in her
garden, for a few minutes, to enjoy the early birdsong, the peace. A black-
bird hopped across the grass, and cocked its head, like Milo had, except
this creature was listening for worms. Small moments like this meant the
world, with the early sun warming her face, her lost in the smells and
noises of nature, a brief escape from other people's expectations. Animals,
plants, the elements, they simply took Tilda at face value.

To her surprise, Milo did indeed appear twenty minutes later, washed,
showered and packed. He'd shaved again and combed back his clean hair.
He looked good in the cheap white T-shirt she'd bought him from the

market. Good as in clean, healthy, that's what Tilda meant – not how it emphasised the firm chest and strong jawline, the brown depths of his eyes that must be hiding so many stories after the last few months. He buttered a slice of toast and slathered jam on top. They ate in silence as Tilda consulted her business phone, skimming through messages from employees and clients. The lack of conversation between them felt unexpectedly comfortable. When he'd finished, Milo pushed away his plate and sipped his coffee. He'd spotted a jar by the kettle and had asked if he could have it instead of tea.

'Right. I'll be off in a minute. Would you like me to wash up first?'

This was new. Shane had never once offered. Not that she was comparing Milo to a love interest, no, Shane was simply the only person who'd been in her house before him, for any length of time. In retrospect Tilda didn't understand why she'd put up with his selfish behaviour. Their split made her realise their relationship had been over weeks before, but she'd kept playing the part of a woman with a boyfriend, telling herself everyone had a partner, that there was something wrong with being single.

Shane made her realise the really wrong thing was putting yourself second to a dickhead who judged instead of celebrating differences.

'No, it's fine. I'll do it. But... thanks,' Tilda replied.

'One question before I go,' said Milo. 'I mean, I've nothing to lose from being nosey. We won't see each other again as I'm moving on, from this street, in case those thugs come back.'

Great news. Couldn't be better. The last thing Tilda needed was him bothering her again. Yet how would he manage next? She chided herself for being remotely invested after such a short time.

'You didn't like me calling you a superstar, even though you've shone a light on my life, these last few days, so I'd like to know—'

'Milo. Let me make this easy for you to understand – whatever you say, you can't stay any longer.'

'There you go again. Why reject a compliment? What – who – has caused you to act like that?'

'No idea what you're talking about...' she said and her cheek twitched.

'Nothing to lose, Tilda. I'm out of your life in ten minutes. Go on, tell me... I'm curious.'

He was right. Milo was a stranger, about to disappear into thin air. What was she so afraid of? Opening up wouldn't make her vulnerable. He wouldn't be staying around to take advantage.

'Okay. Then I get to ask you a question back. Deal?'

He stretched out his arm to shake her hand, but Tilda folded hers. 'Here's your answer... First off, my mum – Dad died when I was nine – even though I didn't want to go, she said I was worth the expense of boarding school, because "you're bright and will blossom there". Years later, I realised that flattery was nothing but bullshit to get rid of me, so she could focus on my brother.' Tilda winced, as if she'd tasted cleaning fluid. 'Secondly, my last boyfriend. Well, my first, that is. I mean, I've never dated anyone that long before. Almost a year. Anyway...' Her cheeks burnt. 'Shane told me I was beautiful. Not before our drunken one-night stand. Nor the morning after. But a couple of days later, after he'd found out something about my life that interested him more than me. I shouldn't have believed him, given that his previous girlfriend was a glamorous flight attendant.'

'But Tilda, you—'

'Please don't patronise me,' she said and ran a hand through her black hair. 'I know what I am. The girls in my dorm called me Wednesday from *The Addams Family*.'

A pained look crossed his face. His chest must still have been aching from days of coughing.

'What was it Shane found out about you?'

'That's two questions,' she said sharply.

'Apologies. I should have explained. My question has parts a and b.' He raised one eyebrow, waggled it slowly. Under any other circumstances she'd have found that funny.

'Fine. That my brother plays for a League One side – Bolton Wanderers. According to Shane, Manchester United were sniffing around him though.' Thinking about the glee on Shane's face when he'd found out about her brother, how he'd come alive in a way he hadn't just being with Tilda, made her want to overindulge in a way she never allowed herself these days: dancing away her worries, half-price shot in hand, before heading to a kebab shop and then sleeping in late, the life of a twenty-something-year-old she'd given up in order to reach her goals.

'Wow...'

'Not surprised you're impressed too, everyone in Manchester drinks and pees football.'

'No. Not much of a football fan here, never been to a game, but wow... that Shane sounds like a right jerk.'

There it was again, Milo, really listening.

'Now it's time for my question,' she said. Tilda put her palms on the table. 'Why are you self-sabotaging?'

Milo put down his mug. He'd not put it on the coaster she'd put out. Tilda picked it up and placed it on one.

'Huh?' he said, not meeting her eye. 'You talk as if I wanted to lose a good job, a great flat, no one would willingly mess that up on purpose.'

'But here you are.' She waved her hand in the air. 'I'm not saying it's a conscious thing but you must be aware, on some level, why you didn't value yourself enough to keep those things.'

His jaw dropped.

'Come on. A deal's a deal.'

Milo stuttered. 'I... I did a bad thing. A long time ago.' Milo's chair scraped back, he got to his feet.

'Part b of my question,' she blurted out, wishing she hadn't but determined to keep things equal between them. 'That photo frame in your bag – it flew out when I was removing your clothes. Is this bad thing you did to do with your daughter?'

Tilda didn't see Milo catch his breath as her phone rang and she answered.

'Oh, great, that's all I need,' she muttered when the call ended.

'What's up?' he said, recovering a little, the colour having returned to his cheeks as he bent down to give Dettol a goodbye stroke.

'Jazz, one of my workers, now *she's* come down with this summer flu. She and Iris clean a large office in Stockport every evening. I've been covering Iris's shift until she gets better, because she's been off with the same bug. The last couple of days with you here, I persuaded one of the others to join Jazz but they can't do it from today. It's a two-person job and I'll never find someone in time for tonight. Guess I'll be burning the midnight oil.' She sighed and reached into her jean pocket. She pulled out the ring and handed it to Milo. 'Now that you are leaving, you'll need this.'

He shook his head. 'That's for you. A thanks for letting me stay.'

Its iridescent colours, its dragon egg shape, captivated Tilda. It would have been easy to agree with Milo but that wouldn't be fair. 'I read a book once. The main character, a young girl, was abandoned in a forest and left starving. She found a dragon egg and had no choice but to eat it or die. She became immortal.'

'*The Dragon Within*? Yeah, loved that story!'

'You've read it too?'

Milo nodded.

'How about that halfway twist when she met the dragon that had laid that egg,' said Tilda, eyes flickering with enthusiasm, 'I couldn't turn the pages quickly enough to find out what happened next. The dragon smelt the girl and accepted her as one of its own. Such a heartwarming story.'

Milo put down his rucksack. 'The girl ended up saving one of the dragon's other young – as if she were paying a debt. It's like you helping me to get better. That's done. But now let me help you.'

'What?' Lines appeared on Tilda's forehead.

'I can clean. I'm not doing anything tonight.'

'You? Work alongside me?' But anyone else would say he was still practically a stranger. A stranger who'd spent five nights at her house.

'Why not? Then I'll head off in the morning. All I ask for is another shower and breakfast.' He took out his phone. 'Today is an opportunity to line up an interview for tomorrow where I could turn up after a wash and shave, and in these new clothes you got me, before they get worn and grubby again.' He picked up Dettol and scratched her head. 'And I promise not to mention your brother.'

Dettol lay on his lap and bared her stomach for a tickle. The stomach was a cat's most vulnerable area, yet she was willing to expose it to Milo.

'Okay... but I'll need the number of this nightclub you worked at. I'll ring up and check your credentials.' Or rather speak to Milo's boss and check out his story for leaving; to get a sense of the man who wanted to stay in her house for another twenty-four hours. Tilda always risk-assessed the premises of new clients she took on, to protect her staff. Risk-assessing Milo, to protect herself, was no different.

'Ring my last employer? Right. Of course.' A flush swept up his neck, as if he'd got a fever again.

'If it comes up, are you happy for me to mention your situation these last few weeks?'

Milo rubbed his forehead. 'You really do cover all the bases, don't you? Yes. I guess so. As long as you realise... I was a bit of mess when I walked out. I let my boss down, I admit it. But I had worked there for four years, worked my way up from barman to the top.'

She reached across the table for the notepad and pen and pushed it towards him, ignoring a sudden urge to squeeze his fingers – a gesture from someone who had once hit a rock bottom too, and understood the challenges that came with getting back on track.

'It's called Shakers. In Wilmslow.' He scribbled down the number.

'Wilmslow? Very nice.'

'For sure, talk about high-end, it's all flash cars and white teeth. Swanky shops too and a great park. If I hadn't been offered a room above the nightclub I could never have afforded to live there. Its poshness made the job easier. The locals are more worried about what they look like, than someone looking at them to pick a fight. Despite the occasional pompous ass who'll ask for an obscure garnish on their drink, like edible flowers, they're polite and up for a laugh.'

She pulled the notebook towards her and jiggled it from side to side, until it lay on the table in front of her perfectly straight. 'One other thing. You must promise not to give me a compliment again.'

Milo gave a small smile. 'Deal. Such a self-assured, successful person as you doesn't need them anyway.'

7

Tilda suggested Milo settle in the lounge to do his job applications. Dettol followed him. She closed the kitchen door and tidied away the breakfast things, wiped down the table and pulled out two portions of dinner from the freezer, for when they got back tonight. Tilda was a batch cooker and stuck to a rota. Wednesday was cottage pie. After shooing a fly out of the utility room door, into the garden that buzzed and fluttered with bees and Red Admirals, she settled at the table, in front of her laptop and rang Shakers' number. A bartender picked up and she passed Tilda onto the owner who introduced himself as Kofi.

'Hello. My name's Tilda Wright. I'm ringing about Milo...' Tilda dug her pen into the notepad. She hated being unprepared and strained to picture his driving license she'd had a quick glimpse of... yes, that was it: 'Milo Campbell. I own a cleaning business and he is... helping out. This isn't the usual procedure, but I'm time-pressed. Could you possibly give me a verbal reference?'

'Milo? He's got a job?' Relief dripped down the line.

'Sort of. Tonight would be his first shift. He's been ill, you see, and...'

The man didn't speak for a moment. 'You know him quite well?'

'No. I mean... I've... it's complicated.'

'Right. Is he still in the Wilmslow area?'

Both Kofi and Tilda were avoiding the obvious. This was unlike the Tilda who'd even been forthright during her childhood, telling her mum how truly bad boarding school was – or trying to, at least, despite knowing she'd not take her daughter seriously and would say Tilda should be grateful for opportunities her mother had never had. Tilda gave up in the end. Dad would have listened, made Mum listen too. During those teen years she'd never felt more alone.

Tilda cleared her throat. 'Milo's been sleeping rough but he stayed with me in Crouchden whilst he got over a bout of flu. Is he trustworthy?'

Kofi let out a low whistle. 'Poor sod. Last I heard he was sofa-surfing at mates' houses, one of them in Reddish. Milo's a good guy. Sure he's got his demons and I tried to get him the support he needed but, in the end, there was no helping him. It happened so quickly.'

'Could you be more specific?' she asked.

Silence filled the line. 'I'm not comfortable discussing this. It's personal to him and doesn't reflect the man I grew to like and yes, trust. All I'll say is, when on top of his game, Milo's a diamond employee and was for almost four years. He got in early, was the first to clean the toilets if someone threw up, he made the team feel like a family. However, in his last month with us, everything fell apart and I had no choice but to let him go – for his sake more than anyone else's.' He paused. Tilda didn't speak, taking in every word. 'Oddly it started when he watched some TV talent show and... I don't understand what happened, but if anyone deserves another chance it's him.' A voice shouted in the background. 'Coming!' Kofi replied. 'Sorry. Got to go. Damn washing machine's leaking again. Milo always knew how to fix it. Give him my best.' The line went dead.

This Kofi still had faith in Milo even though he'd fired him.

The kitchen door opened. Milo looking sheepish. 'I hate to ask but could I make myself a coffee? It's such a luxury to have everything at hand. I want to make the most of it before I leave tomorrow.'

'Of course.' Even though they weren't to her taste, Tilda had coffee and sugar for the guests she never invited in.

He shook the kettle at her. 'Green tea for you, yes?'

'Thanks.' Shane never got that right. Eventually she gave up and would force down the lattes he'd order for her when they were out.

'I've just spoken to Kofi,' she said.

Milo fixed his gaze on the fridge's handle.

'He sang your praises. Didn't say much about why you left, just something about a TV talent show...' Milo flinched as he pulled opened the fridge door. '...he said everything fell apart after that.'

Milo turned around jumpily, as if he'd already drunk too much caffeine. 'Right. Cheers for being transparent. Kofi was great to work for and he didn't judge. When things got... challenging, he did his best to sort me out.'

'But that's never going to work. *You've* got to want to put in the effort.'

He gave her a curious look.

'I've mentioned my parents and school to you,' she said. 'No one else was going to help me make something of my life.'

'Who did then?'

'More like a *what*. I suffered a...' She hadn't talked about this, not even to Shane. But Milo wasn't staying in her life, he was passing through, that must have been why she found it so easy to talk to him. '...a traumatic brush with death that made me reassess my life.'

Milo hung on her every word.

'Up until then I'd simply taken on temporary jobs, partly to spite my mum. It came to a head, once. A phone call though Facebook, I hadn't given her my address or phone number. She asked me to go home for my twenty-first birthday, Logan couldn't make it. I hoped she was going to treat me differently, the two of us getting to know each other as adults and not talk of five-year plans and ambitions. But after a meal she'd had caterers prepare – seafood, her favourite – Mum always forgot I wasn't a fan – she said she hadn't sent me to an expensive school to end up cleaning up after other people.' Tilda cleared her throat. 'Sorry. Rambling.'

'No... carry on,' he said.

'Mum wouldn't budge from her dim view about the work I'd chosen, so I called out her lies, told her what job I did was irrelevant, because I knew the only reason she'd sent me to boarding school was to give her the space to focus on Logan. We've not spoken since.' Tilda put down the phone. 'Anyway, the near-accident I had brought the realisation that, actually, I took great pride in cleaning and loved the flexibility and working in different locations, that life wasn't about living to spite people who'd hurt you. It was about living your best life, in spite *of* them. That's when I set up my own business.'

'You did it on your own, with no support from friends?'

'I became a loner during my teenage years. That made life easy. Guess I've stuck in that groove and I'm fine with that.' Tilda felt herself opening up even more. Was it because Milo had lost everything and she didn't feel she had to impress? She studied his face, the attention he gave her, without interruptions, smirks or yawns. No, it was more than that.

She breathed in the aroma of coffee, breathed in the difference, and it hit her: Tilda would miss the presence of this man who'd wandered into her life... Or rather had been guided that way, by a cat.

'My mates have been lifesavers in recent months,' he said. 'Even when I could tell I'd overstayed my welcome on their sofa, they always tried to insist I stay.'

'But you chose not to.'

'Friends don't take advantage of each other. That's why I'm happy to leave now if you'd rather me not help out tonight.'

'We're friends now?' Tilda teased, surprised at herself.

'In my world... yes.'

Stupid, him saying that shouldn't have meant as much as it did. Though perhaps that's why she kept on messaging Yves, who called her a cauliflower and sent her kisses – any degree of intimacy felt alien, yet compelling.

'We leave at five,' she said and picked up the phone again, busying herself with scrolling emails. 'We should get to the office around six and the job should take two hours with both of us. We'll be back here by nine for dinner.'

Kettle switched on, Milo sat down at the table. 'Thanks Tilda. It's a while since I've had a date.' His eyes twinkled.

Tilda had forced herself to go on many in the last year, since Shane, usually in pubs and restaurants. Apart from the dates with Yves. They'd only been online. He hadn't messaged yesterday which was unusual. She'd checked WhatsApp this morning and went in again now.

> Chère Tilda, sorry I didn't get in touch last night. Really worried about my sister. I'm trying to see if I can borrow two thousand euros from someone reliable. I'd be able to pay it back, with interest next month, after my show. Anyway, enough about me, mon rayon de soleil. Here is a photo of my ginger friend. I didn't know cats liked potato peelings. Yves xxxxx

Tilda smiled at the photo of the cat, on a kitchen unit, eating scraps. A copy of *The Times* lay next to him. That would explain why Yves' English was so good. She googled *mon rayon de soleil*... Yves had called her a ray of sunshine. Tilda looked up and Milo was studying her curiously. She blushed and put the phone down.

'It's even longer since I had a Valentine's Day date,' he said. 'Not complaining, talk about pressure.' Sun rays streaming through the window danced in his eyes. 'I bet you've got some vivid memories of previous ones. I certainly have. Come on, spill. Worst Valentine's Day dates ever. Let's compare.'

'I'm not sure I've been on that many. Often it's just been dinner for one, at home.'

His eyebrows raised. 'I'm surprised. Okay. First dates in general then.'

The dates she'd had in recent months added up to more than she'd been on, in the whole of her life, previous to that. Tilda pulled a face. 'Must I?'

Milo's whole face lit up as he grinned, so different from the man she'd found beaten up on the street. It made her feel good in a way she often didn't.

She sieved through the embarrassing memories and the nights out that left her disheartened. 'You won't beat this one. My date brought his parents. He'd never had a long-term girlfriend. It had been a dream of his to double-date with them.'

'Christ, talk about setting the bar high,' said Milo and he burst out laughing. Rich and warm, his laughter bounced off the walls, creating an energy Tilda hadn't enjoyed in so long. She laughed too. It was good to joke about the disaster that had been her dating life, this last year.

'Okay...' he said. 'On one of mine, my date's hair caught fire. She leant forward to speak and it got caught in a candle.'

'Wow. Was she okay?'

'After I threw a tumbler of water in her face to put it out.'

'You didn't! Wasn't that a bit drastic?'

His voice wavered. 'Probably was but... I let someone down in the past – the bad thing I've spoken about – that happened because of me. Ever since I've been determined that no one would ever get hurt, not when I was around.' As Tilda found her chest pinching, he got up and made the drinks, then sat down again.

'My turn again,' she said, warming to the subject. 'Another date did a runner minutes before the bill arrived. Full story: six months ago, I took on a new cleaner who said straight off I'd be a perfect match for her brother. She wouldn't let it go. Normally I wouldn't engage on any personal level with an employee or their family, but I decided I had nothing to lose by meeting him. Turns out I did. The price of his food. He was an accountant. I should have guessed he'd grab an opportunity to save money.'

'What a loser – but I can still beat that. One date ordered a salad but then ate my chips.'

'Unforgiveable,' said Tilda gravely, chuckling inside. For a second Tilda forgot that Milo was homeless, a rough sleeper. Goodness knows three years ago when her life crashed big time, it could have been Tilda keeping the pavement warm, and an employed, productive Milo walking past. She'd borne that in mind, the last few days. Because he was down on his luck, didn't mean Milo was some miscreant.

'Another guy went to the toilet halfway through and never came back. He messaged me later to say I was quieter in person, than online.'

'Another loser.' Milo shook his head.

'I kind of get it. It's not something I'd do, but I guess there's no point hanging around if it's not working.'

'There's every point,' said Milo, face red. 'What about manners and consideration for the other person? Of course not every first date is going to work out, that's to be expected, but you don't up and leave without saying goodbye. You deserve better than that.'

Tilda shuffled and sat a little taller. Shane was always complaining she didn't talk enough, preferring to read or watch her fantasy series, or to cook. Therefore she did what any twenty-first century woman would do – well, one who didn't talk to her mother, have a sister, a best friend, real or made from AI – and she googled why this might have bothered him. The advice from the screen was that her partner was seeking reassurance in their life and felt unappreciated. She'd always asked Shane about his day, but she increased those efforts, even though his sales job didn't interest her. Tilda asked about his co-workers, complimented his outfits and thanked him profusely on the rare occasions he made breakfast at week-ends. It seemed to work, until it only highlighted how different they were. Shane rarely asked about her job or hobbies. On the day he ditched her, Shane called Tilda boring. She was by the fridge door, about to make an omelette, and had just refused, point blank, for the umpteenth time, to contact Logan. Shane had sneered that the only thing Tilda had going for her was her footballer brother, that running her own business made her act like someone in their forties, not twenties, going to bed early, never getting a hangover. He'd never liked the fact she earned more than him, even though one evening he'd asked and had then insisted on knowing. He'd sulked for the rest of the night.

'Then there were the dates too insignificant to remember,' she continued, 'and all the Saturday nights I've stayed in. Not that I'm complaining. I like my own company. My own space.'

She didn't tell him about her French friend and how her admirer seemed to have hopes he'd be the one to change her situation.

'Not me,' said Milo. 'I don't like to be left alone with too much time to go into my head.' A shadow crossed his face.

'Is this to do with your daughter?' she asked gently. 'Can I see her photo again? She looks lovely.'

Milo pushed his coffee away and stood up. 'I... I've changed my mind. This is a mistake, Tilda. I'm better off on the streets.'

She stood up too as he checked through his rucksack, went into the utility room and picked up the sleeping bag. His shoulders looked tense, the jaw set, his eyes empty of the laughter that they'd shared. For an almost indiscernible moment it was like looking in a mirror from years ago and Tilda covered her mouth.

He's protecting himself.

He is.

From truths.

From his truth, whatever that is.

Like Tilda used to, before the accident that gave her clarity. As she'd discovered, you could run all you liked but that only meant there was never an end point to the despair. Oh, she wouldn't forget her mum's rejection, she'd never forget being parted from her brother, but Tilda had proper roots of her own now, a job she loved – a purpose that had changed everything.

Her mind raced as Milo tied his laces. She couldn't. She could. She shouldn't.

She should.

He went to the side door and glanced back. Tilda had followed him into the utility room. Tilda held out her hand and he went to shake it. Instead, she gripped his fingers tightly and pulled him back into the kitchen.

'No. You aren't running. Not any more. Not on my watch. If you work well on this job tonight then how about I take you on temporarily, at least until I'm back up to my usual quota of staff? I'll keep half your earnings to cover food and rent. I'll draw up house rules.'

'What? But you... you don't know me,' Milo stammered.

A lump formed in her throat. She did. Better than he could ever imagine.

'I did a terrible thing,' he continued. 'I don't deserve this.'

'Rule number one,' she said as if she hadn't heard him. 'You must focus hard on what job you dream of, what future you want to build. Rule number two, no shoes in the house.'

He held her gaze for a few seconds and wiped his nose on his sleeve before a muffled sob escaped his lips. Milo bent down to undo his laces, encouraged by Dettol head-butting his ankles.

8

HOUSE RULES

No shoes indoors
Breakfast is at 7.40 a.m.
Evening meal rota:
Saturday – fajitas
Sunday – chicken roast
Monday – quiche and salad
Tuesday – risotto
Wednesday – cottage pie
Thursday – beef stew
Friday – fish and chips
We do our own laundry – me Saturday morning, you Saturday afternoon whilst I do the weekly shop
Don't leave possessions or clothes lying around
Lights out 11.30 p.m.
I feed Dettol
Speak up if something is bothering you
UNDER NO CIRCUMSTANCES go into my bedroom

Sitting on the train coming back from Stockport that night, Tilda emailed the list over to Milo, all neatly formatted. He'd been subdued but had proved himself to be a more than adept cleaner. The large office was carpeted so needed vacuuming, and the staffroom required a thorough clean every night, after a day of spilt coffees and splattered microwave meals, of sandwich crumbs and crisps tumbling beneath chairs. Milo happily cleaned the toilets, four cubicles, they shone when he'd finished. He'd polished the mirrors too, and refilled the soap dispensers, not things all of Tilda's new recruits took care over. That's why, regardless of their references, she'd always inspect the first job they did, and pass them notes afterwards. The two of them dusted worktops, emptied bins, and Tilda was especially industrious about wiping over those harbingers of germs, keyboards. Milo cleared away discarded takeaway coffee cups and straightened piles of paperwork. When they'd finished Tilda had put her hands on her hips, perspiration running down her back, wishing she was in shorts instead of trousers and the navy Wright Cleaners tunic, and breathed in the smell of disinfectant as if standing in the middle of a fragrant meadow.

The train passed through a station, a hen party on the platform, heading into Manchester no doubt, each member of the group dressed in Barbie-themed summer clothes, a throwback to last year's successful movie probably. Milo's phone vibrated and he tapped on the screen.

'You *were* serious about house rules,' he said.

'Of course. Order and routine, it's the only way to keep on top of life if you're self-employed.'

'Right...' he said uncertainly, and his eyes skimmed the page. 'You have breakfast at the same time each day, even weekends?'

Tilda simply nodded. After breaking up with Shane she made the decision never to apologise again for being herself, never to explain her little ways. To be more like her dear grandmother who unashamedly revelled in her uniqueness. She'd been widowed for years and lived in London, had lots of friends and a life Mum didn't approve of, with tarot card readings and séances. She also wrote romance novels, a career Tilda's mother had never taken seriously. However Dad was protective and proud of Gran's career and would give Mum a pointed look if she started to say something sarcastic. Growing up with a parent who successfully wrote about love had no doubt shaped Dad into the kind, giving man he was. What a welcome splash of colour Gran had been, with her scarves and kaftans, her storytelling, and compliments about the children's English work. Tilda's grandfather had worked in a bank, like Mum and Dad, but her grandmother earned a good living from writing and, in the end, as much as her husband. Despite this, Tilda's mother took every opportunity to refer to her writing as a hobby, unable to comprehend a career that hadn't required formal training.

'Don't you ever veer from the eating plan? No spontaneous pasta meal or pizza?'

'I batch cook. Everything is frozen and ready, apart from the weekend meals, fajitas and roast. It means I don't have to waste time brainstorming dinner each night.'

His eyes scanned the list further and a pool of light flickered in his eyes, his mouth curved upwards. 'A curfew?'

'I need my sleep. If I don't get that everything else falls apart. The lights out rule is important to me.'

'You don't want me to feed Dettol?'

'I don't want her getting overweight. Vets' bills are expensive.'

'Gotcha.' He consulted the screen again. 'I should speak up if there's a problem?'

'Yes. That was Dad's mantra. He was a fair man if I ever complained, and would explain why, say, I had to go to bed early on a school night but now and then would persuade Mum that it was okay to let me and Logan stay up late at the weekend. After he'd gone... he... he got cancer... it was quick in the end...' Tilda took a moment.

'I'm sorry to hear that,' said Milo gently.

'I tried to speak up with my mum, but she never really heard. With Logan I tried too, we were close when we were little, but often the rare holidays we spent together ended in the two of us having shouting matches. We were both teenagers, perhaps that's why. I gave up eventually. Nothing was going to change with them. However, the whole experience has left me believing, stronger than ever, that problems should be aired, otherwise resentment festers and nothing changes. I've made this clear to every cleaner I take on and I like to think communication is good as a result. It means it's easier for me to talk to them about client complaints and vice versa, if they're not happy with a job or the way I run things.'

Milo shook his head. 'Your life is so... so sorted Tilda. You're so on it, so clean-living. It's the opposite to mine. But... don't you ever want to break free from the routine? Stay up late Friday night? Leave the dishes until the morning?'

'No. I meditate. Go running. I cook from scratch. I keep my day-to-day personal life simple. Work is complicated enough.'

'Your bedroom...' He looked up. 'Tilda, I would never go in there without permission. It's locked anyway, right?'

'Glad to hear it,' she said, face tight.

Tilda glanced away, out of the window, able to see Milo's reflection and how he was studying her. It was none of his business as to why exactly the contents of her room were so very private. Conversation petered out until they were back at her house. Dettol greeted them, or rather Milo, by jumping onto his lap as soon as he sat at the kitchen table. Tilda made them each a long, cold cordial and they both knocked the drinks back in one.

'Would you like to eat outside?' she said. 'It's a lovely evening. There are two deckchairs in the shed and a small table. There's a torch in the cupboard to the right of the oven.'

'Say no more,' replied Milo and he grabbed the torch before disappearing into the garden. A few minutes he came back. 'Sure I can't help?' he asked as Tilda heated up the cottage pie and boiled a bag of pre-prepared vegetables.

'All done now,' she replied and passed him a plate. The two of them made their way outside, into the dusk, and sat on the deckchairs. The jasmine plant growing up the fencing had started to bloom the last few days, giving the back garden an extra beautiful quality with the delicate pale pink petals. Tilda used to nab a generous dab of her gran's jasmine perfume. Gran had taken up art in retirement and one time she visited, shortly before Tilda left for boarding school, she brought watercolour kits for the two children, planning to spend a morning painting with them.

However, Mum had said they'd make too much mess. The night before Gran left, Tilda and Logan, sitting on the stairs, in the dark, overheard the two of them row. Their grandmother said *both* children should live at home and go to school locally. Mum called her a hippy in that voice she used, where she was pretending to be joking, and said it was none of her business. Gran said something about a trust and not using her money for school fees. Her grandmother must have been making sure that Tilda and Logan had money of their own, to do with exactly what they wanted. Tilda glanced around the garden, mentally thanking her Gran for the money that had helped her buy her first home.

'Perhaps you could wash up afterwards?' she said, to Milo. 'I want to check some Facebook ads I've been running.'

'Tilda! It's almost nine o'clock. When do you switch off?'

'When I'm reading. Watching TV. But I'm always on the job. I've no one else to lean on. I need to plan for a decent pension, even though keeping up with rising mortgage costs is hard enough. There's always an incentive to work harder, work longer. I don't mind because I'm investing in me, not some boss who's paying their employees the minimum wage.' The two of them tucked into the cottage pie. Milo gave a gasp of pleasure at the first mouthful. Shane always complicated life's pleasures. A stroll in the park had to be selfie-filled, a trip to the coffee shop involved syrups and sprinkles. 'As for those rules, I may not have listed it, but I wasn't joking about the most important one being you planning your future. Do you want to stay in nightclub management?'

He shrugged. They ate in silence, whilst Dettol stretched out on the lawn, showing off her beautiful stripes. Raucous cheers passed by the tall fence and the gate, at the end, and revealed a group of lads in football shirts and jeans, with gelled hair and dog tag necklaces.

'When I nearly had a fatal accident three years ago, it made me take stock,' said Tilda. 'I needed to turn my life around – for me, no one else.'

'I don't deserve a happy future,' he muttered.

'Why not?' Tilda leant forwards. 'Stop running, Milo. Face things head on.'

He pursed his lips. 'What would you know about facing mistakes? You're the one who was wronged, by your family, they were the ones who made the mistakes. It's understandable that your life became hard but even then, you turned it around. I'm not like you Tilda.' He put down his plate and got up. Dettol stretched flirtatiously and he lay down on the grass and tickled the cat's ears. 'You had an accident, Tilda, that's not anyone's fault. Whereas I'm responsible for what happened in my life, the thing that led to me losing my job, that's led to the whole mess.'

'Why exactly did Kofi fire you?' Tilda leant forwards. 'Tell me, Milo.'

'You don't hold back, do you?'

Tilda didn't blink.

He sat up and crossed his legs, picked a long blade of grass and chewed on it. 'I became unreliable. Could have got him closed down. I served underage customers and mouthed off at regulars. I forgot to lock up, once, and almost got into a fight.'

'But why?' she persisted. 'Were you having a mental breakdown? Is that why Kofi's so full of sympathy? What did a TV talent show have to do with it?'

'I'd rather not talk about it, if you don't mind. It's in the past now...'

She got up and went indoors to fetch her laptop, returning a few minutes later.

'Are you sure you want me to stay?' he muttered when she got back. 'I'm only causing you trouble.'

'Wow. This is one big pity party you're having,' she said. 'That won't help either.'

He got to his feet. 'I'm no match for you, with your perfectly run life and professional success, a woman who's emerged victorious from adversity...'

'You make my life sound so easy. I had pity parties too, throughout the teenage years and my early twenties. What a waste of time.'

Milo clenched his jaw, walked past her, the side door creaked open.

'Maybe I see myself in you,' she muttered.

Footsteps came back. He stood in front of her. 'I doubt it.'

'Why?'

'You and I have *nothing* in common.'

'Try me. Go on. Be honest about why your life fell apart. Prove me wrong,' she said, baiting him.

Milo curled his fists. 'Okay.' He took a deep breath. 'I've had a drink problem. For most of my adult life.'

Tilda didn't flinch.

'I haven't touched the stuff for five years but came oh so close when... when that TV show brought back terrible memories. That's why everything went wrong at the club. The chaos came back. It was as if I was dry drunk, that selfish, using, personality taking over me, even though I hadn't had so much as one sip of alcohol. I lost my job, my home, my savings, my health. My sanity too. Once again, my whole life's become a shitshow.' He threw his hands in the air. 'Still reckon we've got stuff in common?'

Still no reaction.

'But I've managed to stay off the booze.'

'What, on your own?'

'You don't seem shocked – about my problem.'

'I worked it out. You just needed a little... encouragement to say it out loud.'

He gasped. 'Get some kick out of it, do you, seeing others down? Is that why you invited me in that night?' he said, pacing the lawn, almost tripping over Dettol who was stalking a shadow. 'I can't work alongside you. Not now.'

'Why not?'

'I think poorly enough of myself. Other people's low opinions, on top, will tip me over the edge. The last thing I want is to drink again.'

'Then don't.'

'Like it's that easy.'

'No.'

'Too right. It's the hardest thing I've ever done.'

'I know.'

He ran a hand in the air, across her house, the sparkling windows, the perfectly square lawn. 'How would you know what it's like for your life to turn into a train wreck?'

Tilda opened her laptop and logged on. 'Because I'm three years sober myself.'

9

Milo stopped dead as a bat swooped over the roof, light from the utility room acting like a lit candle in a restaurant. 'What?'

She met his gaze. 'I get it. The self-loathing, the selfish, risky, offensive, damaging behaviour. The fuck-it button looming large and being unable to stop yourself pressing it.'

He collapsed heavily into his deckchair and it squeaked its protest. Dettol lifted her head and yawned. She strutted across the lawn and jumped onto his lap. 'Nah, I don't believe it, you're joking. Wow. That's some kind of warped humour you've got – taking the piss as a way of helping.'

'Do I strike you as someone with an outlandishly funny side to them? Actually, don't answer that.'

That first year of being sent away to board, young Tilda had suffered a big argument with her mum, not wanting to go, and then also being sent away to summer school. She'd only got through the final term by dreaming of being back in her own bedroom. Mum had snapped and asked why Tilda had to be so miserable, said school holidays had been so boring when *she* was little, said that Tilda should have been grateful for the weeks of planned activities – and that her daughter was completely devoid of a sense of fun and good humour. Tilda had spoken about her unhappiness to her brother, Logan, but he didn't understand either; said he was envious of the fun she'd have. Easy for him to say, when he was spending July and August honing his football skills, in other words doing the one thing he loved most.

Milo studied the tidy garden and peered into the neat utility room. He gazed at Tilda. 'Of course. All this order, the routines… it's your way of keeping sober, isn't it?'

'What if it is?'

'But that's no life – never experiencing spontaneity.'

She turned to him and folded her arms. 'Ending up on the streets and getting beaten up is? No thanks. I'll stick to my methods. I've tasted spontaneity,' she said. 'Didn't like it much. Me turning up late for work, telling a manager to eff off, having sex with a random cleaning colleague in a stockroom, eating leftover pizza out of the bin because I'd got nothing else in. As for the blackouts, I worked two days on a job once, deep cleaning a big, fancy house, and had no memory of it. However, my temping colleagues did. How I'd refused to work with the team and rummaged through the owners' private things, trying on clothes, raiding the fridge.' Her voice was matter of fact, like she was back in group therapy where nothing shocked the others. Milo wouldn't be shocked either. Fellow addicts, despite their faults, were the least judgemental people on the planet.

'You *do* get it,' Milo murmured and shook his head, as he scratched behind Dettol's ears. 'What treatment did you have?'

'Twelve weeks of group therapy, as a day patient in an addiction clinic, followed by twelve weekly sessions at a wellbeing centre, where I had one-to-one therapy and learnt about meditation, about healthy eating, about mindfulness, Buddhism and anger management. It made me aware that part of the reason I got drunk was because my mum wouldn't have approved.' Cheap wine had been her go-to, her mum would have found her choice of label more offensive than her throwing up in the toilet basin. In her bedsit, in private, she'd considered herself to be a civilised drinker, on the sofa with a packet of crisps, watching TV until she fell asleep. Civilised that is, until she woke up and dragged herself to bed in the early hours, hearing voices that weren't there, becoming paranoid about every shadow. Group therapy provided a large dose of enlighten-ment, how there was nothing civilised about the way she behaved at home either, doing so little cleaning that rats appeared, wetting herself during a night time blackout.

'How many AA meetings do you go to a week?' he asked.

Tilda visibly recoiled. 'None. Never been. Trust myself to a higher power? You've got to be kidding. No one's ever looked out for me apart from myself. Being an atheist is practically the only thing I have in common with my mother.'

'But a higher power doesn't have to be God. It can be...'

'I've heard all the arguments. It can be the power of the group or your own idea of some creator – like Mother Nature.' She rolled her eyes. 'As for that touchy-feely hugging and sharing... it's enough listening to my own insidious voices in my head, still telling me to drink, let alone hearing about everyone else's, week in, week out. I got enough of that in treatment.'

'You truly think it's like that?'

'Yep. The addiction clinic did their best to persuade me to go, but the structure of my daily routine is the only support I require. We're not all the same,' she said.

'True,' he said, uncertainly. 'Whatever works for you.' He tilted his head. 'You've never had any faith? Never believed in anything?'

Tilda pursed her lips. When she was little, yes. Tilda believed in doing good, in angels and heaven. Dad and her gran talked about the impor-tance of helping those less fortunate, of kindness, and her father demon-strated that belief through his actions, mowing the lawn for a widowed, elderly neighbour during the summer, always donating to charity boxes, whereas Mum would walk straight past them... but after Dad died, trying to do the right thing, trying to please her mum and failing, it never brought Tilda any happiness. By the time she went to high school, the only thing she had faith in was her relationship with Logan, but then that faltered too.

'What about you?' She unfolded her arms. 'Did AA get you sober at first?'

'No. Four weeks in rehab did. I spent my entire savings, I was so desperate to get off the hamster wheel of waking up each day, promising myself I'd not drink, believing it until the physical cravings kicked in or something irritated or stressed me. As soon as I left the clinic I attended AA several times a week.' He talked about the friends he'd made, how after a couple of months he'd do service and turn up early to help set up, make the drinks, put out biscuits, clear up afterwards.

'Has AA helped keep you on track recently?'

Milo's cheeks burnt red as claret. 'Kind of. I've gone to the occasional meeting in the city centre, when I can afford the bus fare. I miss my old local one, but it is what it is.'

'Why go out of area?'

'Can't face going back to my usual meetings and fessing up that I've lost everything again. I didn't feel so anonymous once I became a regular, and that was great, to be part of something... but it's hard now I've stumbled. I'm less visible at the bigger meetings.'

Tilda took out her phone and tapped into it. 'I'll send you an updated version of my house rules. Right at the top will be "attend a local AA group here twice a week, if you want to stay".'

Milo gasped. 'Talk about hypocritical. You don't go! And I'd rather sleep outside than go to a smaller meeting and risk bumping into someone I know.'

'I'm not prepared to take any risk and share my house with someone who might, at some point, on a whim, bring in alcohol,' she said, more coolly than she felt. The last thing she needed in her life was a relapsing alcoholic. Nor was she prepared to take a risk with someone else's struggles, someone who'd had it tough, like she had, and needed a push to get back onto the right path. What's more, someone who made her laugh, with whom silence was comfortable. Someone with whom she didn't need to be *on stage* all the time.

Milo was... different.

'Come on,' she said, more gently. 'Most of the people in those meetings will have slipped at some point and it's not as if you're actually drinking. If you don't go back now, what's your Plan B, to stop the worst happening?'

'I could give your routine a go, as a safeguard, but honestly, I'm rock solid. I didn't even consider drinking to keep warm, when the nights outside got cold. But no harm in giving your methods a try, if that keeps you happy.'

'You're serious?'

'I mean...'

'I dare you!' She got up and beamed. 'You may as well start now. Let's go in and have a green tea. No coffee for you either, from now on,' she said, airily. 'I'll meet you in the lounge at 7 a.m. sharp for meditation, tomorrow. We'll fit in a mindfulness session at lunch. Then after dinner we could rearrange my crockery cupboards and—'

Milo tapped into his phone, must have been taking notes. Finally, he looked up. 'I've found an AA meeting in a church, the other side of Crouchden. Midday sharp, some of my friends from the other meetings used to go to it. I'll be there.'

Tilda couldn't help giving a small smile. Her plan had worked to get him back to his support system. Clearly Milo wasn't driven by a compulsion to rise to dares, whereas it always had been a mistake to dare Tilda. Like the time Logan told her to wave to strangers from the back of the car and point to their front wheels with a worried face. More than once the driver had pulled over. How he'd dared her to knock on the door of the creepy neighbour, a man who always scowled and got his dog to chase cold callers. Like how Mum told Tilda she'd never amount to anything without going to university. She showed her – eventually. Her smile slipped as she thought back to the night she and Shane broke up and his dare had led to her secret project, the deadline of which was now just three weeks away...

'You're a joke! A born spinster! If I gave you fifty years you'd never find a big enough loser to marry you.' He'd snorted with laughter. 'I dare you to try.'

She'd thought: I'll show him.

That sticky July day, she'd invited him over, fearing his reaction in public. They'd sat in the lounge and she started the speech she'd prepared. His incredulous face had almost made her laugh.

'*You're* breaking up with *me*?' Anger had ripped through his body, insults flying, saying how no one would blame him for being keener to spend time with a footballer instead of a deadbeat cleaner.

It was the closest she'd come to loving Dettol in their months together. To Tilda's surprise the cat had stalked into the lounge and sat at Shane's feet and glared up at him. Her hiss said, *I always knew you were a twat.* That night was the only time Tilda had ever roasted her a chicken breast.

She'd spent enough of her younger life living in the shadow of her mother's rejection, she wouldn't do the same with Shane's, wouldn't let him have the final say on her future and whether she'd ever get married. She didn't need a husband on any practical level. Tilda earned her own money, owned her own house, relied on no one else. That's the way she liked it. She did. But no one had the right to tell her matrimony would never be on the cards. A dare was a dare. And, deep down, she couldn't help believing Shane had proved Tilda wasn't a lovable person. A small part of her truly believed that no man would ever ask for her hand in marriage, would never want that permanence. It was clear to her that she'd need to be proactive if she was to win the bet he'd unwittingly set. She made it her resolution on the day they broke up, the day she found her independence from him, 4 July 2023, that by 4 July 2024, she'd have got to know a man and he'd ask her to marry him – even though it would be a leap year, he could still take the lead.

Because whilst Tilda was as strong as they came, independent, resilient, like a singlehanded sailing dinghy on a rough sea, a small part of her, with a quiet voice that didn't often get heard, just once wanted someone to climb aboard and look after her; someone to be there, to help steer her future.

Tilda had taken to her frivolous project with gusto and did her research online. It taught her the three ways for finding a partner: go online, go out on your own, and don't be too picky. She also drew up a list of the qualities she'd desire in her fantasy husband:

Only half human, wings please or the horns of a goat, or some invisible power like teleportation, or the ability to talk to animals, Dettol might become more obedient.

Or, sadly, seriously...

Respectful of boundaries, must respect me having my own space.

Kind in his treatment of other people.

Doesn't put work before everything else.

Loyal through and through, forever and ever, no matter what.

She wasn't bothered about appearance, she told herself, ignoring the voice in her head that had secretly agreed with the girls at school about Robert Pattinson.

Like any project Tilda took on, over the weeks she became more invested, forcing herself on dates, waiting for them to become easier. They didn't. Although not all were a complete disaster. The occasional one offered her a chink of hope about the sort of thoughtful, caring man she might find. Like the guy who'd put the song 'Matilda' by Harry Styles on the jukebox, as she arrived in the pub; the kind-hearted one who'd said they should stay friends, once it was clear the chemistry wasn't there, and invited her bowling; the chef who'd gifted her a bag of homemade chocolates with her initials on top.

Then it happened. Yves had come into her life six months in, with the strikingly handsome photo on his profile, the glamorous bio of his life. She'd really believed, after a few weeks, that Shane was going to be proved wrong in a really big way. Yves couldn't understand why Tilda was single. He was easy to talk to and fun on their video calls. Well, they'd only had two, along with three short phone calls; he seemed a little cautious, perfectly understandable. But they'd enjoyed lots and lots of text messages and voice notes, Tilda loving the alluring French accent, Yves declaring she was the ideal woman. No one had ever said that before. He told Tilda she was beautiful and his sexy accent came across as... worldly, cultured, coupled with a charming shyness she hadn't expected in someone so accomplished.

And that's when the project, that had started as a bit of a joke, developed a serious note. Despite the relief of having left the toxic relationship with Shane, she missed the idea of having a companion, she couldn't deny that. There had been good times, albeit thinly sprinkled. The cuddling after sex, those times he didn't immediately turn over and go to sleep; the occasional Netflix series they'd both like and binge together, with snacks and drinks. Some of his friends were nice, the girlfriend of his best mate was always interested, asking Tilda about her business and for things like tips on how best to clean her leather sofa. It gave Tilda an insight into being part of a friendship group that was bigger than just a person and their cat.

In the middle of the night, alone in the dark, Tilda had dared to dream that, against the odds, a soulmate did exist for her. And that he came from Paris.

Tilda consulted the kitchen clock. Two in the afternoon. She'd taken dinner out of the freezer for later, it being Thursday meant two portions of beef stew. Milo should be back any minute. Normally she ate her lunch at one but she'd delayed it to eat with him. Why, she didn't know. Two plates were set out exactly the same, each with a cheese and pickle sandwich cut into triangles, a packet of low-fat crisps and an apple. She'd fed Dettol at the normal time, one o'clock, no need to abandon her routine entirely. The cat sat in the utility room now, not asleep in its bed, but squinting in the sunrays that poured through glass panes, staring at the door as if missing the new addition to the household.

That pinch. Inside. Ever so slight. A pinch that reminded Tilda that Dettol had never missed her presence. A pinch that went back to her childhood as she'd walk away from the car when Mum dropped her off for a new term, its radio cheerfully playing. She didn't even wave Tilda off.

A knock made Dettol jump up. Tilda walked into the utility and opened the door. She'd have to give him a spare key. A fawning Dettol meowed loudly and Tilda grimaced at the animal's lack of self-respect. Milo came in and bent down to tickle under her chin and then straightened up. He cleared his throat, raising one eyebrow.

His hair. It had been cut, short at the sides then longer on top, parted to the left and falling down. He ran a hand through the chestnut waves, the scar on his hand visible and ending along his little finger. Without shaggy locks hanging around the sides, the style opened up his face and the square jaw that gave it a determined aspect, the dimples almost too soft, now, for the angles. The girls at school would have crushed big time. Six-foot, dark-haired Robert Pattinson's name had been scrawled in the toilets and on desks, thanks to hormone-led obsessions with *The Twilight Saga*. Tilda loved those movies for a different reason. She related to the theme of being an outsider. She couldn't shape-shift or run at top-speed, Tilda couldn't read minds or live forever, but she could see people for who they truly were. Like the school bitches who were, secretly, as insecure as her, they simply hid it by masking up and pretending to be like the popu-lars. She bumped into one a few years after leaving. One of Tilda's old enemies was the owner of a house she was cleaning. In the midst of her drinking problem, Tilda had braced herself and said hello, wishing she'd brought a filled hip flask to work. However, the woman's face turned puce when she recognised Tilda. She apologised for the bullying, said she wished she'd been strong enough not to join in.

'Do you approve?' asked Milo, turning his head from side to side, smil-ing. 'It's so much cooler in this weather.'

'Seems like AA isn't what I thought it was. Do they offer manicures too? Almost tempted to go.'

'Apparently one of the old-timers has done haircuts at that particular meeting for years, afterwards, out the back. A couple of homeless guys were there today and she also trimmed their beards.'

Milo slipped off his shoes and followed Tilda into the kitchen, ducking slightly as he went through the door frame. He washed his hands, drying them on the small hand towel that hung on a peg at the end of the unit, just past the window. Milo glanced at the plates on the table.

'Is one of those for me?'

'No. Dettol's a bit peckish, she loves a sandwich.'

A wide smile lit up Milo's face. 'I don't like to assume.' He rubbed the back of his neck and sat down. 'Cheers, Tilda.'

'It's no biggie,' she said and shrugged, pushing away her laptop.

'No biggie? After weeks on the streets eating out of wrappers, searching through bins? How neatly you've cut up the bread and I bet that apple's washed too... This is *everything*.'

Tilda shot him a beady stare. 'My oh my. Someone's been dosed up high on gratitude, after that meeting.'

His lips flickered and they both grinned. It felt good, a shared sense of humour, coming from a place that was hard to explain to anyone not in recovery. Tilda had never enjoyed a private joke before, not with anyone since leaving home.

'Yeah. Glad I went. Thanks for pushing me yesterday. AA reminded me of what I've still got,' he said. 'My health, friends, my fantasy books, albeit in storage at a mate's – and my good looks, of course.'

'They are literally the only reason I let you stay.' That grin again. Tilda picked up another sandwich. 'So really, how did it go?' Was living with another alcoholic a risk to her sobriety? *No. She was stronger than that, even if he brought alcohol into the house, she'd be fine, right?*

No answer came to the question in her head. Milo's continued recovery was essential for both their sakes. For his mainly. Yes. Definitely. Tilda was protected by her routines. Her frown disappeared and she bit into the bread.

'Are the smaller meetings that much different to the bigger ones in town?' she asked.

'A little. No one needed to be ejected.'

'For drinking?'

'Yep. Oh, you're allowed to come in drunk, but mustn't cause any disruption. And there weren't any twin sets and pearls like in Wilmslow.'

'It took me by surprise, in group therapy, that some of the group were successful business people, and yes, retired, posh ones too. I had this picture in my head of what an addict would look like.'

'You hadn't accepted that you were one too, then, at that point?'

'No. My near-accident scared the life out of me. I had to stop drinking, but I never called myself an alcoholic. Not until the stories the others told were so similar to mine.' She gave a wry smile. Her personal phone vibrated. Normally she'd ignore any notifications whilst eating, but she couldn't take her eyes off the one that flashed up on the screen. Tilda tapped on it, read, re-read, and sat very still.

'Everything okay?' asked Milo.

'What? Oh... yes... it's just this news app alert, I like to keep up to date with what's going on in the world. Except this item is a bit closer to home.' She put down her sandwich and shook her head. 'What the hell's going on? My brother is retiring from football. Who retires from *any* job, aged twenty-six?'

Milo opened his crisps. 'He's probably loaded and can afford it.'

'No. He must earn decent money playing for a League One club, has a glamorous, comfortable lifestyle from the few articles I've seen, over the years – but he won't be earning anything like as much as Premier League players. He's probably newsworthy because big things had always been forecast for him.' Her eyes narrowed. 'It says "for personal reasons".' Something tugged at her heart. Tug, tug, tug. What if he was ill? Tilda swallowed that fear, forcing it down, and told herself it was none of her business, not any more. 'You know, about one and a half million players take part in organised youth football, that gives you some idea of how good a player has to be, to get into a club,' she said, annoyed at a warm and showy-off tone that had crept into her voice, like when the two of them were little and Logan did well at school. Tilda put down the phone. 'Whatever.'

'May I see?' asked Milo.

Tilda slid the phone across the table. Milo studied the news item, the photo of Logan. He almost choked on his drink, wiped his mouth with the back of his hand and pinched out with his fingers, on the photo, to magnify it.

'*This* is your brother?'

'Yeah, yeah, I've read all the online comments about his movie star looks.' Everyone had said the same growing up – extended family, neighbours, strangers. Tilda's hair had less body, her face less symmetry and unlike hers, his resting expression was smiley. Suddenly her lunch didn't taste so good. Did Milo find her *so* unattractive? Unlike Yves who described her hair and eyes as more bewitching than a full moon. He'd said it on one of their video calls and she'd never heard a man sound more embarrassed. Perhaps the stereotype wasn't true and not all Frenchmen were natural smooth talkers.

Milo couldn't take his eyes off the screen. 'Why don't you get in touch? Find out what's going on?'

His words cut deep. Not Milo as well. 'Starstruck, are you?' Like Shane.

'Are you serious? Tilda. I'm concerned about you, in the aftermath of my meeting where the pain of family estrangement weighed heavily on people's minds.'

She rolled her lips together. 'Sorry. Look. I won't reach out to him. Not ever. I could have done with his support when I left school. I couldn't face moving back home after the sixth form and face the daily pressure to go to university, the cutting comments about my poor A level grades. I needed someone to talk to. I wrote to him, once, in a letter. I couldn't face the immediacy of a text message, things had been distant for a while. But he never replied, obviously too busy since he'd been scouted.'

'You've had no contact at all?'

'He's been in touch twice. About a year later, I got a call through Facebook. It was odd. He said he'd pressed the wrong message, the call was a mistake. Then nothing. Silence down the line, I reckoned he was pretending and really wanted to chat. In that instant I forgot the years apart and pictured him, the little boy, playing hide and seek and tag. I encouraged him to talk, told him about my temporary cleaning jobs, how I'd done up my little bedsit, asked him if everything was all right, could I help. He hung up.'

Milo leant in.

'He contacted me again, the week before my twenty-third birthday, started off with general chat, asked if I was still cleaning... then he said Mum was willing to bury the hatchet if I came home and agreed to go to university as a mature student and become the type of daughter she could be proud of...'

Milo reached across and patted her hand – a small gesture that meant so much.

'Logan said to consider their suggestion. Topped up with Dutch courage, and putting our mother aside, I suggested we met up on my birthday, just him and me. He seemed excited, said he had something to tell me, as if there had been another reason for him ringing.' She gave a sigh. 'But ten minutes into our conversation he asked if I was drinking, it was a morning call and already my words were slurring. Then he said he could pay for me to go into rehab, but that he didn't want to meet up if I wasn't prepared to get treatment.' She shook her head. 'I hadn't hit my rock bottom then so couldn't see I had such a big problem. Perhaps I should have been more grateful, looking back, and more understanding of why he wouldn't want a heavy drinker in his life. When I said no, he snapped that Mum had told him not to bother... It... it hit me hard.' Tilda's voice took on an edge. 'But then Logan put down the phone when I went on to say no to her proposal, the two of them clearly as thick as thieves, as ever. Like Mum, he's kept up the meaningless charade of sending me stupid birthday and Christmas cards ever since.'

'You've always given them your latest address?'

'Only since getting sober. To Logan through social media at any rate – with a note saying that any meeting up would only be due to an emergency. Not my phone number. I didn't want to be hijacked by a patronising, unpleasant call from my mum. He sent me his address.' Sometimes Tilda had wondered, how she'd react, if Logan got in touch saying Mum was in trouble or on her deathbed. Would she drop everything and rush to see her?

'At this point, I would cross the street if I saw him.' She would. Even though he was leaving football. Even though there had to be a monumental reason for that. 'He's played a less real part in my life than the mermen and unicorns I like to read about.' An image jumped into her head of a full wine glass, as if it were a dose of medicine that would take away the pain.

Milo handed the phone back. 'You honestly wouldn't want him back in your life?'

'Sometimes I dream of what it would be like. We were so close. We had this game where we'd spend whole days saying we were reading each other's minds. We'd guess what each other wanted for breakfast, what to play... The magic felt real too, we usually got it right. Logan always loved marmalade on toast with what we called "puddles of butter" – large lumps spread straight onto bread out of the toaster, that would melt and soak in. Whereas he knew my favourite was a bowl of cereal, with the milk in a glass, on the side.' Tilda bit into her apple, chewed more slowly. Her voice hardened. 'But whilst I believe some mythical creatures were once real – like, the Kraken was clearly inspired by giant squid, griffins by dinosaurs – the perfect Logan who never ditched me isn't one.'

Milo went to say something but Tilda interrupted.

'I don't expect you to understand. Although maybe you do, because you've never once mentioned your family as being part of your recovery, let alone your life. I've not pushed about this because I know, first hand, that families can screw you up.'

'It's not like that, in my case,' he said quietly. 'I keep away because I'm the one who screwed them up.'

'Have you got any siblings?'

'Not any more.'

'That makes two of us,' she said.

'But I wish I did. Are you sure about not wanting to see your brother?'

'A sister who's a cleaner wouldn't fit with his exciting lifestyle, going to fancy restaurants, mixing with top sports people, with artists, actors... He might take the route other ex-footballers have chosen and become a boxer instead, or a singer. He must have the contacts. Not that it interests me.' Her voice caught and she stood up to wash the dishes. 'What about you? Would you ever contact your... brother again? Or is it a sister?'

'Sister. No. I could never do that.'

'Same as me, then. Shit, isn't it?' She ran the kitchen taps, drowning out the oh so tiny tremble in her voice that she hoped he hadn't heard.

Milo thought for a moment and then took out his phone. 'I need fresh air. I'll be back by five.' After he'd put on his shoes in the utility room he opened the side door. He closed it behind him and made off, into the sunshine, with steps that became more purposeful with every stride, head down as he tapped on his phone's screen.

11

Milo pushed away the empty bowl of beef stew, perspiration glistening on his forehead. For the first time Tilda considered that she should change her rota of meals to better suit the seasons. He wiped his mouth, downed the rest of his water and gave a satisfied sigh. Milo stood up and set about washing up the dishes. Tilda hadn't needed to prompt him. *This was new.* But Tilda didn't do new, not these days, preferring the security of the repetitive life she'd carved out for herself. Was she accepting of him because he was an alcoholic? The routine of her life felt safe. What if Milo relapsed and introduced all the chaos that would entail, into her home? Tilda ran her eyes over the broad shoulders. The long legs. Despite his imposing physical presence, despite her concerns, he'd slotted so easily into her life, sometimes it was as if he wasn't there at all.

It reminded her of Logan.

What sort of man had her brother grown up to be? Spoilt and entitled? Who would blame him, after a childhood of being hailed as a prodigy? She'd never forgotten one half-term, the first year she was at boarding school, Gran couldn't take Tilda and Logan had been shipped off to a last-minute football camp. Mum kept them apart for the holiday, two home at once being too much. Tilda had overheard her on the phone to her brother. 'Glad you've made a friend, Logan. Just remember, you can achieve anything you want. You're just like me. Tilda's different, she hasn't got that drive. I see an amazing future in you. Don't waste your natural talent. As your sister demonstrates, not everyone has any.'

Tilda took a moment. The pain still seared through her all these years later, over her mother's lack of pride, of belief, in her daughter... Dad never used to compare. He never spoke of expectations. Opposites must have truly attracted when her parents got married, unless the wedding was due to her mum getting pregnant with Tilda. The wedding took place one month before she was born. Her mum didn't have the photos on display, always saying how the baby bump had ruined them.

Logan now... did he have staff, a cleaner? If so, would he treat them as an equal? Tilda was very careful about the new clients she took on, making sure during their initial meeting that they were the type to treat her staff with the respect they deserved. A couple of times she'd terminated contracts. No one spoke to her employees in a superior manner, including the banker who'd referred to Iris as 'the help' and the fashionista who'd clicked his fingers at Adam. One pensioner started following young Jazz around and banged her walking stick to make her jump if she thought Jazz missed dusting an inch. That wouldn't do.

'There's a werewolf drama series premiering on Netflix tonight,' said Tilda. 'It's called *Were Is the Wolf?* Like, "where" without the letter h. I might give it a go.'

Milo reached for the gingham tea towel. '*An American Werewolf in London* is one of my all-time favourite movies. Such a classic. You'll have to let me know what this show's like.'

'Watch it with me, if you want? Not that I mind either way.' She broke eye contact and her cheeks glowed as if her insides had captured the June sun and were releasing it in bursts.

Milo turned around. 'Are you serious? Tilda, I'd love to!'

'It's only a TV series,' she said, unable to suppress a smile. 'It's not like I've offered you a visit to the *Game of Thrones* set.'

'But it's ages since I've watched TV – and not only because I've been on the streets. In my flat, at the end, I'd either fall asleep or end up shouting at the screen.' He smiled. 'Talking of unskilful traits like that – good thing I didn't have neighbours, they'd have often been complaining about the noise – I've got another AA meeting tomorrow morning to keep them in check. Same place, same time. Why not come along?'

Tilda pulled a face and his rich laugh bounced off the walls. He didn't push it. Not like Shane who'd use all his powers of persuasion to get her to go to football matches and on pub crawls with his mates.

'We can't watch a new fantasy series without snacks though,' he said. 'Seriously. We need to veer a little away from the weekly menu.'

She got up and reached into a cupboard to the right of the cooker and pulled down a large bag of popcorn with a rubber band tight around the top and a sticker on the side, indicating when she'd first opened it. 'I'm not a complete robot,' she said.

That laugh again. Bounce, bounce.

She poured the popcorn into a bowl and then pulled out two Cokes from the fridge, replacing them with two more from a six pack in a cupboard by her feet. Normally she only treated herself to fizzy drinks at weekends. Milo followed Tilda into the lounge and after pulling the curtains and switching on a small lamp, then straightening a pile of magazines and wiping imaginary dust off the old electric fire that had belonged to the previous owners, she sat down on the sofa, next to him. Dettol, already on his lap, washing herself, didn't even look up. A guilty conscience, Tilda told herself. Dettol knew she wasn't allowed to settle in the lounge.

'How do you do that?' she asked Milo. 'Click with the cat? She's never climbed onto me. Not that I'd want her to, what with that moulting fur,' she added hastily. She'd have to brush down the sofa, later.

'I follow my instincts,' he said, and tickled Dettol's cheek.

'I've literally only stroked her a few times. She always swipes me away.'

'Show me how you do it.'

'What's to show?' she said, and went to touch the top of Dettol's head. Sure enough, the animal swiped.

'You're coming at her from above. That's threatening,' he said. 'Cats fear predators swooping in the air, like birds of prey. Come in from the side instead. In fact, let her smell your hand first.'

'It's that complex?'

Milo grinned. 'It's easy for me, I was around a lot of animals when I was younger – next door were never without a pet.'

Tentatively Tilda held her fingers in front of Dettol's nose. The cat touched her thumb, cold, wet.

'Now tickle her cheek,' Milo said.

Tilda moved her fingers around to the side and scratched. Dettol gave her a wary glance before closing her eyes and tilting her head.

'Keep going until you find her sweet spot,' whispered Milo.

Tilda moved her hand around. Dettol lifted her neck right up and... Tilda's eyebrows shot into her hairline. A purr? A sense of achievement vibrated through Tilda.

'Tell her she's beautiful,' murmured Milo.

'No. I'll feel stupid.'

'You'd only be telling the truth,' he said. 'There's nothing ever stupid about that. Those stunning dark stripes contrasting with the white bib. As for the M marking above her eyes, it's as if she was made for an owner called Matilda.'

Oh, an M, hiding in plain sight on Dettol's forehead. She agreed, it was as if the universe had allocated her to Matilda for some reason. Milo had thought about her name enough to realise Tilda was a shortened version. That was down to Dad, although Mum never approved and always used Matilda if she was cross with her daughter, which became more often after her husband died. Tilda would brace herself, not flinching an inch when Mum spat out her full name, reminding herself of how Dad said her name meant *mighty in battle*.

Tilda's fingers moved to the cat's head, and she ran them over the letter's marking. Dettol purred even louder. She took her hand away and pressed the remote control, not looking at her feline flatmate who, she was sure, would be as surprised as her. The credits rolled and Milo placed the popcorn bowl in between them. Her fingers dived in at the same time as Milo's. Their skin brushed and the sensation overwhelmed her, the urge to run her hand across his arm, across the small hairs, the smooth skin. She fixed her gaze on the screen and hardly moved as a familiar longing washed over her, that she hadn't experienced for three years, the desire that would surge through her, after a few drinks, that led her more than once to have a one-night stand.

Except she wasn't drunk, nor was Milo. Not to mention the fact that flattering, attentive Yves might get hurt. He'd sent her a photo of his coq au vin last night, oddly bright red and not like the one she'd once seen made on a cookery show. She'd said as much, adding a smiley face, and he'd messaged back:

> Chère Tilda, a client took me out to dinner tonight. You are right, the sauce looks odd and tasted too tomatoey. But I was grateful for the free meal, I'm trying to save all my pennies to raise this money for Beatrice. I hate to ask, ma coccinelle, really I do, but is there any way you could help? Mon dieu, I feel like a grifter. Forget I said anything. Your friendship is too important to me for it to be stained with problems over money. Please forgive me. Yves xxxxx

A fashion designer with no savings in the bank? But Tilda got it, she ploughed everything into her business. Independence and security excited her more than flash cars or holidays. She'd read his message several times. *Saving pennies... grifter...* his English really was excellent. *Ma coccinelle* meant my ladybird, she'd read about them once, how their spots were a warning that they tasted foul. Tilda sometimes wondered if she should come with a warning, too. Tilda didn't do relationships well. If she said no to Yves, about the money, would he stop messaging? She didn't think so, because he apologised again, later, in another message, accompanied by a photo of his stray cat, asleep on his couch with a back leg in the air. Yves sent a photo of his leg doing the same, photoshopped with zzzz for snoring, by the side. Tilda had laughed out loud. She'd been downstairs making a hot chocolate and Milo had raised his eyebrows and looked as if he was trying, hard, not to be inquisitive. She'd muttered something about a friend telling a bad joke.

Milo. She'd never experienced that strong pull with Shane, Tilda could see that even more clearly now. Sex with him had been more... mindful. Not in the sense that she was more in the present, but that it was planned, intended, controlled, level-headed. She always had protection in, had changed the sheets, cooked a nice meal first, cleaned her teeth, put on a laundered and ironed skimpy nightdress she saved for those occasions. She'd set up the spare room with dimmed lights, always told Shane their closeness in the single bed made it more fun. There was no way she was letting him see her bedroom. When they'd broken up, he'd called her a weirdo, said maybe she'd got a dead ex in her wardrobe and that he'd had a lucky escape. Shane's jokes never had been funny.

Whereas images flashed through her mind, like a movie on fast-forward, of her and Milo tearing off each other's clothes, of smiles, of laughs, of his lips on hers, the urgent yet tender touches, the curling up in each other's arms afterwards, duvet on the floor.

Tilda needed to get a grip.

This was pure lust. Any alcoholic would recognise that. Lust didn't make for a calm, safe, life, its beats steady and evenly spaced. It didn't sell itself, as Yves did, he came across as a family man, looking after his sister, reliable in a way her mum hadn't been.

When the episode finished, she turned off the television and took their empty cans and the bowl into the kitchen, without saying a word.

'How do you rate it?' Milo appeared, Dettol asleep in his arms.

'It was good. Right. I'm off to bed. Could you settle Dettol in the utility room and check everything's turned off in the kitchen? Thank you.'

She hurried past and Milo put the cat on a chair. 'What's the matter?'

'Nothing,' she replied, without stopping. 'I'm just tired.' Tilda climbed the stairs two at a time and went into her bedroom. Crap, she should have got using the bathroom out of the way, then she wouldn't risk bumping into him again. Tilda went to clean her teeth. She washed her face. Less than five minutes later she came back onto the landing and froze. Mouth open, Milo stood, staring... into her bedroom. She'd accidentally left the door open.

Clothes sprawled across the bed.

Dirty crockery piled on a dressing table.

A wet towel crumpled in a heap under the rail on the radiator.

Crumbs and used tissues strewn across the carpet.

A hardback book in the middle of the floor, open, cover half off and torn.

A powerful whiff of jasmine filling the landing, due to a knocked-over perfume bottle, right next to the hardback.

No... no, no. He had no right to stick his nose in. Tilda clenched her fists and charged past him. She hurtled into her bedroom and slammed the door behind her, before turning the key in the lock.

12

Tilda woke up at seven the next morning and checked WhatsApp.

> Chère Tilda, I wouldn't ask unless I was desperate, but, as my friend
> pointed out, Beatrice's life could be at stake. Today is Friday 14 June, I
> only have a couple of weeks now, until the deadline of July. You'd think
> a fashion designer would have lots of people he could ask, but I have
> my reputation to think of. If I can tell the cartel the money is on the
> way, they might even relax their deadline. I'd be so very grateful.
> Yves xxxxx
> > P.S. Sorry, don't hate me.
> > P.P.S. I've named my stray friend: Cantaloupe.

Despite the seriousness of his message, Tilda couldn't help smiling.
He'd named the cat after an orange melon. Two thousand euros. Yves
really was in trouble. But it was a large sum to lend anyone.

> Hi Yves. I'm sorry you and your sister are struggling. I am sympathetic
> but it's a lot of money. Love the cat's name. Tilda

She cleared a space on her messy bedroom floor and sat cross-legged to do ten minutes of meditation. Or tried to. Intrusive thoughts kept ruining her focus, about Yves, about Milo's gobsmacked expression as he'd stared into her bedroom the night before. Eventually she gave up and took a cold shower, brushed her hair, and then changed into trousers and a cream T-shirt. Tilda applied her favourite jasmine scent, there was just a bit left in the bottom of the bottle after it had fallen over. Her gran had always said Tilda and Logan had inherited her writing genes and with gusto she'd read their stories, raving about the imagery they created. Since getting sober, now and then, during a quiet moment, Tilda would have a go at writing a short story. Gran wrote romance and the escapist aspect of that genre appealed. Tilda had written several set in fantasy worlds, but always had the same problem. She never knew how to end them. Her gran believed in Happy Ever Afters. Tilda didn't.

At seven thirty precisely she arrived in the kitchen. Indignant meowing floated in from the utility room. She let the cat into the kitchen and tipped its food into a bowl. Twenty to eight and it was time for Tilda's breakfast, cereal flakes with fruit, five walnut halves, a small handful of raisins and two tablespoons of probiotic yogurt on top. Except the raisins had run out. Milo had big hands.

A door opening sounded from the top floor and she braced herself. Slow walking downstairs. He appeared already dressed and washed, hair slicked back in its appealing new style.

'Help yourself to food,' she said, not meeting his gaze. 'I need to get straight on with work.'

'Tilda, about last night—'

'Sorry, Milo. I must get on.' She sat in front of the laptop, with her bowl, pretending to read the screen. What must Milo think? Why did she care? He didn't even have a bedroom of his own. If he did, his might have been messy as well. However, the voice of her dorm parent, at boarding school, rang in her ears, from the days when she had to make her bed in a certain way, fold every clothing item, set out her possessions neatly.

A tidy living space means a tidy mind. A busy day keeps us happy and bright. Uncluttered personal areas mean uncluttered minds, leaving plenty of room for growth. Success in life is all in the detail, so we straighten our pillows and time our tooth-brushing. You'll thank me in years to come when, during periods of strife, routine and discipline will be your constants and give you strength.

Tilda shook her head, ever so slightly, if only she could lose the mantra of that woman who grew up in a military family. The other girls scoffed and pulled faces, sometimes skipping the tooth cleaning and hiding creased clothes in the bedcovers. But parental guidance was lacking in Tilda's life, so she lapped up the advice, lapped up the praise, even if it meant the other pupils saw her as even more of an outsider.

Nowadays her bedroom was her one release.

Milo washed up both their dishes and scrolled his phone, taking notes, presumably about job applications. He played with Dettol using a kitchen roll tube. A couple of times he started a conversation but Tilda answered in monosyllables and took a break mid-morning, standing alone in the back garden, face lifted to the sun. Before coming in she plucked one of the blush jasmine flowers and stood it in a tiny vase, on her desk. She exhaled with relief when Milo left for his meeting.

When he got back, lunch was on the table. Two plates, each with a ham sandwich cut into four triangles, and a packet of low-fat crisps and apple for each of them as well. Milo washed his hands and sat down and waited for Tilda to finish an email, before eating.

'How was AA?' she asked.

'Good. Friday meetings are always full, with the weekend vibes and temptation looming. It reminded me why it's so important to live a transparent, honest life. In the spirit of that, and of one of your house rules, I've decided to speak up about something that's bothering me.'

'Look, Milo...'

'Why is the rest of your house such a stark, clinical contrast to your bedroom?'

'You say that as if it's the tidy rooms that are the problem,' she muttered.

'That's how I see it. Your bedroom is you. Why mask it?'

Oh.

But her bedroom was a mess, unhygienic in places, the towel also smelt and she'd damaged numerous book covers. How could that be preferable to the rest of the house, where everything had its place, where the air smelt of disinfectant?

'It's none of your business,' she said tightly and picked up a sandwich.

'But it is. I like you, Tilda. You're a good person.'

'You would say that because you want to stay.'

'I'm a liar?'

She bit into the sandwich, it felt dry in her mouth, even though the bread was fresh.

'You should have seen my flat before I had to give it up,' he continued. 'I'd regularly find an old coffee cup with mould in the bottom. But that's me,' he said, gently. 'As long as I'm not hurting anyone else, why should I give a damn? Why work so hard to make the rest of the house appear like a showroom just to please a bunch of strangers?'

Her face burnt.

'Tell me. Come on. Us reformed souls are both old hands at sharing our truth.'

Shane had never asked her these sorts of questions. He'd caught sight of her bedroom once when she'd thought he was having a lie-in. He couldn't stop laughing and said he was impressed that his girlfriend was human after all, and then he'd danced in a robotic manner. Although he agreed it was just as well, when he was over, that she'd always made sure they slept in the spare room – he reckoned her room must smell bad and wrinkled his nose, eyes sneering. Conversations with Yves were more jokey than deep and yet... sometimes he gave a little of himself away. He called her beautiful in his very first message, and could have left the compliment like that, but made some comment about him having problems accepting flattery too, after years of being bullied at his own school for being short.

Tilda took a deep breath. 'Okay. If you must know – school dorm rules gave me a sense of control, when everything else about those years was such a shitshow. I carried them onto my life at home, the brief times I was there during the holidays, and not at Gran's, hoping Mum would be impressed at how grown up and organised I was, cleaning the house, and I took on the laundry. What with work and chauffeuring Logan to the latest practice session or match, none of my efforts registered.' Her voice faltered. 'It seemed pointless, eventually, in trying to make her proud of *me*.'

'So who are you trying to impress now?'

'I do have visitors,' she snapped.

He folded his arms and raised his eyebrows.

'I do! Delivery men. The gas meter reader.' She sighed. 'I mean, anyone might call by.'

Dettol jumped onto his lap. 'Tilda. Look at me. Look at us two over here.'

She gazed across the table.

'You're a successful woman, who – in spite of a difficult start in life – has a kind heart, even though you don't like to admit it, who is an ace cook and a person with great taste in books and movies... You don't have to impress anyone, least of all a rough sleeper and this furry interloper.'

She bit into the apple, eating easier now. Much as AA was her idea of hell, she'd got to know regulars years ago, workers at the addiction clinic, and some of her peers who'd relapsed big time. They all had one thing in common – honesty, about themselves, about other people. They didn't bullshit and didn't take crap from others either. It had made her want to open up in a way that caused discomfort. She'd resisted the urge in treatment and not let everything spill out about her childhood. She'd given the group leaders just enough to satisfy them that she'd purged her soul. It was one reason Tilda had avoided AA. Making friends who were kindred spirits would make it harder to keep the bad stuff in.

However, with Milo it was different.

The bad stuff had loomed again since he moved in, rubbing her insides, making her twitch, willing her to release it, making the urge hard to resist.

'The disciplined ways, entrenched at boarding school, somehow helped me cope with the bullying.'

'What?'

She opened up more fully about the pinches and slaps, the nasty comments, the ganging up, and how that was the reason she kept her door locked.

Milo's face turned an ugly shade of red. 'I'm so sorry you went through that.'

Tilda shrugged. 'Eventually I found the strength to stand up for myself and I established a way of living that gave me a safe structure. That went to pot when my drinking got bad, so in recovery I doubled down, taking them to the next level. I worry, if I let... let go of the order, I'll drink again.'

'Slacking off when it comes to housework, never turned anyone into an alcoholic.' He gave one of those smiles she found hard not to return, that made her want to take him in her arms. He brushed back the side fringe that had flopped forwards. Once again images flashed through her head of him and Tilda close, their legs intertwined, her kissing his neck, his fingers exploring parts of her tantalisingly slowly, of them skipping in the rain, dancing on table tops, binge-watching Netflix from sunset to sunrise.

Was his presence feeding into the old impulsive, reckless behaviour?

That could be dangerous.

A shiver ran down her spine.

Dangerous because these days she had so much more to lose. A house. A business. Roots.

Dettol would hate her and so would the house, because these last few days it had felt even more like a home. But there was no alternative – even though she never wanted him to stop, once he started talking, listening to those warm tones emanating humour... even though she found it hard to tear away her gaze when he walked in the room, due to that long, broad, loyal, principled, protective aura he carried... Sensible Tilda, not ruled by hormones, nor instincts, nor primeval urges, had made up her mind: she'd pay Milo tonight for his three evenings' work and then first thing tomorrow would tell him to move out.

13

Saturday morning, and Tilda had given up on her meditation, having not slept well, with one leg out of the covers, due to the heat and the screeching of foxes outside. For once, Tilda couldn't face a cold shower and felt like she'd needed the comfort of warm water. Stupid. She owed Milo nothing. Tilda had done everything to help him. She gazed out of the lounge window and onto the street and the cars already whizzing past, some with the drivers' windows down. Last night Tilda had paid Milo for the three shifts, half as they agreed, the rest covered food and rent. That left him with thirty-six pounds.

A meow sounded at her feet. Dettol. No doubt she wanted more biscuits. Tilda hadn't been so precise about the amount in her bowl this morning. She went to follow her upright tail into the kitchen but then stopped. She crouched down and cleared her throat.

'Dettol? Aren't you... a beautiful girl?' Slowly the cat's head turned around. Tilda reached out her hand, being careful not to raise it above Dettol's head. The cat came over and sniffed her fingers, paused, and then rubbed her cheek against them. Tilda scratched the fur and Dettol directed her to the sweet spot. Purrs filled the room and Tilda risked a stroke, with her palm, down Dettol's side. 'Don't you feel... soft,' she said.

Dettol butted her head against Tilda's hand, the two Ms making contact. Tilda stood up. All this time the cat had simply been waiting for affection, not being willing to give it up first, acting wary. Tilda related and filled with genuine respect for an animal she'd felt like she'd only tolerated up until recently. Dettol was a savvy survivor, with boundaries and an air of distrust that kept her safe. People had to earn her love. She'd been abandoned too.

Tilda went into the kitchen and hesitated. She opened a cupboard and took out a small tin of tuna, pulled off the lid and before she could change her mind, forked half into the cat bowl. Dettol did a double take. Footsteps sounded upstairs and Tilda quickly tipped the rest into a cup, covered it with cling film and put it at the back of the fridge. She rinsed out the tin and hid it behind the kettle as Milo came down. Dettol seemed to understand, scoffing the tuna in record time and licking away any traces of evidence.

The two of them exchanged a conspiratorial glance as Milo entered the kitchen, bed hair contrasting with his neater day clothes, he must have forgotten to brush it. Tilda's fingers twitched as if they longed to skim through it. He held the bank notes in the air, that Tilda had given him. 'Pathetic, isn't it, that so little money means so much? Don't get me wrong, I'm grateful, but...' His voice wavered. 'I'm thirty. I should be earning hundreds to pay a mortgage, to build up a pension.' He sat at the wooden table, head in his hands. 'I'm not ungrateful Tilda. For this.' He shook the notes. 'I'm starting from scratch again, I know that. It's hard, but at least my life is now moving in the right direction. It's down to you giving me a roof over my head.'

'About that...' she said.

'Right. You've got laundry to do,' he said and jumped up. 'I'll make breakfast. Then later on, say, midday... fancy a walk in Crouchden Park? I could do with some... what do you call it? Mindfulness. You could give me tips on how to practice it.'

'It's due to be even hotter today, midday is a bad time,' she said. It would be boiling sleeping on the pavement. Not her problem.

'All the better,' he said, hopefully. 'I could do with topping up my tan.'

'I want to chill over lunch before doing the afternoon shop, Milo. Why don't you go on your own? Mindfulness is simply about focusing on the detail.'

'I'd walk around there when I was rough sleeping – away from the traffic, it relaxed me. But I'm worried I'll be recognised from the street and locals will think I'm there to cause trouble,' he said, running one hand around the other arm's wrist in a stressed manner.

He hadn't appeared bothered walking to and from the station the last few days, smiling at pedestrians, saying hello to passing pensioners. But maybe it would be easier to tell him her decision away from her house where he'd been settling in. The park always calmed Tilda down too. In the colder months she'd gone there with bird seed and sprinkled it on the hard ground, near one of the benches. Despite the crisp air, warmth had surged through Tilda as she sat near the hungry birds that pecked with enthusiasm.

As midday approached Milo became more and more quiet. He consulted his phone several times. Perhaps he'd had a few job rejections. Tilda would take the ring out when they went for their walk, give it back to him in the park. She'd searched online and found a pawn shop on the outskirts of Crouchden that was open until six. Tilda would drive him over. That way, for a couple of nights at least, he'd have enough cash for a B & B.

Side by side they walked down the street, past the familiar litter and overflowing wheelie bins that smelt of rotten scraps. A couple of metres before the dingy launderette they turned right and into a large square of park with a winding path going around, lined at the sides by bushes and trees with wooden benches in the middle. Tilda took a moment, taking in the plants gently swaying in the breeze, the buzz of bees at a nearby lavender bush, the shouts of children roller-skating at the far end.

Breathe.

For a few seconds her problems slipped away as if the nearby oak tree had lowered its branches and told her to pin them to its shoulders. They veered left and began the lap. Milo kept looking at his phone and the time.

'First things first, put your phone away,' said Tilda. 'Mindfulness means stepping away from the modern world with its many distractions.' She pointed to the oak. 'Notice the bark, the different shaped scales, the range of shades. Often my mindfulness journey has led me to research. Bark is amazing, it does so many jobs – keeps...' She blushed. 'Sorry. Probably boring you.'

'Go on,' he said, 'it's interesting.'

'Bark keeps too much moisture out, keeps moisture in, and it protects the tree from heat and cold, also from insect damage... It's actually the outermost layer of stems and roots.'

Milo stepped onto the grass and ran his hand over the tree's trunk. 'Incredible.'

Tilda had often wished her skin had been more like bark, especially when she was younger. She didn't mind insects, could tolerate heat and cold. Tilda would have needed it to keep out mean words.

They carried on to a bush with elegant, bright pink fuchsia blooms. Milo stopped and leant forwards for more detail. 'It's relatable, isn't it?' he mumbled. 'How they hang their heads. I've done that so many times in recent weeks.' He reached out and lifted up one of the flowers. When he let go it happily dropped down again. 'Perhaps fuchsias have the right idea, turning away from the noise, the commotion.' He stood up. 'Why don't we sit down on one of the benches?' he said, in a strained voice. They sat down, comfortable in silence for a few minutes. 'You've helped me so much,' he said. 'I'd do anything to repay your generosity.'

He kept looking around. Where was this going? Had he sensed she was about to tell him to move out? An elderly couple walked past, shooting the two of them smile. A teenager skateboarded around the park, followed by a jogger with earphones on. A young man approached the benches. Tilda yawned. With Milo gone she was bound to sleep better tonight. Tomorrow morning she'd get back to her meditation and cold shower and...

Milo had got to his feet. She was about to join him when an unfamiliar voice cut in. 'Tilda.'

She raised her head.

Everything swayed, as if the trees were doing the rumba, yet the breeze was hardly noticeable. She gripped onto the wooden slats by her sides.

'Logan?'

Same movie star looks. Same wiry frame. Yet dark shadows hung under his eyes and he hadn't shaved. He'd probably been out clubbing for several nights straight, celebrating whatever new career he'd chosen. But how had he found her there?

Then she realised. Of course.

She glared at Milo. 'How *could* you? How did you even know how to contact him?'

'Twitter. You see, your brother and I have...'

She shook her head. 'I've been so stupid. You're just another football fan.' She pointed to her brother, not catching his eye, not talking to him, he didn't deserve her attention. 'All I've been is an "in" for you to get to him.'

Milo inhaled and breathed out long and hard. 'Tilda. No. I'd met your brother before you and I crossed paths.'

Logan stood, mouth agape. 'I wasn't sure what to think when this man contacted me, but now I recognise him and... Sis, I—'

Tilda got to her feet. 'Wowwww. Entitled or what, to call me that after what... five years? After you refused to meet me, point blank, because I was having a drink? After I'd reached out to help you, previously, when you "accidentally" rang.' She shook her head, got up and went to walk away.

Milo took her arm, gently. 'He's here now, isn't he?'

'Only because of you,' she said. 'He must want something.'

'No... that dragon egg's ring...'

She reached into her back pocket. 'You mean this?' She pushed it into his palm.

'Your brother, Logan, he was the passer-by who gave it to me. I recognised him when you showed me the photo on your phone.'

What? But... that was why Milo was so surprised, when he saw the photo on her phone, that he was her brother?

Yeah, well, so what? She turned to Logan, nose wrinkling. 'Isn't a huge diamond more of a footballer's thing, for a proposal? And you, slumming it in Crouchden?'

Her brother's forehead furrowed.

'He wasn't proposing, Tilda, I got that wrong. This was a present for you. He was coming to *your* house.'

Tilda's breath cut short.

Logan nodded vigorously. 'It's true, Tilda. I spent ages choosing it. I thought it looked like a dragon's egg too, that's why I bought it.'

'You remembered that I liked fantasy fiction?' she asked in a faint voice.

He gave a nervous smile. 'I'll never forget the games we played. Me sitting on your back pretending to ride a dragon through the sky. You were brilliant at acting out breathing fire! Us crawling across the grass holding a wooden spoon each, to our heads, pretending to be unicorns. Whenever we went swimming, you said we had to pretend to be a mermaid and merman. Then there were the stories we wrote about fairy kings and queens. Do you remember how much Gran loved them?'

Gran. Yes. She was always so encouraging, just like Dad had been. 'What do you want, Logan?' she said coldly. 'I'm not ever going to university. Mum needs to realise that, so if you're here on her behalf... although I imagine she's given up on me by now.'

'This isn't about her. I've got something I want to show you.' He took his rucksack off his shoulder. 'She's taken a sabbatical from work and is going on a long holiday to France, testing it out for retirement, an idea she's had for a while. Several friends of hers moved there and love the expat community. The house is too big for her now and she might sell up. But I've been sorting through boxes in the loft. And I found—'

'Wait... Mum might be moving abroad? *That's* what it's taken for you to reach out? Yes, of course it is, you've always been in her pocket. Can't you imagine a life without her in your life, without family? Well try coping with it, like I had to, when I was a teen.' She strode away.

'Tilda,' he called, running to catch up. 'It's not like that. Please. Just look at—'

She swung around. 'No. Don't do this Logan, don't mess up a life I've finally created that makes me happy.' Her voice hitched. It was too late to make up, despite the disappointment on his face, despite the hurt in his eyes. 'It's too late to start over,' she said in a steadier tone and glared at her brother and then at Milo.

Eyes glistening, Logan rubbed his forehead. Milo mouthed, 'Sorry.'

'You had no right. Either of you,' she choked out. A sob rose in her throat and she ran out of the park.

14

Tilda sat in her garden, slumped on the ground by the jasmine climber, comforted by its scent and the carefree appearance of a sparrow who hopped happily across the grass. Dettol studied her, from a few feet away. Tears streamed down her face, the audacity of Logan, to call her 'sis', as if they hadn't become strangers. She spotted a nettle sprouting in the soil. That meant there had to be a dock leaf nearby, to salve the sting – nature's way. Fantasy fiction, be it on the screen or on the page, had been the equivalent of dock leaves over the years, every time Tilda had been stung by others' words or actions. It had enabled her to keep going on, to build a business, buy a house – fiction had created a reality she'd become fond of. *Labyrinth* was one of her favourite movies. Forget the Saturday shop. Tilda would spend the afternoon watching it with the rest of the popcorn and a can of Coke. Even two. Three. Four. The image of a wine bottle loomed into her mind. Cold, crisp, with a buzz no fizzy drink could match. She was about to get to her feet when the gate creaked and Milo appeared. She jumped up and brushed down her trousers. Lips pursed, she folded her arms.

'I'm sorry,' he said, in a quiet voice. 'I messed up big time. Over-stepped. I gave the ring back to Logan.'

Fool. That was an investment in his future. Not her concern. Without saying a word, she opened the side door and busied herself feeding Dettol, too angry to talk to him. Milo disappeared upstairs. Good, he needed to keep out of her way for the time being. However, when he came back down he'd packed his belongings.

'Thanks again for everything,' he said. 'I've stripped the bed.'

'What were you thinking?' she muttered. 'How would you like it if I reached out to your sister?'

He flinched.

'Exactly.'

'I only did it because it's obvious you still care.'

Tilda stopped emptying the popcorn into a bowl and put the bag down. 'I've hardly ever mentioned my brother.'

'You've set up Google alerts to specifically inform you of news items about him. That notification you received about him ending his football career didn't come from a general news app, did it?'

Tilda's jaw tightened. 'As they say – keep your enemies closer than friends.'

'But when you talked about how many kids go into youth football but how few make it to the big time, you couldn't hide the pride from your voice. And I could tell you were worried about why he was giving up his career. I wanted to surprise you, just assumed you were simply nervous about getting in touch and that me doing it for you would instigate a reconciliation.' He picked up his rucksack. 'It was arrogant, I can see that now. Your business is your business.'

Tilda *was* proud of Logan, that was the annoying thing. She'd secretly gone to a match once, managed to get a ticket for his first appearance with Bolton Wanderers. How the crowd had roared with joy when the new signing scored a goal. Tilda had wanted to jump up in the air with them and holler, until she was hoarse, the words 'that's my brother', how she'd imagined how thrilled their dad would have been with his success, if he was still alive. Instead, she'd sneaked out, tears in the corners of her eyes, not wanting to bump into her mum who was no doubt there taking videos and photos.

Milo went into the utility room and crouched as he did up his shoes. Dettol followed and lay on her back, stretching in front of him. Milo ruffled her stomach and called the cat gorgeous. Dettol licked his hand and playfully he grabbed her paw and shook it. Misplaced as Milo's surprise for Tilda had been, it had genuinely been about her. Whereas Shane's surprises were always, underneath the surface, about himself, like the toastie maker he bought for her kitchen because toasties were his favourite snack. Or the surprise date night he'd booked at the sports bar in town, even though he knew she didn't like all the noise, food to be followed by cinema tickets to see a niche martial arts movie, a genre he loved. She'd suggested a new fantasy release, once, and he'd said it was a kids' movie.

Her work phone buzzed and she glanced at the notification, then clicked on the email. A satisfied nod before she looked up again. Milo gripped the side door's handle. An emptiness washed over Tilda, like a wave from the most tropical ocean that should have been teaming with life: fish, krill, plankton, but instead was clearer than sterilised swimming pool water – a familiar sensation, like an old friend you don't really want to hang out with any more.

Empty? Her life in Crouchden, running a business, making a home?

No. Absolutely not. Every day was full. With Milo gone, order would be restored. That's what she wanted.

It was.

'There's no need to be dramatic,' she found herself saying. 'Another job has come in. A client I visited in your neck of the woods, Wilmslow, would you believe, a couple of weeks ago. Residential. Big house. The owner was interviewing various cleaning companies, without realising I was interviewing him too. How about I make this client yours? Four hours a week should do it. The client suggested Monday mornings, after the weekend. He has five bedrooms, three bathrooms and a downstairs toilet, a large kitchen, several reception rooms. He often throws parties at the weekend and the guests stay over. As you know, I pay my staff twelve pounds an hour. That's forty-eight for you – minus half to cover rent and food here. So twenty-four, on top of the other shifts you're doing with me in Stockport, that earn you thirty-six. Per week, for the time being, you'd be on...'

'Sixty pounds,' he cut in. His rucksack dropped to the floor.

'You doing a job on your own would be on a trial basis for now, of course. The first Monday morning I'd go too – show you the ropes. You've experience of cleaning from the nightclub but residential work is slightly different. Then... we'll see how you go. A casual arrangement, if you like, whilst you're applying for jobs.'

'I don't know what to say.'

'I need to set up a cleaner for Monday pronto, so the sooner you can say something, the better.'

'What I meant to say was yes! Yes! Yes!' He raced into the kitchen and grabbed her hands. 'You're sure? About me staying here?'

She nodded as his large hands easily enveloped hers.

'I won't let you down.' He twirled her around.

'Stop it,' she said, shyly, and pulled away, willing the smile on her face to dissipate. 'I'm still angry with you.' She gazed pointedly at his feet. 'And you've still got your shoes on.'

Milo took them off in the utility room and carried his rucksack back upstairs, saying something about making the bed. She went to the side door and the nettle outside caught her eye. What had Logan wanted to show her, in his rucksack? She shook herself. Let it go, Tilda. You're only going to get stung again.

A small meow caught her attention. She hesitated and then picked up Dettol, something she'd only ever done before if she had to get her into the pet carrier for a trip to the vets. She positioned the cat over her shoulder and tentatively ran a hand down the furry back. The cat's body relaxed. Tilda's did too. She leant her head into the fur, closed her eyes and her heartbeat slowed as the purring vibrated through to her own chest.

A door closed upstairs and quickly Tilda put down Dettol and went back into the kitchen as Milo entered the room too.

'I'm going to watch *Labyrinth* this afternoon, after I've set things up with that new client. Fancy joining me?' she asked.

'Love to. Cheers, Tilda.' Milo's lips twitched and he leant forwards to pick a wisp of fur from Tilda's shoulder. 'But first things first. There's an empty tuna tin behind the kettle. I'll put it in the recycling bin. Most odd. There's half of the contents in the fridge. Must have been a tiny sandwich.' He looked at Dettol and back to Tilda before heading towards the kettle, grinning.

15

They ended up sitting through *Labyrinth* twice. Then binge-watched the whole season of *Were Is the Wolf?* It had felt comfortable, warm, even... homely, a first for Tilda, those sensations in someone else's company. Tilda had rarely missed doing the weekly shop on its designated day. Fortunately she'd had peppers and onions in, because Saturday's meal was fajitas and she had chicken in the freezer. All they'd eaten for lunch was popcorn and crisps. Appropriate because there had been nothing normal about yesterday. It was as if she'd been living in a video game and the brother was a player who'd been killed off several rounds ago, but popped up again, as if he had nine lives, like Dettol.

Tilda reached for her bedside clock. She'd slept through her alarm and woken up at eight instead of seven? She jumped out of bed and sat cross-legged on the floor and did one minute of meditation before losing interest. She took a hot shower in the name of pure pleasure, brushed her hair, and then changed into trousers and... no, actually, today it would be jogging bottoms and a baggy shirt she hadn't worn for years. Tilda applied the last drops of her perfume. At roughly eight thirty she arrived in the kitchen.

Indignant meowing floated into the kitchen and she hurried to open the utility room and picked Dettol up for... wait... a morning cuddle?

Then she filled the cat bowl and at quarter to nine, made breakfast – cereal flakes with fruit, five walnut halves, a small handful of raisins and two tablespoons of...

No. She put the cereal box back, experiencing a sudden craving for pancakes – with lashings of syrup.

Milo walked into the kitchen and stretched. 'Those pancakes smell delicious.' A pile of them sat, stacked like meditation stones, in the middle of the table, flanked by syrup and jam. He filled up the kettle. 'Your usual green tea?'

'Coffee for a change,' she said. Once wouldn't hurt. She checked WhatsApp and grinned at the photo Yves had sent her of Cantaloupe, sitting like a human, washing his face.

'What's so funny?' asked Milo and he smiled.

'Oh. Um... a friend, Yves, he's sent me a photo of his cat. Well, it's not his, you see...'

'Yves? So he's French?' Milo's voice sounded artificially bright.

'Oh, it's complicated,' she said in a distracted voice, reading Yves' message.

Ma chère Tilda, Cantaloupe has practically moved in and unfortunately prefers to sleep either in my favourite chair or on my designs. I have to keep all my garment prototypes hidden. Dettol sounds very well behaved. Cantaloupe is mischievous. I kind of admire him. Mon ciel étoilé, I hate to mention this again. Beatrice came around last night, crying. Never has she looked so ill, with bloodshot eyes, she couldn't stop shaking. I wanted to turn her away but I'm her brother. I can't. Have you thought about lending me the money? Free clothes for life if you agree. Honest. Yves xxxxx

'*Mon ciel étoilé*,' murmured Tilda.

Milo turned around. 'This Yves calls you his starry sky?'

Her cheeks pinked up.

'Sorry, sticking my nose in again,' he said. 'Just amazed I've remembered anything of my French GCSE.' He cleared his throat. 'You two must be close?'

She raised an eyebrow.

He gave a sheepish smile. 'Okay, learning when to back off...' The doorbell rang. 'Want me to get it?' he asked, as if keen to leave the kitchen.

Tilda switched off the hob and placed the last pancakes on the stack. 'No. It's okay. Won't be a minute. Must be a cold caller hoping to sell something. I'll get rid of them.'

She went to the front door and pulled it open. Her chest contracted as if a wintry gust had snuck in and couldn't speak, as if she'd crammed in too much pancake.

'Didn't I make myself clear yesterday?' she said, stiffly. 'I've nothing more to say to you.' She went to close the door but a head popped around its wooden frame. It belonged to a small person with a mop of black curls and wearing bright red cotton dungarees. The little girl held out her hand in a solemn manner.

'Hello Auntie Tilda. I'm Riley. I'm six years old, I don't like eggs, red is my favourite colour and *Puss in Boots* is the best movie ever.'

Auntie Tilda? Wait... she had a niece? That meant... Logan had a daughter. With a move she felt powerless to resist, Tilda bent down and held out her hand, chest tighter than ever.

Tilda was an aunt.

Logan was a dad.

The little girl squeezed her hand tightly.

'I told you to let me do the talking first,' Logan hissed.

Riley folded her arms and shook her head. 'Silly Daddy. It would be rude to keep hiding around the corner.' She gave Tilda an impish grin. Tilda gave a small smile, secretly pleased Logan had been admonished by his daughter as well.

His daughter. He'd done a good job of keeping his private life away from the news apps. She met Logan's eyes. No, she wouldn't tear up, wouldn't show how much it hurt that they'd missed out on so many of each other's adult years.

'Logan, you can't turn up when you want and—'

Riley squealed and crouched down. Dettol had appeared at Tilda's feet. Riley reached out and tickled under the furry chin.

'What's its name?' she asked and raised her head, eyes half-hidden by an uneven fringe.

'Dettol,' Tilda said. 'She is a tabby cat and was living here when I moved in.' She added that information so that Logan didn't suspect she'd become a soppy animal lover. She felt vulnerable enough without showing anything that could be perceived as a weakness. She didn't know what his motives were, for suddenly wanting contact. And...

Tilda exhaled.

The little girl tilted her head. 'Why is she called that?'

'I found out she used to be called Dotty. Silly name for a cat, if you ask me.'

'Names are mega important. One of my friends has two cats called Sparkles and Glitter.' Riley pretended to be sick.

'So I changed it to Dettol,' continued Tilda. 'I'm a cleaner. Dettol comes in a bottle and in something that helps me do my job...'

Riley ran a hand along Dettol's back, cooing to the animal. 'It suits her. It sounds like kettle and Cameron and Daddy love their teas and coffees.'

'Cameron is my partner,' Logan explained.

How very modern, Riley calling her mum by her first name. Immediately Tilda pictured the ultimate WAG, with the blonde good looks of Cameron Diaz.

'Kettles used to hang over fires, we learnt that in school,' she said proudly. 'Daddy won't let me get a pet. Dettol is such a cool name.' She turned to Logan. 'Auntie Tilda has one. A cat might cheer Mummy up, when she has those days in bed.'

Oh, so she called Cameron Mummy as well, and she... wasn't well? Logan, the favourite child, the successful footballer, that image of him slipped for a second, hanging crooked, not so perfect, letting in the bags under the eyes and the stubble – and the possibility that neither of those things were due to partying, after all. But then she spotted the Armani logo on his jacket. His world was vastly different to hers, set against a backdrop of adoration. Not that she'd change her bargain basement clothes. Outfits had never interested her much. She'd told Yves that once and he'd sent smiley faces, saying sometimes he likes nothing more than wearing jeans and a T-shirt. Tilda was surprised her French friend had heard of Primark. Whereas Logan always had a certain flair. She'd teased him when he was little and refused to go out unless the colour of his T-shirt matched either his trousers or socks.

A car backfired and Dettol charged back into the house. Riley raced after her, past Tilda's legs. Logan opened his mouth but before he could say anything Riley was back, standing in front of Tilda.

'Please can I go after her?' she asked, out of breath. Another impish grin.

Tilda sighed. 'Okay. For a few minutes.'

Riley whooped and immediately took off her shoes. Tilda liked the girl already.

'You'd better come in,' she said tightly to Logan. 'But only until your daughter has finished playing with the cat.' She closed the door and pointed to the lounge. 'I'll be back in a minute.' She hurried into the kitchen. Riley was chatting to Milo about how cats sleep thirteen hours a day; she'd also learnt that in lessons.

'Milo, this is...'

He smiled. 'Riley has already introduced herself. She says... you're her Auntie Tilda.'

Tilda couldn't meet his eye. Having a niece she knew nothing about seemed like a stain on Tilda's character. Riley sat cross-legged on the floor, talking to Dettol about how her neighbour's cat would make the perfect best friend for her.

'He's called Ash and is grey. Much bigger than you. If he sits on my lap I can't get up, and when he sees a bird in the back garden he makes this funny chattering noise.'

'Logan is in the lounge,' said Tilda. 'We won't be long. Would you mind...?'

Milo gave the thumbs up. 'No problem. Perhaps Riley would like to have some pancakes?'

Riley shot up, a wide grin across her face. The button nose was the same as Tilda's had been at that age, along with the black curls. This physical familiarity between niece and aunt overwhelmed Tilda with a sense of sadness because, effectively, the two of them were strangers and not familiar at all. The little girl had Logan's smiley expression, with a dash of something else thrown in – a strong spirit, a confidence Tilda's mum would have called cheekiness. She very much believed in children being seen and not heard, and as Tilda got older she often thought her mother was channelling parenting from a bygone decade. 'Don't question me', 'Don't do what I do, do what I say', 'If you say another word, it'll mean bed without dinner'... These weren't responses to bad language or insults, Tilda's mum simply didn't like her children disagreeing with her. Tilda always swore that if she had kids, she'd be more like Dad and bring them up to be allowed to express their views and question everything. She went into the lounge. Logan sat on the sofa, the rucksack from the other day at his feet. 'Riley's having pancakes. Is that okay?'

'Great, thanks,' he said. 'She won't want to leave.'

Tilda sat down in an armchair by the window, opposite him, focusing on anything but her brother. The *Labyrinth* DVD hadn't been put back in its alphabetical position. Unusually this didn't bother her.

'Nice place,' he said.

'What do you want, Logan? Didn't I make myself clear enough yesterday?'

'If nothing else, I want to warn you about Milo. You hardly know the guy and took him in off the streets, right? He could be anyone.'

Tilda shook her head. 'Un. Effing. Believable. You waltz into my life, acting as if you know better.'

His cheeks flushed. 'It's not like that... I've just met his type before. I've had so many losers try to be my friend since becoming even a bit famous.'

'He gave your ring back!'

'Maybe he's got a bigger plan.' He sighed. 'My new neighbour couldn't have been more friendly when he moved in, a few months ago. When he found out who I was, the favours rolled in. He took me out for drinks, always insisting on paying. It was refreshing to have a mate away from the football scene. Then he offered me a great investment deal, in the foreign exchange market, said my team mates would benefit too. The night before I was about to sign on the dotted line, with a chunk of my savings, the police turned up outside his house. It was all a scam. He'd acted so genuine. You can't be careful enough.'

Tilda folded her arms. 'I'm more than capable of looking after myself.'

His shoulders sagged. 'Sorry, but his texts rang alarm bells. He's an intelligent, personable guy. How did someone like him end up homeless? You've got to admit, it's a bit suss.'

Riley's laughter came from the kitchen. Milo's too. Logan was wrong.

'You have a daughter, then? Became a father when you were what... twenty?' Tilda had been an aunt since she was twenty-two.

'Scared the life out of me. Best thing to ever happen.'

'Are you married?' Tilda hadn't seen any hint of this on the news app.

Logan shook his head. 'No... it's complicated. I hope to get married in the next year or two, with Riley as a flower girl.'

'She doesn't strike me as someone who'd want to wear frills and pastels.'

He smiled. 'Too right. We've already discussed it. She wants to wear her Spiderman outfit.'

'Mum must be thrilled to be a grandmother,' said Tilda. All the pleasure, none of the responsibility.

'Haven't seen her much.'

'What, in the last six years?'

'Oh, she's come to football games, the occasional Sunday dinner, but... well... her work's always time-consuming. My job is too. Was.'

'But Riley's mother... Is she okay? Mum's helped out with Riley, right?'

Logan's eyebrows shot up. 'Are you serious? Remember Mum's mantra? *Mind over matter.*'

Yes. Every time she broached the subject of leaving boarding school. Every time she opened up about the misery around going back at the beginning of a term, Mum told her to toughen up. She said it was character building and that Tilda would thank the more challenging times for making her strong, when she was older.

'Dad would have spoilt Riley to bits,' mumbled Logan and looked at Tilda.

Tilda met his gaze and bit her lip. Logan still missed him too?

He picked up the rucksack. 'There's something you must see, from the loft.'

'Don't bother unpacking it,' she said in a measured tone. 'You might be interested in helping our mum sort out her belongings, before she sells up, but there's nothing I want from my past. Keep any heirlooms for your-self. That's what she'll want.'

He frowned. 'I wasn't helping her out, Tilda. She's not even aware I've been up there. Riley wanted me to hunt out my old toys. Found my light-up sabres.'

Her face softened for a second. 'We'd fight with them in the dark. Your pirate ship was great too and we'd play with my mini plastic dogs on it.'

'Captain Woof and the Wag Tail Crew.' Logan smiled, a toothy grin, straight and white these days, with no gaps. The Tooth Fairy stopped visiting when Dad died. Mum made it clear you had to work hard for rewards in life, as an adult or child. He took a plastic bag out of the ruck-sack and passed it over but Tilda kept her hands by her sides. Nostalgia, happy memories, they were too much, a stark contrast to the siblings' relationship now.

'You won't even hear me out?'

Tilda got up.

Shoulders hunched, Logan followed her out of the lounge. He called Riley.

'But I'm eating pancakes, Daddy.'

Mum would have hollered for Tilda to do as she was told.

'Sorry sweetie, we'll have a nice lunch.'

Footsteps. 'McDonald's?'

Logan gave a tired smile. 'Maybe. Seeing as it's the weekend.'

Tilda stood by the front door. Her brother walked past. Stopped. Went to say something but changed his mind.

Whereas she couldn't help asking a question she could contain no longer. 'Why have you given up football?'

Riley sat on the doorstep, humming to herself.

'There are more important things. Riley's mum's health, Riley's stability.'

'I see. You wanted me to help? Just like that? That way you can pick up your career again.'

'Wow. That's one low opinion you've got of me.'

Tilda pursed her lips.

'No, of course not. Riley is more than happy spending time after school with our neighbour, who's a trained childminder. What I found, in the loft, made me realise that you and I, we've misunderstood each other.'

Tilda wanted to lean forwards and whisper *there's nothing to misunderstand about a brother who ditched his sister for fame and fortune.* But something in Logan's face made her stop. She must have been turning soppy after all. That wouldn't do. Logan would be fine. He had Mum. Money in the bank, no doubt. A daughter who clearly loved him to bits. A partner. Tilda firmly pressed her lips together.

Logan stepped outside. 'Come on, Riley.'

Having put her shoes back on, Riley threw herself at Tilda and hugged her tightly around the waist. Tilda stood stock still, not sure how to react. She placed her palms on the little girl's shoulders and gave a squeeze, not wanting to ever let go of that brief moment where she felt... a connection.

Riley stood back. 'I've promised Dettol that next time we visit, I'll bring her a toy. Poor thing hasn't got any.' She went out of the house and into a world of her own, practicing a dance move.

'I would say give my best to Mum but, well... I'm sure you understand if I don't,' Tilda said to Logan.

'Don't worry, I'm in no rush to speak to her again...' His voice caught. 'Not after what I've seen in that plastic bag.' He reached out and brushed her arm. 'I never stopped loving my older sister.'

Tilda covered her mouth with her hand, taken aback, she gulped. 'Why are you doing this? Can't you see how selfish, how wrong it is, to only contact me now because you happen to be having a hard time? Why couldn't you have reached out when you first had a baby, when you were shooting winning goals? It's like you didn't need me then, like you didn't need me when I got sent away as a child.'

'It wasn't like that, Tilda. Not like that at all.'

'Come on Dad!' Riley danced up the road.

'Goodbye Logan. Please don't come here again.'

'Just be wary of Milo,' he said and gave her a pained look before hurrying after his daughter.

16

Milo stood at the lounge door, light anorak over his arm. It had spotted with rain a few hours earlier.

'Just off for my meeting.' It started at midday. He intended on going to AA on Tuesday every week, along with the other meetings on Thursday and Friday. He fiddled with the coat's zip. 'About this Yves... I don't know the details – and it's not my place to ask...' he added quickly. 'But if... if you and him... I wouldn't want to cause any problems by living here...'

Oh. My. God. Heat flooded up her neck. 'Milo. It's fine. No one tells me who I can or cannot invite into my home. And Yves... he doesn't live in England.'

Milo's let go of the zip. 'Oh. So, he's in France?' He sounded relieved, must have been because he was worried about finding himself homeless again.

'He was born in Paris. Studied clothes design in Milan then moved back.'

'Wow. Impressive. I've never lived anywhere but Manchester. But if he ever wanted to visit, I'd be happy to... I'd understand...'

'That won't be happening any time soon.' He had his sister's two thousand-euro debt to pay. Tilda couldn't afford to meet the cartel's demands either. She was holding out to her July deadline to give him her final, negative answer, the deadline of finding a man to propose, the deadline set by herself after Shane's belittling comments. The day, one way or another, she'd have to face the truth about her future.

The utility room door slammed shut. Monday's job in Wilmslow had gone well. Tilda had enjoyed losing herself in the cleaning after Logan and Riley's visit the day before. Milo had proved himself to be an industrious worker, thorough, paying attention to the detail, like the wall tiles in the bathroom and underneath the lounge furniture. He didn't balk at the grimier tasks, either. The owner had held a party over the weekend, a wild one by the looks of it. Nothing much fazed Tilda, including the joint butts on the kitchen floor, the traces of vomit around the toilet bowl, and crisps and nuts that had got lost down the sides of upholstered furniture. Milo had seen it all before, in the night club.

Iris and Jazz were both due back next week – the flu had hit them harder than Milo – so Tilda and Milo's evening shifts in Stockport would stop after Friday. Another job had come in, residential, in affluent Bramhall. A former, retired client had gone to Australia for three months, to stay with her son. She was back and wanted a deep clean of her sprawling bungalow next week, before returning to the usual once every Friday arrangement. Milo would be a perfect match. Mrs Hudson and her late husband used to own a bar in Spinningfields.

Tilda stretched. She sat in the lounge, not knowing why. It wasn't as if she had no work, there were ads to run and a client base to grow. Her next blog post was also overdue. Feeling unable to leave the lounge was nothing to do with Logan's plastic bag shoved behind the armchair. He'd left it, on purpose, no doubt. Milo had planned to catch the bus yesterday after lunch, to pick up some clothes he'd been storing at a friend's house. Cautiously, he mentioned it to Tilda, not wanting her to worry he intended to stay permanently, and no doubt not wanting that himself. Life in Crouchden, in Tilda's modest house, must have been very different to the glitzy vibe of Wilmslow. But glad for the distraction, she'd driven him over. Then last night she and Milo re-watched several episodes from *Lucifer*, season one, on Netflix, a favourite series for both of them. Tilda loved the concept that the devil wasn't bad, he simply punished those who were; the concept that a person was sent to hell by their own guilt.

Whereas Milo was most taken by a demon character who eventually grew a soul. He'd seen in AA how much people could change, himself included, and reconnect with the goodness in them, growing to care about others as much as themselves. They'd gone through her whole DVD collection, chatting about each one, before they'd stuffed them back onto the shelf, in any old order.

Tilda stretched again as Dettol strode in. She stood on the floor, eyeing the sofa.

'Go on,' said Tilda, gently. 'I'll brush it down afterwards.'

Dettol didn't move so Tilda patted the cushions next to her. The cat jumped up. It stared at Tilda. Tilda stared back. Dettol yawned. Milo had told her cats do that when they are embarrassed. Up until then she'd believed the cat had simply been bored with Tilda's company.

After a few strokes, Dettol curled up and went to sleep. Tilda wouldn't examine the bag. Stuff Logan. She got up and went to the door. However, Riley's adventurous manner came into her mind. That little girl would take a peek, no doubt about it. A younger Tilda would have as well. When they were little, when Dad was alive, she and Logan would go what they called, 'exploring'. They'd creep down the stairs at night, once their parents had put them to bed, in the dark with torches, and spy on Mum and Dad through a gap in the lounge door. Soon they'd lose interest due to the news channel their parents loved, and would tiptoe into the kitchen and sneak a couple of digestives from the biscuit tin. Sucking in their cheeks, trying not to laugh, they'd make their way upstairs, avoiding the step that always creaked. The best game ever was hide and seek, in the house or out in the massive garden. The gardener who visited once a week was good fun and would sometimes agree to play once he'd finished his work.

One of the reasons Tilda fell into cleaning, and eventually set up her own business, was their cleaner, Shirley, who took such pride in making the stainless-steel kitchen sink sparkle, expressed such gusto as she'd pull on her rubber gloves, with a smile. She whistled while she vacuumed the carpets and stuck her tongue out, concentrating hard, as she got a stubborn stain off the hob top. To Tilda it seemed like a happy job, rewarding too, and one where you didn't have someone constantly telling you what to do. Shirley also bought Tilda and Logan chocolate at Easter and books at Christmas. One of her mum's redeeming qualities was that she appreciated Shirley's work ethic and bought her flowers on her birthday and gave her a Christmas bonus.

Logan and Tilda would make her a card. Her brother would scrawl rows of kisses.

He gave the tightest hugs. Opened up about his problems. Would rub Tilda's back whenever she cried. He'd been a good brother. She liked to think she'd been a good sister.

Tilda went to the armchair and peered around its side, she pulled out the plastic bag and opened it. Tilda frowned as she took in the contents.

* * *

'I'll make lunch,' hollered Milo.

Heart thumping, Tilda tore herself away from the contents of the bag, not realising Milo had got back from his meeting. The DVD player clock indicated how much she'd lost track of time. Her hands trembled as she put it back behind the armchair. Tilda stood up and went to the window, hardly noticing people walk past in sunhats, dogs on leads panting, music belting out of cars with open windows. When she arrived in the kitchen Milo had made sandwiches, put out the crisps and apples along with two glasses of water.

'Good meeting?' she asked.

'Yep. I'm getting to know the regulars. One member is bringing in a number for me on Thursday of a shop that sells cut-price second-hand furniture, for when I get my own place. Another has a mate who runs a bar in the Village, said they are advertising for temporary staff. He's going to ask if there are any positions left.'

Milo, working in a bar? Pushing away what she'd seen in Logan's bag, for a second, Tilda wondered if that was the best, the wisest, option.

Tilda sat quietly as she ate, hardly replying to Milo's conversation. Slowly the shock of what she'd seen in the lounge settled, deep within. Deeper, deeper, until she shut it off and told him about the client in Bramhall, and how Iris had mentioned that she and Jazz had both been nervous Tilda would have given their shifts permanently to someone else, seeing as their flu became prolonged.

'They should know me better than that,' she said.

Milo wiped his mouth. 'How? They only meet you during interview, and then for their first ever shift when they are stressed about impressing you. Have you ever got the whole team together? For a night out? To show your appreciation?'

Tilda looked aghast. 'Why would I do that?'

Milo grinned. 'Team building, that's a big part of my management ethos, and it makes you more approachable. I used to arrange loads of events for my staff. Kofi would come along too – meals out, bowling nights, Laser Tag, Escape Room afternoons.'

'I can't think of anything worse.'

He laughed. 'A meal. How about that? In a pub. You foot the bill. In return it will motivate them, it will improve communication, the quality of their work will go up – I've seen it all before. Their job satisfaction will massively increase if, every now and again, they feel truly appreciated – in person. They could have worries about the job they don't want to put down in an email. Go on. Do it. Say the weekend after next. A Saturday night dinner out. In Manchester. I dare you, Tilda Wright.'

'What if they say no?'

'What if they don't? Come on. It makes sense from a business point of view, if nothing else. Could be fun. How many people do you employ?'

'Ten.'

'Oh.'

'You thought it would be more?'

'This is a decent-sized house, so yes. But to be fair, I have zero experience of running my own business.'

'The staff I take on want to do two shifts a day, out of morning, afternoon and evening shifts. For each four-hour shift, I earn twelve pounds, as I charge my clients fifteen per hour and pay my staff three less than that. In total that's twenty-four per employee each day, and with ten of them, that's two hundred and forty pounds to me per day, slightly less at the weekend. And there are always some shifts I have to work myself. Plus

I don't lose money, once a client has signed the contract. For example, I charge cancellation fees if not given fair notice.'

'Wow. That soon adds up.'

She'd never talked business with anyone before apart from the bank's employees. She'd tried with Yves, to find common ground, but it soon became clear he knew little about the practical side of being a fashion designer and said he employed an accountant. 'I have costs, of course, for the website and various subscription fees. Public Liability Insurance, as well, but I don't rent office premises, don't have admin staff. My overheads are minimal.'

'A night out for eleven people. It wouldn't cost that much.'

'Twelve if you came,' she said.

Milo smiled.

'My personal costs are low, I love my job, I don't go on holiday much. I was able to save a phenomenal amount the first two years; the company took off quickly. There are always plenty of new clients out there, disgruntled with their current cleaners. That's why I only take on the best workers. It enabled me to save enough to pay for a deposit on this place, along with some money from my grandmother.'

'You could double your profit if you took on an admin assistant to advertise and chase leads, if you got someone keen. My last job was great, Kofi gave me the freedom to use my own initiative. We hired brilliant staff but they often left, so in my second year there I suggested we paid them more – and that paid off within months. We landed people fully invested in the job, wanting to build a career and, like me, keen to use their own initiative to improve profits. They were enthusiastic about working overtime, to cover colleagues who were sick... Also, I had great fun brainstorming and introduced theme nights, tying them into bar snacks. People need carbs when they're dancing and drinking. I was confident that even the higher end Wilmslow crowd would enjoy Dirty Fries Friday and Buffalo Wings Wednesday.' He pulled a face. 'Sorry. Rambling. God, though, I loved the creative side.'

Tilda couldn't take her eyes off his face, the animation, the sparkle in his eyes, the passion was infectious. 'I suppose if a night out raised productivity and loyalty...' Arranging it would make for a super busy afternoon, finding a location, sending out emails... Exactly what she needed after discovering what was in Logan's bag in the lounge earlier, before Milo had called her for lunch. A meal in two weeks was late notice but here was to being spontaneous.

However, Logan's bag kept bobbing into her mind. She pushed away her apple, trying to identify the emotions coursing through her veins. She could be angry about what she'd seen, or so, so sad. Ashamed. Confused. In fact, forget mere anger, she was dripping with rage. Then this mix of emotions left her numb. She studied the screen but her mind shifted to the first of the unaddressed, unposted letters she'd opened amongst the bundle her brother had left behind. Tilda forgot Milo was there, didn't hear Dettol meowing, wasn't aware of her house guest washing up, didn't respond when he said he was off to do job applications in the lounge. The letter, its words, its sentiments, kept going around, and around, and around.

Saturday 20 Sept 2008

> *Big Sissy Sis,*
>
> *How is High School? Feels like ages ago you went, but it's only one week. Is it like Hogwarts? Wish I could get an owl to deliver this letter. Mum said she'd write the address on and post it.*
>
> *Maybe I sound like a baby, but I wish you were still here. It's really quiet after school, and boring with Mum reading and watching telly about news, about banks and wars. She's talked about some football thing at half-term. Five days away, studying tackling, kicking, food to eat and video analay... anala... Whatever. It sounds cool but I'd rather see you. I can't talk to anyone else, not about the important stuff. You know we were practicing riding our bikes without holding on? Did it, sis! Last night. I wanted to ring you, but Mum said you'd be too busy with your new friends.*
>
> *What are the teachers like? Your bedroom? I'm dreading sleeping over at this football thing. I won't know anyone. Got any tips?*
>
> *Don't forget me :)*
>
> *Little Bro Lo*

17

Tilda got up Wednesday at six thirty; she hadn't been able to sleep. After accidentally knocking over her alarm clock, she shivered and sat cross-legged on the floor. She went into WhatsApp and hesitated before starting to type.

Hi Yves. Problems here too with siblings. My brother. He's turned up out of the blue, wanting a reconciliation. I've mentioned that we are estranged. I'm so angry with him. But now something's happened that has made me realise maybe... things aren't as black and white as I thought. That bacon and eggs from last night's photo looked good. An English staple, I didn't know the French liked them too. Tilda

She pressed send, waiting to feel better. Nothing changed.

A knock at the door made her jump. She opened it, pulling the door closed behind her. Milo stood on the landing in jogging trousers and a sweat top. He held up a pair of old trainers.

'Heard you were awake. I haven't been jogging for months. Fancy giving it a go, with me? We could do a few laps around the park.'

Her eyes narrowed. Was this because she was quiet last night? Some ruse to get her to open up? She pursed her lips.

'I'm afraid I won't be up for much conversation though,' he said. 'I'm likely to be 100 per cent out of breath.'

He'd done it again. Read her so well. Her frown softened. 'Not sure what I'd wear,' she muttered.

'Don't worry, nobody will be looking at what you're wearing, running with me, with my unfit legs wobbling, dribble down my chin...'

'You're making this whole idea so appealing.'

'And I promise... no surprises.' His cheeks flushed.

'Okay. Give me ten minutes.' She'd never jogged before. Nothing could be less fun – apart from sitting indoors, alone, with that plastic bag calling from the lounge.

Twenty minutes later, Tilda appeared in the garden wearing a pair of old black leggings she'd dug out from the back of her wardrobe, and a T-shirt. She stopped, for a second, immediately cheered by uplifting sunshine and dew making the grass sparkle. With no gusto, Tilda did a couple of lunges, put her hands on her hips and turned side to side, following Milo's lead.

Her phone buzzed.

Sorry to hear that Tilda. I feel bad asking for your help now, you've got problems of your own. I'm hardly sleeping. The sibling bond's a strong one, isn't it? However much you want to let go, it keeps hold, through the decades. I... I dated an English girl once. She taught me a lot about England's food. It's not as bad as the French think :) She intro-duced me to English biscuits too, although her calling me her little Hobnob was a step too far... Yves xxxxx

Tilda gave a small smile, looked up and spotted Milo watching her.

'Have you ever actually met this Yves?' he asked.

'No, but we've had a couple of video calls,' she snapped.

Milo held up his hands. 'I wasn't criticising. I think it's great that you're getting to know someone thoroughly before... well... whatever happens.'

'Sorry I snapped,' she said. 'I thought you were implying that...'

'I'm implying nothing,' he said. 'Lots of people get to know each other online these days and you're the most sensible person I've ever met. I'd trust your judgement any day.'

Tilda stretched upwards for a second, as if the morning sun had made her grow.

They started jogging. Very slowly. She glanced at Milo. So much for wobbling legs. Years of dancing in clubs must have kept him fit. A young female passer-by shot him an appreciative look.

They turned into the park and passed the large, black, spiked metal gates. She slowed, breathing not coming so easily for herself. Tilda drank in the early morning hush disturbed only by the birdsong, crisp and melodic, hopeful, generous, ever so friendly, as if the birds remembered her feeding them seed. A couple of ducks quacked by the circular pond edged with reeds and bull rushes in the distance. Grateful to be outdoors, she ran faster and faster and overtook Milo. Her calves hurt now, nausea built; she was hoping to forget about the bundle of letters.

> *Saturday 5 Oct 2008*
>
> *Big Sissy Sis,*
>
> *Did you get my letter two weeks ago? How's school? Bet the evenings are fun. Have you taught your new friends our favourite card games? Mum says she is too tired to play in the evenings – but not too tired to work on her laptop. Guess what? After all the times you've told me to actually read the Harry Potter story, I've started the first book from your bedroom. Have you got friends like Ron and Hermione? Enemies like Draco? Does your school have houses with cool names? Any pets like Hedwig?*
>
> *Gotta go. Mum's calling. I've got a football match. Wish I didn't. Outside it's rainy and cold. For just one Saturday, I wish I could stay in bed and watch cartoons. But I can't let Mum down. She makes such a fuss if I score a goal and puts it on Facebook. Mega cringe.*
>
> *Write to me sis.*
>
> *Don't forget me*
>
> *Little Bro Lo*

Big Sissy Sis. Little Bro Lo. Their nicknames for each other. Tilda closed her eyes, long enough to miss a large stone in her way. She tripped over it and crashed onto the ground, yelping as her elbows took the brunt of her weight. Tilda ended up in a pile of soil, raised her head and spat out the dirt. Strong arms easily lifted her up and one slipped around her waist. Tilda resisted, went to push Milo away. Instincts told her to accept no help, because that was how falls played out in her childhood. Her mum would leave Tilda on the ground, waiting for her to get to her feet on her own. Briefly she'd check her over and remind Tilda that big boys and girls didn't cry, that you had to be able to manage on your own in this world. It was a phrase Mum had become even more fond of after Dad passed. However, Tilda's heart spoke in a different way, a language she'd learnt from her dad and gran about kindness, and helping others. She always rushed to pick Logan up if he tripped, even though Mum scolded her. She'd wipe his eyes and give him a hug.

'I'm fine,' she groaned and rubbed her elbows. Milo held firm and led her to a nearby bench, by the pond. A duck jumped down from the bank, onto the water, and glided into the middle before disappearing under the surface. The sun had risen further now. Sweat marks stained Milo's top, his face was red. What a sight the pair of them must have made, streaks of mud across Tilda's clothes and face. She couldn't blame a nearby black-bird for giving its alarm call. She rubbed her elbows again and gently Milo turned her arms to take a look.

'There's blood everywhere and bruises already appearing. Those grazes need washing,' he said. 'Come on. It's my turn to look after you. Let's get back.'

Hobbling, she leant into him. The first commuters were on their way by the time they arrived. Once back, she stood, under hot water wincing as it touched grazed skin, losing herself to the sound of the shower's gushing water, before more written words reappeared in her head, drowning out the splashes.

Saturday 25 Oct 2008

Big Sissy Sis,

I'm just about to leave for that half-term football thing. Secretly wish I wasn't. I'm missing two birthday parties, and don't want to sleep away *from home. And I won't get to see you tomorrow, when Mum picks you up. Perhaps it won't be so bad sleeping in a strange bed cos you must love it, in your dorm at boarding school, as you never reply to my letters. I was hoping we could catch up when I heard you were coming home for half-term, because Gran couldn't look after you like Mum wanted her to. But Mum booked me in for this football camp instead, and I'll be the one not here, I'll be having adventures. Hope you are writing a diary, then I can read it when you get back at Christmas. We are still best buds, right?*

It's raining again here, today. Mum says rain won't matter when I'm earning millions a year, in the Premier League. Bet Ronaldo doesn't like Manchester as much as Madeira, where he grew up. Remember that time we stuffed Madeira cake in our mouths and couldn't talk without blowing crumbs? We laughed so much. I nearly choked! Mum doesn't understand fun like that.

You haven't forgotten me, have you?

Little Bro Lo

Milo jumped into the shower, after Tilda. A heavy metal song pulsated downstairs whilst he changed; Milo had penchant for Iron Maiden and Judas Priest. They shared the same taste in books and movies, but Tilda was more pop than rock when it came to music. She did a double take when he came downstairs, smart in a shirt of his; white and striped, it complimented his dark hair and eyes, and the chinos struck exactly the right balance between business and casual. He smelt good, too. Pine, fresh, his aftershave had a rawness about it.

'I just got an email,' he said, and beamed. 'A last-minute interview for a bar management job in Stockport. You may not have to put up with me much longer.'

'Great,' she said, baffled as to why her voice sounded flat. There was nothing better than personal space. Tilda couldn't wait to be alone. She couldn't. Perhaps it was flat because of the obvious concern. 'But are you sure, Milo? A job in a bar... you aren't worried that...?'.

Milo shook his head. 'No. I'm not. Me... me falling apart at Shakers had nothing to do with the litres of alcohol in the bar, underneath my flat. I'm 100 per cent rock solid.'

Tilda looked him in the eye and a sheepish expression crossed his face. Milo had been through rehab like her, he knew you were only ever sober for one day at a time. No recovering alcoholic could say 100 per cent that drinking wouldn't ever happen again. He'll have gone through treatment, like she had, alongside some people who'd fallen off the wagon after years, after decades, without booze.

Tilda prepared toast, an easy replacement for the more complex cereal meal she'd made for so many mornings. *Alone.* In the evenings, she used to spend time with her meditation tapes, her gratitude journal, her inspirational postcards, companions that had been nudged to one side by Milo moving in. She thought back to the evenings alone when she'd been drinking. Reading those letters would have meant blacking out, walking down in the morning to spilt alcohol and greasy takeout boxes. Tilda sat down and shuffled in the chair. The image in her head of herself hungover, a mess, didn't disgust her in the way it used to. She grabbed the jam jar and made polite conversation before turning to work, whilst Milo went over his notes about the company who was interviewing him just before lunch.

'I'm amazed,' she said. 'Everyone has replied straight back about the night out. Saturday 6 July it is.'

The sixth – two days after her project's deadline, two days after it was time to open her heart to Yves, who'd wooed her in a way other men never had.

'Two are gutted they're not free,' she continued. 'That means a table for eight, or rather ten with you and me. Stockport is central to most people. The Windmill is only a twenty-minute walk from the station. It's a lovely pub. It was one of the temporary cleaning jobs I had, a few years back. Decent manager. I took them on recently again as well, after I went in to see if they were happy with their current cleaners, so I might be able to wangle a good deal on, say, wine for the table, for the others. It worked out well as I'd just lost a client, a coffee shop in Davenport was cutting costs and pushed the cleaning onto their baristas. Happens a lot.'

'Are you still growing the business?'

'I'd like to. The potential client base is certainly out there and my pricing has hit the mark. Trouble is, if Wright Cleaners gets much bigger it won't feel as manageable. As you mentioned, yesterday, I'd have to...' Her voice trailed off. Milo raised an eyebrow. 'I'd have to take on an admin assistant and... I'm not sure about working with someone else at such close quarters,' she blurted out.

Milo tilted his head. 'I get it.'

'You do? But working in hospitality you've had to be so sociable.'

Milo sat down. 'In my experience, most addicts they... get used to loneliness. More than that, they crave isolation, especially when using. It's easier, they don't have to hide their drug and the deeper you get stuck, the louder those voices in your head talk, telling you no one understands, that you're better off on your own. The drunken one-night stands, the shouting matches, the verbal fights, the embarrassing behaviour, that's all a front for a very quiet addict inside, who wants nothing but to hide.' He stood up. 'But you're in recovery now, Tilda. You don't need to keep hiding.'

Was that what she'd been doing?

He consulted his watch and disappeared upstairs and came down wearing a light jacket, saluted Tilda and then strode into the utility room.

It was good to see him stride, it had been more of an apologetic shuffle when she'd first taken him in. An unfamiliar emotion rose in her chest. Maybe, just maybe, she'd made a difference. She experienced that warm feeling in her job – oh, she loved creating a spick and span space, that always produced a sense of satisfaction, but not one as deep as when she'd work with clients with additional requirements. Often she'd do those shifts herself. Like the woman who'd been diagnosed with dementia. Tilda helped her reorganise her rooms with Post-it notes and no trip hazards.

'Good luck,' she called, not wanting to fear the worst happening if he got the position.

'Cheers,' he called, 'I'm keeping my fingers crossed.'

The side door closed.

Lonely? Isolated? Hiding? No, Tilda simply enjoyed her own company. It was safer.

Tilda got up, went into the lounge and collapsed onto the sofa. Dettol followed her in and, still unsure about this new type of owner, sat at her feet and tilted her head. Tilda patted her lap. Dettol hesitated until Tilda gave her a second invitation.

Riley had called Dettol a 'poor thing' for not having any toys. The elasticated Buddhist bead bracelet on her wrist caught her eye. Since getting sober, she'd put it on every morning, without fail. Tilda pulled it off. Now how did this work? She dangled it in the air, swinging it from side to side. Dettol's eyes widened, pupils dilated, she swiped the bracelet. Hypnotised, Tilda watched the bracelet rocking to and fro.

Saturday 8 Nov 2008

Hello Tilda,

It's bonfire night at school today, with a huge display. It's going to be awesome. I suppose you are having great times with your new friends. I worked out it's two months since I started writing to you, and haven't got a reply. But I don't care any more, cos I'm really, really busy too. I made a friend in my dorm at half-term, at that football camp. He wants to be a famous footballer like Mum wants me to be. His parents have got a Porsche and I'm going to stay with him for a bit, in the Christmas holidays. We'll be doing grown-up stuff like looking after his family's horses. So I won't be around much when you are next home.

This is my last letter. Guess you forgot about me. No matter.

Logan

Dettol swiped the bracelet another time, caught it and jumped back, arching her back, as it broke and beads tumbled onto the carpet.

18

Monday and Tuesday passed, then Wednesday came. Every day Tilda had stared at Logan's phone number. He'd left it on a scrap of paper, in the plastic bag, and she'd added it to her list of contacts. An early run with Milo yesterday had helped distract her; the morning chill, the park's dewy smells from grass, flowers and soil, the focus on not tripping over. They'd agreed to make a habit of it. He'd be back from AA any minute and then, after lunch, the two of them were going to deep clean Mrs Hudson's bungalow in Bramhall. The side door went, a voice chatted to Dettol who'd jumped down from the wooden chair next to Tilda and run into the utility room, a voice now as familiar as the furniture itself.

'Dettol needs her lunch... You could feed her,' said Tilda as Milo came into the kitchen.

'Rule-breaking?' he said and smiled.

'Being flexible,' she replied. 'How was your meeting?'

'One poor sod has relapsed, after ten years. Reminded me that we must always be wary.'

Tilda felt an itch inside, an itch that wanted to be scratched, an itch that had become stronger in recent weeks that, nevertheless, she'd become good at ignoring, refusing to admit where it came from and what it meant.

'I'll make lunch in a minute,' she said, changing the subject. 'Must finish this email first.' They'd got into a routine of taking it in turns to prepare the food – a routine that hadn't been formally established by any verbal or written agreement. This was new for a woman who lived according to rotas and schedules. It made her think about her and Yves' routine of swapping dinner photos. That had felt real, as if it meant something, until she and Milo shared actual cooking.

Over the week Milo had spent more time in the kitchen, at the table, in front of the old laptop that he'd borrowed from the same friend who'd been storing his clothes. He must have found lots of jobs to apply for, as he'd spent more time typing than Tilda. She wasn't used to talking on the phone, with someone else listening – calls including that first contact with new staff or clients, keeping patient whilst dealing with a mistake made by the tax office, firmly chasing the late delivery of a new cleaning product she was keen to test out, and challenging the price rise on the tunics she ordered in for staff – Milo's being in the recent batch, along with a new one for Jazz, a spill of bleach had ruined her current one. However, soon she hardly felt his presence. Cups of coffee would magically appear by her side. Purring would float through the air when Dettol crept onto his lap. The amicable, easy company didn't intrude and had dulled the pain caused by reading the letters, including one that, unlike the others, wasn't to Tilda from Logan.

She pressed send on her email and her chair scraped the floor as she stood up. She stretched and went over to the bread bin. Milo pressed send too and looked up nervously.

'Everything okay?' she asked.

Gently he placed Dettol on the tiled floor. 'I've emailed you.' He stood up and rubbed the back of his neck. 'You don't have to read the attachment. It's up to you.'

Tilda put back the bread bin's lid and sat at her laptop. She clicked into her inbox.

'It's sent with best of intentions. I did a lot of research.' Excitement bubbled in his voice.

Tilda opened the document headed – *Wright Cleaners. The Next Step.* Her eyes scanned the page. 'What's this about?'

Milo stood up and paced up and down. 'The Stockport bar offered me the job – manager, full-time, pension perks, the lot.'

'That's great!' she said and beamed, her face aching with the fakeness as she pictured Milo working with spirits and beers, those bottles' voices calling to the man who not so very long ago, lay in a broken heap on the pavement with a bloody nose. 'So...?' She studied the document.

'This is my way of saying thank you, before I leave.'

'Tips on how to improve my business?'

'Not tips. Concrete ideas. And not to improve, it's amazing as it is. More on how you could expand. I'll summarise – if that's okay?'

Milo was leaving. She was just upset because Dettol would miss him, she decided.

He pressed his palms together, intertwining his fingers. 'Firstly – you could focus on either residential or commercial jobs. Specialise, so you aren't managing and overseeing three shifts. Residential are morning and afternoon, commercial mainly the evening. Restricting your hours to the nine till six might make sense, targeting your energies on those individual clients.'

'No. My workers have different needs. Iris likes the evening as she's busy with grandchildren during the day.'

'Oh.' He looked crestfallen. 'Okay. My second point... to stand out, because that's the way to increase profit, you need to diversify your services. How about carpet and upholstery cleaning, that would suit both residential and commercial clients? Pressure washing too – making driveways and entrances to buildings sparkle.'

Tilda sat up. The furniture of some of her older clients could definitely do with a refresh, and the outside too, a tricky job for clients who'd lost their strength or mobility.

'Thirdly... I've watched you working this last week, your online ads are important... but not everyone stops to read when they're scrolling... How about, hand in hand with the digital marketing, you do flyer drops around areas where you'd like to acquire clients? Have you ever done offline advertising?'

'No... No, I haven't.' He could have a point. It was easy to flick past an online ad whereas flyers always had to at least be picked up, even if they did also often end up in the bin.

'Those online posts play an important part, and whilst I believe you do an incredible job, there's always room for improvement. You gave the company a great name but don't play on it enough. How about more about "Getting it Wright" – upselling how your business is reliable, thorough, competitive and flexible? You could list what other companies do wrong...' The ideas flowed, like looking into selling clients basic cleaning products. 'Of course, some of this would require upfront investment, but slowly, slowly – the best cleaning business in Manchester isn't going to be built overnight.'

'I'm lost for words.'

His face fell. 'Am I an interfering idiot?'

'No... quite the opposite... You... you've given up your time to study my company and see how it could grow. Thank you, Milo. No one's ever taken that much interest in what I do, before.'

He rubbed the back of his neck again. 'You deserve it.'

'Of course, it probably won't happen. To take these ideas forward, I'd definitely need an admin assistant and I've told you how I feel about working closely with someone I hardly know. Unless—' She'd become used to Milo in the house, in a way she couldn't imagine getting used to any other person. But working alongside him, formally? Would he even be interested? Someone else to share the responsibility of running her business would certainly fit in with her plans regarding Yves, and just in time too, as her plans came to fruition soon, what with 4 July only being about one week away, the deadline she'd set for asking a man to marry her. The words were already prepared in her head. She wondered how romantic, good-looking, sweet Yves would react.

'Unless what?' he asked and shrugged.

'...You came on board,' she blurted out.

'*Me*? But you've been encouraging me literally every day to go back to bar work and—'

'Wait... what? No. Not at all.' Working around alcohol? Not ever if possible. 'A job, yes, but not necessarily in the profession you're used to. You know about cleaning.'

'Blimey. Right. Well...' Milo shook his head. 'That's an amazing offer... have to say I'm tempted. Working at Wright Cleaners, I'd really be part of something.' His eyes sparkled. 'The bar was initially keen for two managers to job-share, they find that works better, so offered me part-time hours if I preferred. That could work, me combining the two jobs, at first.'

'I'd pay you the going admin assistant rate, alongside what you earn from cleaning shifts. And part-time would be perfect. Unless the expansion of the business took off quickly, there wouldn't be enough admin for us to both work at it, full-time, not to start with. I could even do a cleaning shift myself now and again, with you on board... I miss getting stuck into the practical side. I can't promise when your earnings would substantially rise. That would depend on our success.'

The smile fell from his face. 'Of course, it's not possible. I... I'll only let you down in the end.'

Tilda frowned. 'Why?'

'If you knew the truth about me... about my sister... you wouldn't want me anywhere near your business. I'm not to be trusted.'

Tilda stood up and took his hands, unable to resist the need to touch him. She squeezed his fingers. 'What happened with your sister, Milo? Tell me. Or fill me in about your daughter. You've never talked about either.'

He swallowed. 'Because of me, my sister... she lost her chance of a career she wanted. I messed it up. Big time. You see... that's why everything fell apart at work. I watched a talent TV dance show. To my amazement, her best friend from primary school was on there. But then I shouldn't have been surprised, Julie was always an incredible dancer. She and my sister, Grace...' He flinched at saying her name. 'They'd go to dance classes together. Grace always came top of the class with exams in ballet and tap. She had big dreams, from a young age, of being on stage in the West End. Because of me, her talent never came to fruition...'

His voice sounded so sad Tilda didn't like to push about his daughter as well. She leant forwards and gave him a hug, before coming to her senses and pulling back in an awkward manner. 'I'm so sorry you two are estranged, whatever happened. But as for you letting your sister down, here you are helping me develop my future, so the universe clearly doesn't agree with your fear that history might recur.'

'You don't understand...' he cut in.

Tilda held up her hand. 'Kofi called you a diamond employee. Come on, Milo, let's do it. To be honest I'm not 100 per cent sure either. I could let *you* down. Working alongside someone, I'm not used to it, and might call it all off in a few weeks, so you'd be taking a risk as well. No guarantees.'

'You're serious, aren't you?'

She glanced at Dettol, washing herself by her food bowl. 'We could come to some agreement about rent. You'd get full wages from me, instead of me taking a cut for costs upfront. You'd become more of a standard lodger. We'll go through the basics today. I'll take you through the apps I use on the business phone.'

'This is crazy. Wonderful. So unexpected. Thanks. Thank you. You're certain about this?'

No. But then Tilda didn't have anyone to talk to about it. Yves had enough problems of his own. Logan was once a great sounding board, back when they were kids. It was one of the things she'd missed about him most. His reassurance, his belief in her. Tilda's hands curled into fists. But she didn't need anyone to back her up. She'd got by, for this long, trusting her own instincts.

She went over to the bread bin. 'Do you want your own food cupboard? Would you prefer to cook your own dinners?'

'I like eating together. How about we split the food bill, but...'

'We could vary the rota? Swap off some of the meals for your favourites?' She could read him too.

'I love cooking from scratch, always found it relaxing after work – even if it was sometimes at one in the morning. We could use your meals a few times a week and I'll rustle up the others. Take tonight, it's supposed to be your delicious cottage pie but, for a change, what about a spicy chicken couscous? I'll nip out and get the ingredients, after I've rung up to accept the part-time bar job, and researched flyer companies. What do you say?'

'I say we need to have lunch first. Sandwiches as usual?'

'How about fried eggs on toast? Sunny side up.'

Yes. No.

Milo and Dettol stared at her face.

Okay. She'd go for it; go for change. It was scary but recently other thoughts had crossed her mind – like how even scarier, maybe, was the prospect of staying the same, and living a lonely life, as she had done, without a single other soul to witness it.

19

What a week it had been, since Tilda offered Milo a job. They'd brainstormed every evening, chatting and making notes till late, making big plans for Wright Cleaners. Last night she hadn't gone to bed until one. However, Tilda woke up early. It was deadline date: 4 July. The culmination of a year's efforts and the last week of knots in her stomach. This was it. A message was waiting from Yves. Another written communication. They still hadn't had a video call since the second one two months ago. He'd been especially busy in recent days, having landed a contract with a big department store. At this stage he couldn't give Tilda details, but said he'd be able to pay her back any loan within days. She'd succeeded in not committing to lending him the money, waiting to tell him her answer today.

She took a deep breath. Tapped out the words. Tilda had them all ready, literally at her fingertips. But they wouldn't come. She needed to say them out loud. So instead she simply messaged:

We need to speak, Yves. About the money. Tilda

She pressed dial. Yves picked up straightaway.
'Tilda, ma chérie, I am so glad you rang. My sister—'

'Yves. I haven't got the money. I'm sorry. It's all tied up in the business. I'm sure you understand.'

Silence.

'I do. Of course. No matter. I'll work something out. Family is everything.'

Tilda paused. 'It is. And on that note... I need to know where this is going, Yves, you and me. I'm serious about us. I want the whole shebang: marriage, kids... do you feel the same?'

'Of course I do...' His voice wavered.

'But you're always too busy to video call and now with having to help your sister, it could be a while before we can meet up for real. Until then, I need something more concrete. Proof that I'm the one for you. I need... commitment.'

'Ma chérie, of... of course I want you to marry me, I've known that since the first time you messaged back.' Yves gave a nervous laugh. 'Is that proof enough? Say yes and make me the happiest man in Paris.'

There, she'd done it. Got her proposal. Proved Shane wrong, her plan had worked. So why did Tilda feel like crying?

'Enough. Stop this charade, please. It ends now,' she said quietly.

Silence. 'What do you mean?'

'You can drop the accent. Yves St Laurence? Really? You thought I'd fall for that?'

'I don't know what you mean...' The French lilt faltered.

Tilda sat in bed, hugging her knees, stomach churning. 'The English lamppost in the background of a photo you sent, and the one with the British newspaper on your kitchen unit, the very familiar meals like beans on toast and bacon and eggs, the odd looking coq au vin, your incredibly good English, say, talking about "saving the pennies"... saying you'd met President Macron and spoken – as if! And not sending me a photo of one of your supposed designs... Please. What is your real name?'

A strange noise came down the line.

He knew that she knew.

Tilda should have been angry, and had been at first, but as time passed his photos of dinners and Cantaloupe the cat, his apologies for asking for money, his low self-esteem comments – those signs of sincerity came to mean more than being called a starry sky or little cauliflower. Then there was the matter of the times in her life when she'd felt utterly desperate, as he must have been to try and dupe her. Ingrained in her memory, she'd never forget the dehumanising effects of hitting a rock bottom.

All this time Yves believed he'd been successfully catfishing her. Logan didn't need to worry about Milo. Tilda could spot a con artist a mile off, especially when the clues were so obvious.

'Well?'

'I'm sorry. Truly.' His voice cracked.

He didn't even deny it.

'You must have thought me some idiot, not to suspect why you'd only agree to video call with me twice, and then with sunglasses on, or practically in the dark.'

'I lost my wife. Lost my job. I can't face going out the house. I'm in debt. My friend suggested I try a romantic scam.'

'Ripping someone else off, making their life a misery too, that's your answer to your problems? What sort of friend would recommend you do that?' Her voice sounded harsher than her heart.

His breath hitched. 'Meg would be so ashamed of me. I'm ashamed of myself.'

Tilda used to be ashamed of herself too. She paused. 'Has she been gone long?'

'A year today, as it turns out. I'm visiting her grave later.'

He'd lost her on the same day Tilda had lost Shane, and she was glad it ended but the separation had still hurt.

'My name's Ian.'

Ian.

Tilda's eyes pricked, they did. Her big romance with 'Yves St Laurence' was well and truly over. A tiny part of her had held onto the initial excitement of being wooed by a Parisian fashion designer, held onto the prospect of a life in the City of Lights. But it wouldn't have been real, in any case; she didn't have true feelings for him.

'Ian... a few years ago I had nothing, but I've rebuilt my life, you can do that too. Find a new friend. See the doctor. Cantaloupe is real, right?'

His voice perked up. 'Yes. He's on my lap right now. You... you aren't going to report me?'

'No. Crap things happen and that's okay, as long as we learn from them... It'll get better, Ian, life, grief... I wish you luck but don't message again.' She went to put down the phone.

'Why are you being so kind?'

'Because... sometimes kindness is the answer. Go out today, Ian, do something kind... Pay someone a compliment, do an elderly neighbour's shopping – you'll feel so much better. Those things are actually doing something kind for yourself as well.'

She put the phone down before he could reply and blocked his number.

Oh, for the first few weeks she'd been fooled, flattered by the handsome man who she'd met online in January. It was six months into the year of her quest to find a man to propose to her, six months of unsuccessful, cringeworthy dates in England. Yves had given her a little hope that Tilda's path to happiness was there, just different from the one her family members, her employees, most people, had followed. But doubts quickly set in, like the professional photos of his meals, some looking as if they'd been lifted off a website. Also his sketchy knowledge about the fashion business and a big red flag was his ridiculous name, aping the great Yves St Laurent. In that first phone call he'd apologised for wearing big sunglasses, said it was an especially bright day and the sun gave him headaches – even though he sat inside. In the second one the screen was practically pitch black, he'd insisted she ring him at night time, and said, at the last minute his electricity had gone out. He probably looked nothing like his handsome profile picture. After that first call Yves started calling Tilda by pet names, and adding lots of kisses to messages, only a couple of weeks into their friendship.

Fooling him back became a game. A game she was glad to play because it stopped her thinking about how Shane was right. The six months of real-life dating had brought disappointments, like the guy who'd played 'Matilda' on the jukebox when she'd arrived at the pub. He'd held out her hand to twirl her around but, out of her comfort zone, she'd shrunk back. To her sorrow, the date never recovered, yet he was funny and kind, despite her initial offhand manner, and he could have been a good match. And boy, she'd fancied the man who, at the end of their meal, had declared they'd be great friends only and invited her bowling. As for the chef who made her personalised chocolates, their chat was non-stop, she even made him laugh... until, so used to her routines, she declined one of the chocolates in front of him, said she only ate sweets at the weekend.

However, soon Yves'... Ian's... genuine personality had come through, a naivety that appealed to Tilda, a gentle humour, a shared interest in the simple things like food. She'd even felt able to open up a little, about her family rift.

He'd felt like a friend.

A tear rolled down Tilda's cheek as she dropped her phone onto the duvet, lay down and pulled the covers over her face. Despite having known she was being catfished, she hadn't been able to end things earlier, hoping, secretly, that perhaps she was wrong, he really was French, that his sister genuinely needed money and that he had every intention of paying Tilda back. Because in the beginning she'd fallen a little in love.

With a fake man.

But still... it had felt better than nothing.

Ending this secret project of finding a husband now did tie in well with taking on Milo, a person who could share the responsibility of her business, because... she rolled her lips together. Because, it was obvious, no one ever would give her that permanence marriage represented. The last year had proved that.

Shane was right.

She gulped under the covers, in the dark, where no one could see the hurt. Then she sat up, sniffed and rubbed her eyes. Tilda's stability would come from her job, so now was the time to focus even more on her cleaning business. To expand it. Establish it. Secure a comfortable old age. Wright Cleaners was the only 'forever' Tilda needed. Perhaps today, 4 July, really was a celebration of her independence.

The independence she'd always known. Tilda looking after Tilda.

An overwhelming sense of emptiness washed over her, but fortunately Tilda knew how to fill that vacuum. Or *un*fortunately. The idea had grown and grown these last weeks, as it became obvious her project was failing. Despite her being so firm with Milo about his sobriety, Tilda had sensed a relapse of her own coming, sharpened by the appearance of her brother. A relapse had been *in the post* as they said in treatment, and she'd known it would be delivered after her last message to Yves.

That was the itch, inside, that she'd been ignoring. The itch of drinking again. The itch of seeking oblivion.

She'd been worried for Milo, yes, and also worried for herself.

Worse than sensing she was about to reach for the bottle, Tilda had actually planned it – even though she was in denial about that. Despite the risk that she could lose everything, Tilda had got drink in.

Hello fuck-it button. It had been a while. Three years and almost five months, to be exact, since the day of that traumatic accident, when a passer-by had saved her life. She'd been seconds away from death and been overwhelmed not by fear, nor sadness, but by a heart-ripping realisation that she'd wasted the precious years she'd been given, wallowing in self-pity, blaming her mum for everything, not taking charge of her own destiny. Thanks to that passer-by who'd pulled her to safety, Tilda had a second chance to build a successful, content, productive future.

But now she felt weak, when it came to her old favourite poison – white wine, dry, refrigerated, in a fancy glass; favourite, until the end, when she'd drink anything, the higher the volume the better, straight from the bottle.

Tilda got up, showered and ate breakfast. She started work, went through the motions, even though she knew what was going to happen as soon as Milo went out the door, at eleven thirty, to walk to his Thursday midday AA meeting. The side door clicked shut. She stood up and he disappeared up the road. She waited until midday, to be sure of his absence, unable to sit still, unable to work. Then Tilda went to the cupboard under the sink and reached to the back, past the cleaning sponges, air freshener, anti-bacterial wash and bleach. Her fingers curled around the top of a bottle.

However a loud meowing disturbed her and she turned around. Dettol had come in, from the lounge. She'd nipped indoors quickly this morning, after being let out, due to the light summer rain, but the sun was out again now. Dettol nudged Tilda's ankles. A sob exploded from her chest. She collapsed on the floor, tears running down her face. Dettol clambered onto her lap and stared Tilda straight in the face. Shoulders shaking, Tilda cried, as if she were nine again, standing by Dad's coffin, nose running, eyes swollen. She reached out and touched Dettol's cheek.

'I'm sorry,' she said and gulped. 'I'm not strong enough to stay sober, not any more. Mum, Logan, Shane, Yves... What's wrong with me?' Another gulp, painful, sharp. 'Is it my fault Mum always pushed me away? Is there something about me that's so deeply, so completely unlovable?' Dettol licked Tilda's hand. She'd never done that before. It helped. A little. But not enough. Gently, Tilda pushed the cat away and it ran into the utility room. Tilda let it into the garden, locked the door again, and came back, almost tripping as she hurried. Heart beating, she pulled out the Chardonnay with a blue label, more expensive now than three years ago. She couldn't refrigerate it overnight, what with Milo being here. No matter. It would still hit the spot, cold or not.

Hand shaking, she reached into a top cupboard for a wine glass, its narrow stem feeling sophisticated. She put it on the table and took a deep breath. Tilda was about to open the bottle but steadied herself, took a moment. Shook her head. How could she risk turning her life upside down? She threw the bottle and the wine glass into the bin, pushing them down, and went into the lounge and switched on the television. She re-watched the first episode of a favourite show, none of the dialogue or action registering. However, as the credits rolled, Tilda practically ran back into the kitchen and pulled out the glass, slammed it on the table top, before retrieving the bottle. She unscrewed the cap and poured out the wine, filling the glass right to the top.

Chest heaving, she sat at the table, the glass in front of her. The smell wafted into the air. Tilda shivered.

Was she going to say goodbye to her business, her house, her security, for the rush of that first mouthful that would lead to glass, after glass, desperate to rediscover that initial hit? Sunlight streamed through the window, caught the glass, its contents winking at Tilda. It looked like a day on the beach with golden sands and turquoise waters, glamorous, escapist. A rush of excitement infused her as she picked up the wine and lifted the glass into the air. Cheers Mum. Cheers Logan. Cheers Shane and so-called Yves.

A muffled voice outside the side door made her jump. Tilda dropped the glass. It smashed. Wine everywhere.

Crap! Two o'clock already? That would be Milo, talking to Dettol. Panicking, she glanced at the table, thank God the lid had been down on her laptop, and the wine had missed her jumper and trousers, she'd pulled away in time. Rivers of Chardonnay ran off the table, onto the floor, amongst shards of glass. More knocking on the door. Milo called her name. She still hadn't sorted out giving him his own key.

Tilda hurried into the utility room. Opened the door a crack.

'I've dropped a glass... it's smashed into tiny pieces. I'm worried about Dettol's paws. Can you keep her outside, and... would you mind nipping to the corner shop? I'm... we're out of milk.'

'Really?' He frowned. 'There was a new pint in the fridge when I left.'

'Oh... yes... I made pancakes and a hot chocolate. I was starving and fancied something different for lunch. I...I put the drink in a glass for a change, like they do in coffee shops, but it slipped out of my hand,' she continued, rambling, heart pumping. 'I should be cleared up by the time you get back. There's sticky chocolate everywhere.'

Milo gave her an odd look. 'Sure I can't help clean it up?'

'No. Honestly. So much glass. Probably best there's only one of us in there.'

Once he'd gone through the gate she ran into the kitchen, got out the dustpan and brush, and swept up the pieces of wet glass. She rolled them into newspaper and tied that into a plastic bag, pushing it into the bin. Then Tilda washed the brush that stank of wine and ran aromatic anti-bacterial wipes over the floor. Seconds before Milo knocked again, she'd sprayed air freshener everywhere and emptied the pint of milk that had been in the fridge, down the sink.

Twenty-four hours had passed since the smashed glass. Milo's presence had irritated her this morning and she'd longed for the house to herself – and the other bottle of wine she'd stashed at the back of the cupboard. However that first drink of a relapse would be a special occasion, not chugged back in the bathroom or under the duvet. Special because, this time, despite her fears about risking losing everything, she was determined not to let the drinking spiral. She *could* drink in moderation, regardless of what they used to say in treatment. Tilda had learnt so much about alcoholism. So she would wait until this evening and set up the lounge with Netflix on, pour wine into one of her other wine glasses, this time it would be chilled. A packet of her favourite crisps would be tipped into a bowl and Tilda would sip with sophistication. She probably wouldn't even finish the whole bottle.

She just needed to get Milo out of the house, tonight, to fit in with her plan. Tilda had managed not to drink this afternoon, even though Milo had finally gone out for a couple of hours, because Logan and Riley were due, at six, any minute now – she'd texted him yesterday. It was a Friday. She could tell Milo a friend was coming around later, after her brother had left. Tilda winced. Milo would doubt that. Perhaps, instead, an upset employee. But then they were all going out for that meal tomorrow night, he'd ask who it was and want to help. Tilda sighed. Well, it was her house. Sod it. She'd tell him she'd had some upsetting news and needed the space. Which was true... her whole life felt upset, turned upside down, tilted askew.

Tilda sat on the sofa, holding the letter from the bag, the one that wasn't to her from Logan. Milo had just got back from the bar in Stockport, and was filling in paperwork after having been shown around and introduced to the staff. He was in the kitchen now, writing notes. Industrious. Conscientious. In fact, he'd rung the Windmill to double-check the booking for the Wright Cleaners meal tomorrow.

Tilda read the letter again, from almost exactly ten years ago, the sheet of paper shaking slightly in her hand.

Thursday 3 July 2014

Hi Logan.

How are things? Hardly saw you when I came home for the Easter holidays, but then you had football academy and Mum had worked out that revision timetable for me – that I ignored. My last A level was on Monday. For sure, I failed. Is it bad that I don't much care?

I'm sorry that, on the one day we had together, we had that shouting match about us not caring about each other, about you giving up writing to me because I never answered your letters. I wasn't lying, Logan, I never got them, and I hope one day you'll believe me. They must have got lost in the post, or I wouldn't be surprised if the other girls hid them, or... maybe you didn't write them and are just angry at how our relationship has changed and... you want to blame something, even if that means making up a reason. I get it. I don't understand either. We used to be so close, didn't we? I have called you during term-time, over the years, but you're never at home. Mum's always passed on my messages though, right? So you could have rung me back. This isn't all down to me.

Mum thinks I'm coming home this weekend. She's in for a shock. I'll be long gone by Saturday and by the time you get this. You will know, by now, that instead of revising these last weeks, I focused on setting up my own life instead – away from the pressures, away from the criti-

cism. I've signed up with a temp agency, got myself a bedsit and managed to pay a month's rent upfront with my savings.

I was going to leave a note with the school for Mum, but that would embarrass her and I know what it's like to be humiliated. Like, at the end of every term, over the years, with the other girls excitedly packing to go home, but the Head coming to see me after Mum had rung to say she was running late. I was always the last man standing, like an unwanted piece of luggage. So I'm calling Mum directly, once I'm gone. Because I'm not like her.

I move into my new place this afternoon. Am all packed. My new home is pretty basic. You can see through the curtains, the mattress is knackered and it's above a noisy launderette. Mum won't approve of my decision. Nor will the school's head. But I'm eighteen now, so to hell everyone else.

I'm scared, though. There, I've said it. Do you reckon I've done the right thing? You always used to know what to say. But it's like we've got nothing in common any more. Whatever. The bedsit can't be worse than living at school as the outsider; can't be worse than living at home as the disappointment.

Well done on getting scouted, you deserve it.

We had fun, didn't we, when we were little? No one can take away those memories.

I miss Big Sissy Sis and Little Bro Lo.

Tilda X

Five minutes to go until her brother's arrival, except keen rapping already sounded. She put the letter back in the bag, took a deep breath and went into the hallway. Tilda opened the door. Small arms wrapped around her waist. Riley hugging tighter than tight. Physical contact. Tilda wasn't used to it. She stood tense for a few seconds, before her body relaxed and she found herself patting the little girl's shoulders.

Riley stood back, put her hands up to her head and waggled them like bunny ears. 'I've been practicing for the school end-of-term play. I'm a rabbit, called Carrot.' Her nose twitched. 'You've got to do it back, Auntie,' she said firmly.

Auntie. How had that happened? Tilda paused before following her niece's command. Feeling a little bit silly, her nose twitched, until Riley's face split into an even bigger grin and warmth infused Tilda from her toes to her own ears. The little girl slipped off her shoes and ran into the kitchen calling for Dettol, holding a small rod with a feather on the end that Logan had passed to her. Milo's voice boomed her a hello. Logan waited on the doorstep.

'Come in,' said Tilda. 'Do you want a drink? Tea? Coffee?'

'No. No thanks.'

He put down his rucksack in the hallway.

'Shall we sit in the garden?' she asked.

'Why not?'

She fetched the plastic bag from the lounge and they walked past Riley's chatter and laughter, into the utility room and out to two deckchairs. Tilda and her brother sat down.

'You've read the letters?' he said.

'Yes.' Tilda breathed in the jasmine scent, the summer heat kissing her cheeks, but neither eased the pain in her chest caused by the post that had remained unopened all those years.

'I rang Mum last weekend. Had it out with her, in a Zoom call,' he continued.

She raised her eyebrows. 'Wow. And?'

'What you'd expect... bold as brass, she explained that she didn't pass my letters on because they would distract you from settling into boarding school. She didn't give me the letter you sent because I'd just been scouted and needed to focus. She'd never passed on your messages over the years because...' His cheeks reddened.

'What?'

'She said you were a bad influence. Mum overheard us talking once, just before you left for the first time, for boarding school. I must have expressed doubts about football because you'd told me I could be anything I wanted, that Mum didn't know me best, I did, and I should never forget that.' He sighed. 'Mum was worried I'd listen to you and – in her words – *throw away my chances.*'

'Christ. It's like we were employees, not children. In fact, scrub that, I wouldn't treat my staff in such a way.' Her voice wavered. 'Had she opened my letter?'

Logan shook his head. 'It was sealed when I found it in the loft. She hadn't bothered opening mine either.'

'She must have been fuming about me taking control of my own destiny.'

'That letter of yours... I had no idea you hated boarding school so much,' he said, quietly. 'If it helps... I was never into the football as much as Mum was and, over the years, I did think about what you'd said to me.'

'You're joking, right? What about the hours you put in, all the praise? If your heart wasn't in it, you're a great actor.'

'It's true. Must be hard to believe.'

Ya think? Tilda couldn't hide her shock.

'I played my part so well. In your letter you talked about pressure, about criticism... I got that too, but with the added emotional blackmail that I couldn't "waste my talent", that "thousands of lads would be thrilled" to be in my position.' He frowned. 'I also hated the way she'd introduce you to her friends, rolling her eyes, saying you were the child who "still had to find her way".'

Tilda gave her brother a quizzical look. He had?

'But I hated being paraded like some trophy too, fucking despised that amount of attention. I was a young lad who wanted, most of all, to be tucked away in his room playing with Lego or... you. Talk about cringey, all her comments about how I was going to be the "next Messi".'

But Logan was the star of the family, he'd always shone so brightly, so happily, or that's what Tilda had assumed since moving away. Yet thinking back, over the years, on the rare occasions she hadn't been at Gran's or at a summer camp, during the holidays, and he hadn't been away taking part in a football programme, she recalled sullen scowls, directed at no one in particular, along with yawns and a reluctance to turn off the television, pursed lips on one of the countless nights he was told "lights out" early because he was getting up first thing. But that had just been teenage moods, right? He'd had it lucky. At least Logan hadn't gone to bed at boarding school and found a mouldy piece of fish from dinner days before, in the sheets, or the pillow missing, the rest of the dorm giggling.

'Sounds like first world problems to me. You've no idea what my life's been like. I'd have done anything for Mum to even have a scrap of that pride in me. That first year I tried hard at boarding school – but it was never good enough. Until I realised there was no point. I'd never match what you had – a God-given gift.'

Logan winced. 'Please. Don't call it that. I've worked my guts out to get into a League One club. Training all hours, minding every mouthful of food I eat, barely drinking, never smoking. Every term break was taken up with practice or learning when I was younger. Holidays happened less and less.'

'But you can make up for it now with the money, the lifestyle, the celebrity freebies, surely. The possibility of real fame and fortune...' She looked confused. 'Talk about privileged. You've clearly lost complete touch with reality. You want to live a day in your average person's shoes, ones without your designer labels.'

'Tilda. I literally didn't have a childhood,' he replied, an edge to his tone. 'Not after you left. It's like I was treated like an adult as soon as I turned ten, with responsibilities, expectations, schedules.' His voice swelled with emotion. 'I worked bloody hard – and doing that was crap, especially when I was younger. At least you got away from it all at boarding school, away from Mum's gaze. I remember overhearing a conversation once about you having trouble settling to start with, Mum was on the phone to a friend. But that's normal, right? And you did okay in the end – you got to choose what you wanted to do with life.'

'Oh, come on, Logan. Don't be such a dick. You've got to live every bloke's dream.'

'Then why have I ditched my career?' he asked and threw his hands in the air. '*You* were the one who had choices.'

Tilda blinked several times. None of what he said made sense.

'Yeah. My teen years were a real Enid Blyton story, sharing a dorm for years with the more popular, more trendy girls who bullied me with all the classic moves. Tripping me up. Signs stuck to my back. Head down the toilet. I toughened up eventually and gave as good as I got. Mum didn't want to hear about my problems. I gave up trying to tell her because her only response was to say I needed to make more effort to fit in, that I was the problem. She told me to be...' Her voice caught. 'To be "more Logan".'

His jaw dropped. The colour drained from his face. Logan stood up and paced up and down the lawn.

'Actually bullied? I assumed it was the teachers, the study, the rules you didn't like, but that you found your own tribe of friends to have midnight feasts with, sneaking out for cigarettes and booze, having the time of your life.'

'What? Learning to fly on broomsticks?' She shook her head.

'And Mum really said that? About me?'

Biting the insides of her cheeks, Tilda refused to cry, over her mother.

'Oh Tilda. That's unforgiveable.' He reached out but pulled back his hand just before touching her. 'Mum told me the same, about fitting in,' he said in a tired voice. 'I never truly felt as if I belonged with the lads.' He reached into the plastic bag and pulled out the letters, ever so carefully as if they were precious. 'A proper Dursley, wasn't she, our mum, keeping letters from us, like those characters did from *Harry Potter*? Except we had no Hagrid to intervene.'

'Did you really read the whole *Harry Potter* series?'

'Yes. I carried on, even when I got angry that you weren't replying to me. It got me into reading. I'd have done an English degree, given the chance. Some of my happiest memories are of the writing you and I did, creating plots and characters, Gran giving us tips. I've actually read a couple of her romance novels now. They left me feeling better about the world.'

'Really? Me too! Gran was a great writer, her words were full of love and hope.'

Logan went over to the jasmine plant and smelt one of the flowers. He looked at Tilda. She nodded. A dragonfly landed on the grass, it must have come from the pond in the park. She lost herself, just for second, staring at its iridescent wings before it flew off, over the fence. Everything she'd believed about her brother had broken into pieces, like a jigsaw that had painted a false picture. He sat down next to her again.

'Why did you ring me about a year after my letter?' she said. 'You pretended you'd accidentally called me, it was through Facebook. I sensed something was wrong so rang you back, but you clammed up.'

'I... needed to talk to someone, yes. Didn't trust anyone else, even though things were so distant between us. But when the moment came, I couldn't do it. I was going through a crisis, you see, about... my sexuality.'

Tilda peered deep into his eyes. *Oh, Little Bro Lo*, if only she'd been there.

'I didn't know a single player who was gay and out, so I kept my confusion to myself, but questions loomed bigger and bigger. I was seventeen and had been so focused on my football, I'd not gone through any phase of... experimenting.' His cheeks flushed.

'Me neither, being unpopular and at an all-girls school, and being more into unicorns and fairies than anything human.'

They exchanged tentative smiles.

'Long and short of it, I eventually worked out I was bi.' He paused as if waiting for a reaction.

'Okay... and you're in a good place, now?'

Logan's eyes shone. 'Yes. Yes, I am. Cameron's my first long-term boyfriend – and I'm hoping it turns into a forever relationship. He's been so supportive of me reaching out to you, after all this time. When I'm not feeling brave it's... it's like he frees the tiger that's hiding in me. It used to be like that when you and me were close.'

Tilda's throat felt sore, as if the truth she was having to swallow, about the years of misunderstandings between them, was covered with spikes and needles. So Cameron was a man? 'So... who's Riley's mum?'

'Patsy. A sports journalist. She's thirty now and suffered badly with post-natal depression. We'd been going out for a year, I was nineteen, she was twenty-three. Patsy had never wanted kids but we were so in love, the accidental pregnancy didn't rattle us for long.' He explained how, after much effort of living together, they now shared parenting, Cameron helped when Logan had Riley, and Patsy's parents helped at her end, especially as she was back at work, her depression vastly improved and just the occasional day spent in bed, now.

'When you called me shortly before my twenty-third birthday...' Tilda did the maths. 'It was to tell me about the baby, wasn't it?'

'Yes. I wanted to. But it became obvious that you had a drink problem. You wouldn't agree to go into rehab – not judging, but I couldn't cope, Tilda, with any more stress at that point. I could already tell something was up with Patsy, I had my career, Mum's expectations, then a new baby...'

He sat down again, put the letters back in the bag, and she slipped her fingers over his and almost filled up. The last time she'd done that, *her* hand had been the biggest. Logan turned his palm up and intertwined his fingers with hers, the two of them holding hands in the way they always used to.

'How's it going? The not drinking?' he asked. 'I'm... so proud of you. I can't imagine how difficult it must have been.'

Tilda's throat hurt again, she couldn't speak, unaccustomed to praise, feeling like a traitor because she was counting down the hours to pouring that wine. They sat, in silence, for a few seconds before Tilda pulled her hand away. She stretched both arms out and leant towards him. Logan hugged her back. Tears ran down her cheeks, and when she eventually pulled away her shoulder was damp where Logan's head had rested.

'I miss Dad,' she whispered.

'Me too,' said Logan, his voice thick. 'Every single day. What do you think he'd have made of all this?'

'He'd have been very sad. I don't think he and Mum were ever a good match. I've always wondered if they only got married because she got pregnant. Perhaps she resented me, an accident, whereas they decided to have you so that our age gap wasn't big, I remember Mum told you that once. I was too little, at the time, to realise that maybe that meant she loved me less.' Tears streamed down both their faces again, speedily wiped away when the door flew open and Riley charged onto the small patio. She put her hands on her hips and tutted at Tilda. 'Milo told me about your night out tomorrow and said you still weren't sure what to wear.' Riley held out her hand in a determined manner. 'Show me your bedroom. I'll choose something. Anything in red will be pretty. You're the boss and must look like a superhero.'

21

Tilda wiped her eyes and followed Riley into the house and upstairs. Hesitantly, she stood outside her bedroom. Was she actually going to let someone into her private space?

'Why is it locked?' Riley asked as Tilda took out her key.

'Because... Dettol's fur makes me itchy and I don't want her creeping in and sleeping on my bed sheets.' She took a deep breath and ignored the strange look Riley gave her. They went in. Tilda braced herself, waiting for Riley to exclaim about the mess. Quickly Tilda closed the door behind them.

Riley exhaled as she surveyed the discarded clothes, the hairbrush on the floor and books messily piled on top of each other in the corner. 'Cool! Daddy and Mummy are always getting me to tidy. When I'm grown up, I'm going to have a bedroom like yours.' She picked up the hairbrush and pretended to sing into it.

Tilda's shoulders relaxed. It was an unfamiliar sensation, being accepted for everything.

Humming, Riley sat on the bed and bounced up and down. She went to the window and stared down at the garden, before pushing her finger into the soil in a pot. 'This plant is thirsty.' She headed for the wardrobe, grinned at Tilda and then pulled the doors wide open. Her head turned from left to right, the grin slipped. 'All dark colours.'

'I like it that way,' said Tilda. 'It's easier to decide what to wear in the morning.'

'But bright colours are the best thing! Red is for strawberries! And poppies! I like wearing my yellow T-shirt when it's sunny, and purple is the colour of my favourite drink.' She peered into the wardrobe again and studied the trousers. 'Black, brown, grey... what do they mean? Nice stuff like... a good night's sleep and chocolate and cute dolphins?' she asked hopefully.

Tilda cleared a space on the bed and sat down. 'No... I guess it's because they make me feel... ready for work and... Well, that's it.' She swallowed.

Riley went over and put her nose on Tilda's, staring directly into her eyes. 'There's something you aren't telling me.'

A bubble rose in Tilda's chest and, as Riley pulled back, she laughed. Riley joined in and touched Tilda's nose again, with her finger. 'I always do that to Daddy and Mummy when I can tell they are keeping something from me. Like the time Daddy said the bird on our lawn was having a nap. But birds don't sleep on their backs. I put my nose on his and he said it was actually dead! It's like a magic trick that makes people be honest. We buried the bird and I made a cross out of two lolly sticks.' She folded her arms. 'Go on, why do you really wear dark colours?'

Tilda stared into those little black eyes; inquisitive, curious eyes that reminded her of Logan as a little boy when she'd explain a new game to him. 'I went away to boarding school. Like a school where you live there. Most children love it but... the girls in my bedroom were mean and would tease me. Dark colours make me feel... invisible, as if I can hide, like I'm... safe, I guess.'

Riley plonked herself on the bed, next to Tilda. 'Is that the real reason you lock the door too?'

'Yes. Sorry, I lied.'

'S'okay. Sometimes I do that. I was just playing with Dettol, with the cat fishing rod I brought. I told her she had the strongest paws ever.' Riley lowered her voice. 'But she hasn't. My neighbour's cat, Ash, has paws as big as tablespoons.' She cocked her head. 'But you are all grown up now.' She linked her arm through Tilda's. 'You don't need to hide any more.'

Tilda gave a shiver. Milo had said that too.

Riley jumped up. 'Back in a minute.' She raced out of the room. Five minutes later running footsteps thudded up the stairs. She came in, holding a smartly folded white shirt covered in flowers. Riley held it up in the air like a game bird she'd hunted.

'What's that?' asked Tilda.

'Daddy's shirt. On the way here he saw it in a shop at half price and bought it. I asked if you could borrow it. You could wear it over a pair of trousers with a belt around it. Mummy wears big tops like that.'

'I can't do that! What did he say?'

'I gave him one of my looks, so he did what I asked,' she said proudly.

Tilda laughed again. Riley shook the shirt in the air. 'Try it on, Auntie Tilda.'

Tilda took the shirt as Riley sat on the bed and covered her eyes with her hands. 'I want it to be a surprise. You have to do your hair, and everything. Make-up if you've got any.'

Make-up? Was she joking? Under any other circumstances, with anyone else, Tilda would have replied *no*, outright. But Riley's enthusiasm was so infectious. She pulled on a pair of black jeans and slipped on the shirt. Tilda stood in front of the wardrobe's long mirror. Riley was right. With the shirt hanging out and a belt hung around her waist, it looked... almost stylish. The printed flowers were red and blue. She ran a brush through her hair and rummaged in a toiletry bag she didn't get out often. There it was. A coral-coloured lipstick that would match nicely. She'd bought it to please Shane. He'd said it would suit her even more if she had lip filler. Funny how you don't always notice the red flags until it's the end of the race, and they are waving wildly. Tilda picked up a full perfume bottle, a new one she'd bought, and generously applied the familiar scent.

'Hurry up, Auntie Tilda,' said Riley, legs banging against the end of the bed.

Tilda consulted the mirror again. Turned side to side. She used the lipstick as blusher too, and found a pair of gold hoop earrings her grand-mother had given her, on her sixteenth birthday. Mum had called them tacky.

'Ready,' she said, nervously.

Riley's hands fell to her sides. Her eyes widened. Tilda's niece hated her new look, of course she did.

'I love it,' said Riley, in awe. 'You are soooo pretty.'

She was?

'Daddy says I look like you,' she said and puffed out her chest.

The comment made Tilda want to puff out hers too. Her, look like this gorgeous little girl? Perhaps the other pupils' cruel comments at school had been off the mark.

'And you smell like a bunch of flowers, like last time I saw you, too. That shirt is wayyy better on you than on Daddy,' she whispered.

Granted she looked less like a figure in a sepia print, less like a member of the Addams family.

Riley grabbed her hands. 'Now I need to teach you my latest dance moves for your night out.'

'But it's a meal, not a dance,' Tilda protested.

The little girl's face took on a stern expression. 'Always be prepared, that's what my Rainbows leader says. Right. Arms in front. Move your feet like me, left to right. One, two, one, two...'

As the routine progressed, with an additional spinning move, and kick in the air, Tilda's chest tightened. Not because of the physical exertion, but because dancing with her niece took her right back to her childhood, and how she and Logan would make up steps to their favourite songs. 'Doctor Pressure', that came out when Tilda was eight, Logan six, was a mashup that contained 'Dr Beat' by Miami Sound Machine, one of their Dad's favourite songs. It remained a firm favourite for several years and they had a routine the two of them kept adding to.

Logan's voice called upstairs and Riley stopped. 'Better go. Dad's drop-ping me off at Mummy's tonight. Can we show them your outfit first, pleeease!'

Tilda folded her arms.

'Okay, you don't have to, Auntie. I don't mind. But you look cool. Cross my heart.' She drew a big cross on her chest, face as solemn as if she were giving a church sermon.

Tilda allowed herself to be dragged downstairs. As they reached the hallway, Tilda became aware of her brother and Milo talking, something about Logan's plans for the future, about sport, of course. Logan's voice mainly dominated but only because Milo was prompting. He was good like that. Generous. Interested. The scent of garlic filled the air. He was cooking too, he'd muttered something about making salmon with garlic potatoes, a twist on Tilda's usual Friday night meal of fish and chips. She'd not replied, needing time to work out how to convince him to go out after her brother left. But now, since speaking to Logan, since spending time with Riley, the itch of that relapse wasn't as strong.

Riley gave her a little push. Cheeks burning, Tilda walked into the kitchen. The men stopped talking. Milo was wearing her yellow Marigold gloves, having done some leftover washing up. *Leftover* washing up. How things had changed.

'Wow,' said Milo. 'Love it. Riley had better help me pick out an outfit.'

Riley grinned.

'Love the shirt, Tilda, wherever did you get it?' asked Logan.

'Silly Daddy,' said Riley and she giggled.

'Great lipstick,' Logan continued. 'Reminds me of that time we ransacked Mum's dressing table and put on her make-up. The lipstick might have been the exact same colour.'

'Shirley, the cleaner, found out and helped us tidy up,' said Tilda. 'She washed our faces. I don't think she ever told Mum about it.'

'Right, Riley, we'd better go or we'll be late for *your* mum... And late for your bedtime, Missy,' said Logan.

Riley played on the pavement whilst Logan slipped into his shoes, in the doorway. 'Milo tells me he's joining your business,' he said, in a loaded voice.

'Logan. Don't ruin things,' she said. 'He's a good guy.'

He was clenching his jaw, she could tell, Logan always did that as a little boy when he wanted to say something but thought he shouldn't.

'You and me... where do we go from here?' he asked Tilda a few seconds later.

'Sunday lunch? You and Riley too, if she's back from her mum's? We've got a lot to catch up on.'

22

Tilda stood outside the Windmill, a greystone pub, framed against a sapphire blue sky, marred only by a few puffs of cloud, or industrial smoke, she could never be sure. Traffic whizzed by; the pub was just off a main road, practical and urban, like Stockport itself, like Crouchden too. Tilda had never yearned for the suburban prettiness of her childhood. There was an honesty about much of Stockport centre's architecture; the pub building solid, reliable, like the food. Her thoroughness meant she'd eaten there incognito, one lunchtime, before introducing herself and taking the pub on as a client, to see if it had changed since she'd worked there as a temporary cleaner. The members of staff were still conscientious and if there was a spill did their best to tidy it up. That would help Tilda's employees. Otherwise spilled soft drinks left difficult sticky marks on tabletops and carpets, and the reek of stale beer could be time-consuming to remove. They also swept up fallen food and wiped the tables down in between guests. Tilda wasn't trying to avoid earning what she charged, but had made the mistake once of not checking out a small coffee shop. She'd quoted one hour's work to clean the dining area and toilets. It turned out no member of the shop's staff had checked the latter even once, during the day, and there was a blockage, toilet paper everywhere, and worse. It had required a deep clean. As for the room where customers sat, the cobwebs hung, covered in fluff, as if they'd been there for decades, covered in layer upon layer of dust. To get the place how she'd want, to protect Wright Cleaners' reputation, the job had required three hours' work that first evening, and still she and her employee weren't entirely satisfied. The owner had refused point blank to pay, deciding he was better off with his current regime of pressurising his staff to quickly clean up after their shift.

Tilda pulled at the collar of Logan's shirt around her neck, moving the scratchy label. Hair combs pushed against her scalp. The creamy coral lipstick felt glutinous. She exhaled as Milo pushed open the wooden door. The two of them had sat opposite each other on the train and Tilda had tried not to cast an obvious eye over his long frame, the chinos that cut in in all the right places and, visible behind his open jacket, the buttoned-up collared shirt, navy and crisply ironed. To her he was a friend, a colleague, that's all. Definitely. It was best that way.

Tilda stole glances from the train's window, his reflection apparent now the evening sun wasn't as bright. He'd shaved, and gelled his hair and the tight shirt was tucked in, emphasising his waist, and he wore that expression of his, the one that had appeared when he'd declared himself disappointed she wasn't called Cillit Bang. Unlike her parents, the girls at school, unlike Shane, Milo laughed *with* Tilda, not at her. He teased about her idiosyncrasies, only gently questioning them, never dismissing them outright with scorn. Like the way she used Post-it notes to clean in between the keys of her keyboard at the end of each day, and how she liked symmetry in every room, apart from her own, regarding the placing of objects and how pairs of curtains were pulled. Shane would roll his eyes and call her a neat freak.

Other people had been kind over the years, she could see that now, through the lens of her lodger. But back then she hadn't been in the position to appreciate the positives. Like the fellow cleaning temps who'd admired her skills and asked her out on girls' nights. Like the neighbours when she'd first moved in to her Crouchden house, who'd come around to introduce themselves. Internally, Tilda had always gone on the defence, waiting for the sucker punch.

A wave of pain crossed her chest.

What a waste.

Deep, deep down, the truth had stuck, that she'd unearthed from treatment, from fellow addicts... She couldn't blame her mum, couldn't blame boarding school, Tilda had no one to blame but herself for the way she'd reacted to her situation and held onto resentment. Now could be the time for change, starting with tonight, her having organised a social event.

More than ever, she needed something to numb the nerves.

She glanced at her watch. Quarter to seven. She and Milo had turned up early to check the table. He'd expressed surprise that she wasn't going to drive; a welcome summer shower was forecast for later. However, she'd insisted she needed the walk. But Tilda had another reason for not taking the car. In the old days, if she ever went out with the other temps, Tilda couldn't recount anecdotes about family or boyfriends, so alcohol had filled the gaps in her conversation, giving her the confidence to come up with banter.

One drink, that's all she needed. Tilda was a different person these days. Responsible. In charge. The bottle wouldn't get a grip like it had before. It wouldn't.

They walked into the pub, welcomed by the smell of fried meat and yeasty ale, by the hubbub made up of chatting friends and clinking glasses, by the relaxing mint-coloured walls and highly polished wooden tables. Tilda stopped. At least half her guests were already there, at the bar, including Adam, Connie, Iris and Jazz. They waved, and Tilda put on her best smile, stiffly waving back.

'It's going to be a great evening,' Milo said and squeezed her shoulder, reading her as he always did.

Logan had also always been sensitive to her moods. He could tell when she'd had a fallout in the playground, when she hadn't slept well. As she walked over to her employees, Tilda passed a man who reminded her of him. She used to think she read her brother well, too, but it turned out she... she'd let him down. There. Those words had been waiting in the shadows since she'd read Logan's letters, since the two of them had met up and talked honestly. She'd let down her little brother. Apart from that time just before Tilda left for boarding school, when he'd expressed doubts about playing football, she'd never spotted the signs that he wasn't happy, that the game truly wasn't the be all and end all for him. Tilda was the older sibling, she'd been that little lad's older sister. She should have stood up for him.

In contrast to Tilda's dark thoughts, along with the landlord, the bar twinkled in a welcoming way, with its mirrored backdrop, the glistening wedges of citrus fruit, the glossy straws and upside-down spirit bottles. Any one of those drinks would take the edge off the guilt that gnawed at her stomach.

'Hello, everyone. Great to see you.' She smiled. 'Please let me introduce my, well, assistant manager. Or rather... the new brains in the company, that is, a business partner as such, or...'

'Just Milo will do,' he said and grinned with the others.

The rest of the team arrived, and Tilda made sure they all knew each other by name, at least, before they sat down on the maroon upholstered seats. They worked alone, apart from Iris and Jazz, and Adam and Callum. Milo sat at the far end of the table opposite Jazz, Tilda the other end next to Iris, which was a relief; there was plenty to chat about. Had she recovered fully from the bronchitis? How were the grandchildren? What was she having to eat? Wine for the table arrived, along with the starters. Tilda had stuck with soup, but couldn't help fixating on Adam's plate, opposite and, laughing, he insisted she have one of his bacon and cheese croquettes – fuel for a half-marathon he was running tomorrow. She mentioned her and Milo's plans to expand the business and Callum, next to Adam, explained how he used to help out on his uncle's window-cleaning round and, if she was interested, he'd be happy to offer advice such as the best equipment to buy, for gutter clearing too. News of their plans spread down the table and ideas for growing Wright Cleaners became their talking point. Milo caught her eye and smiled. Team work and being collaborative lifted Tilda. Connie suggested a wider service for the elderly, her Tuesday morning client needed help with her laundry and the Friday afternoon gentleman was finding it increasingly hard to change the beds, especially when his family visited. Adam suggested shed and garage clean-ups. Jazz proposed advertising deep cleans for people about to move into a new property.

The main meals arrived and Tilda raised the orange juice she'd barely touched. 'I can't thank you all enough.' She smiled down the table. 'Please, email me with any ideas you have.'

'We had a suggestions box in my last job,' said Milo. 'Each idea went into a prize draw once a month. People could enter as many times as they liked. You could do that – via emails with "Ideas Box" written in the subject line.'

Heads nodded up and down enthusiastically.

'It could include tips on how to improve our current service, or... the way things are run,' she said with questioning eyebrows.

'Love a prize draw, count me in,' said Iris. 'A friend of mine owns her own online make-up company. She started small, a couple of years, ago, and says discounts for new customers really work. If you were going for a bigger client, where there was competition, you could offer a discounted rate for say, the first six months. By the end of that time hopefully they realise the quality of our service.'

'We should participate in community events,' said Adam. 'Charity runs or walks with the business's name on our tops. It's free advertising, gives you content for the website... and will raise money for a good cause.'

Tilda sat back, their eagerness washing over like the pleasant first glass on a night out. Hunger eventually took over brainstorming and Tilda caught Adam admiring her onion rings. She smiled and tipped her plate towards him. Conversation moved away from work and towards summer holidays.

Down the other end of the table Milo and Jazz were deep in chat. They'd been laughing a minute ago, but now the conversation was serious. A familiarity existed between them. Tilda had never been able to quickly create that easiness with strangers. Or was it chemistry? Jazz laughed at something he said. Milo patted her hand. Tilda had only been able to let go of her reservations so quickly when she was drunk and searching for a meaningless physical connection. He'd asked her about Yves last night. Embarrassed to say a man had tried to catfish her, to admit that she must look like someone gullible, desperate enough to respond to such a ridiculous French name in the first place, she simply said he was fine and smiled. Milo had looked thoughtful afterwards, been quiet for a while, and now here he was, going for it with Jazz. Perhaps Milo thinking Tilda had found romantic fun online had inspired him to be bold tonight.

'What about you, Tilda?' asked Iris. 'Going away this summer? I'm guessing with that lovely soft, pale skin, you aren't much of a beach bod? More of a sightseeing person?'

Iris was around the age of Tilda's mum, who'd never paid her any compliment. An ache swelled in her chest and she sipped the orange juice. Tilda looked around shyly. Adam loved Ibiza, Callum Greece, Iris the South of France with the grandchildren. 'I haven't been on holiday since I left home at eighteen.'

'Afraid of flying?' asked Iris.

'Too busy working; must be hard running your own business?' said Adam.

'Do you grab weekends away instead, throughout the year?' asked Callum.

Team building was important, Milo had said. Tilda guessed that meant opening up a little...

'I had... a difficult time in my teens and early twenties. This business saved me. I haven't left it alone for three years. It's all I need.'

Adam went to pour Tilda a glass of wine. She put her hand over the top. If Milo wasn't here, she wouldn't have been so coy.

'No thanks, I'm... on antibiotics.' There were limits to her honesty. On the rare occasion she had gone out, during the last three years, driving was her usual excuse for not drinking.

'Talk about management not joining in,' said Kat, a younger worker sitting next to Jazz. Playfully she shook her finger at Milo.

'Not a wine fan, Milo?' asked Callum.

'More of a whiskey after dinner man?' said Connie.

'On a health-kick?' asked Kat.

The questions weren't unfamiliar. Tilda never ceased to marvel at why people pressed others about not drinking a liquid that could leave you with headaches, sickness and dodgy hook-ups.

'A life-kick,' he answered. 'I'm five years sober.'

Tilda didn't move. Wow. He'd told them the truth.

'That's epic. Credit to you,' said Callum. 'Must have been hard.'

'Five years. What an achievement,' said Iris. 'Wish my uncle had managed that. He died of alcoholism.'

'We had a teacher at school who got fired in the end for turning up drunk,' said Ellie, one of Tilda's newest recruits. 'He couldn't cope after his husband died. The whole class signed a petition for him to come back.'

Tilda had never told anyone about her past habit. The supportive reaction of the table surprised her.

'Don't you find it a challenge, out socialising?' asked Adam.

'Depends on the crowd. Some people don't get it and keep pushing, telling me one won't hurt. But it's the first that's the most dangerous.'

Tilda wrinkled her nose. She'd prove that didn't always have to be true. She asked if anyone wanted another drink, aside from the wine. Jazz wasn't drinking either and asked for another Coke. Milo asked for a surprise. Callum had a pint. She took her orange juice with her, pretending to drain it as she went. Instead she asked the barman to add a shot of vodka. No, two. Her stomach fizzed. She carried the tray back to the table.

'Elderflower spritz,' she said to Milo and handed him the drink. 'It smells delicious.'

She handed out the other drinks and sat in her seat. She swirled the orange juice around and around and then put it down. Milo was staring at her. He got up and came over.

'I can tell you'd rather have my drink. Here. Let's swap.'

'No. No way!' She said. 'I... I got that elderflower drink for you. Orange juice is fine.' Oh God, what if he drank it and broke his five years of sobriety without even realising it?

'Nonsense.' He placed his glass in front of her, picked up her glass and lifted the vodka-laden fruit juice to his mouth.

'No! Don't drink that!'

Everyone at the table turned to Tilda. She grabbed the orange juice, spilling some onto his shirt. She stood up and peered into it, and dipped her fingers in, pulling them out quickly and shaking them. 'One of my hairs.' She pulled a disgusted face and the others laughed.

'A near miss. Thank you, Tilda.' Milo wiped his shirt. 'You were like a mythical angel sweeping in to save the day – or rather my digestion.'

Hurriedly she took the drink back to the bar and came back with a juice, minus the alcohol.

A couple of hours later, after dessert and coffee, after too many risqué jokes about vacuum cleaners, Tilda and Milo ran for the right platform and caught the last train back to Crouchden, having walked through a refreshing shower of rain that eased the July humidity. He yawned and scrolled down his phone. As they left the Windmill, Tilda had overheard him say to Jazz, 'See you next week.' Good for Milo, getting back into dating. She was pleased. Her job of helping him out, emotionally, was almost done. Soon he'd have a special someone, a conclusion that left her feeling surprisingly cold, hollow.

Love wasn't just about a partner causing a warm, fuzzy feeling, surely? It was also about them sticking out the tough times by your side. But then Milo was that sort of man as well.

Not that she loved Milo, that was ridiculous. She stared out of the train window, berating the line of her illogical, inner thoughts.

Whatever. Nothing would ruin tonight. Tilda was on a high, for two reasons. Firstly the evening had been a huge success. Tilda Wright had enjoyed a social life and the others had all agreed to come up with activities they'd like to do as a team. Adam suggested crazy golf. Kat a night out dancing. The suggestion box idea had been keenly embraced, too. Everyone had hugged her at the end, thanking Tilda for a great meal. She'd stood stiffly at first, overwhelmed, but by the end held out her arms as well.

The second reason she was in good spirits was that building excitement at the prospect of drinking. Being around alcohol tonight had fuelled her desire and she wallowed in pleasurable anticipation about tomorrow evening. Logan and Riley were around for Sunday lunch, she'd ask Milo to give her a bit of space after they left and would say she was exhausted and wanted to be quiet, alone, in the lounge.

It was lined up. The perfect evening of escape. For the first time in months she'd be free from stress. Tilda almost rubbed her hands with glee. Tomorrow night the tight knots inside her would unfurl in a happy glow. She ignored the voice in her head, from the treatment centre, from three years ago in group therapy, pointing out that seeing a glass of wine as a means of escape was a big warning sign that spelt nothing but trouble – with a capital T.

23

Tilda had never made Sunday lunch for four people. Shane hadn't introduced her to his parents and she'd only ever met his sister and friends on pub crawls or at restaurants. 'Roast chicken with all the trimmings, you couldn't go wrong with that,' said Milo, 'as long as no one was vegetarian.' But then they were in the middle of a long, hot summer, so he came up with an equally appealing option: a barbecue. Appealing but scary, Tilda had never hosted one of those either. But there was a weather-beaten barbecue set left in the shed by the previous owners and Milo insisted he could clean it up. He bought a charcoal bag and offered to take charge of the meat and cooking. For her part, Tilda spent the morning preparing side dishes – rice, with saffron and peas added at Milo's suggestion, a potato salad, and she'd bought coleslaw, burger buns, dips and fancy crisps. After cleaning up, she changed into a green checked shirt from the bottom of one of her drawers, Riley would love it. Last year she'd got caught in an unexpected summer downpour, on the way to a cleaning job. Soaking wet, Tilda had stopped off in a charity shop to buy a dry top. This brightly coloured one was the cheapest.

The doorbell rang. Tilda charged downstairs, not locking her bedroom door for the first time since moving in. She stopped halfway but didn't go back. Neither Milo nor Riley had castigated her for the mess, quite the opposite in fact. The bell rang again and she arrived in the hallway, took a breath, smoothed down her clothes and then opened the door.

Pow! Riley sped in and flung her arms around Tilda's waist. She couldn't help grinning and bent down to say hello to her niece, hugging her back.

'Like your shirt, Auntie, I've got a green top! Next time I'll wear it. We'll be like twins.' She kicked off her shoes and called out Dettol's name, speeding along the hallway and into the kitchen. Logan gave a sheepish smile. He and Tilda did the dance of awkwardness that only the very British knew, before a mutual decision to embrace, pulling apart almost as soon as they touched.

Milo appeared holding two glasses of Coke, hands in Marigold gloves again. 'Why don't you two chill in the lounge? Riley is going to help wash lettuce and tomatoes, and she can keep me company in the garden whilst I cook.'

'Is *help* the right word, mate?' asked Logan. 'My little superstar might take over.'

Milo laughed and passed them the drinks. 'I'm sure that young lady can teach me a thing or two, although I've already had to be firm about us not frying eggs on the coal.'

Logan and Tilda stood awkwardly again.

'In the summer we'd sit on the front door step and natter, remember? It drove Mum crazy, in case a bluebottle got in the house or the neighbours saw that we weren't using our time productively,' said Logan.

Tilda pursed her lips. Opened the front door again, and beckoned to her brother as she sat on the step. Grinning, he joined her. Unlike the old days it was a bit of a squeeze. A young woman walked past with her dog. The Labradoodle came over and Logan ruffled its head. Tilda placed her drink on the pavement and hugged her knees.

'I've been mulling everything over. A lot,' she said. 'I'm sorry that...' She exhaled. Saying the words out loud would make them real; that she'd let her brother down. No. She couldn't do it. 'I'm sorry I've missed out on Riley's first six years, so if you ever need a babysitter, I'd be happy to help. You can tell Patsy that too.'

'Honestly? That would be great. She's really taken to you.'

'Or the cat, more like.'

On cue, Dettol appeared, pressing her body between Tilda and the door. She stared at Tilda and then stepped onto her lap. It reminded Tilda of the time Dettol had sat with Milo on the street.

'Babysitting might help me out occasionally because there's something I want to discuss... I could do with your advice,' said Logan and he tickled the cat's ears.

Tilda plonked Dettol on the floor and excused herself, dashed up to the bathroom and closed the door. She squeezed her eyes oh so tightly shut and bit on her fist; she mustn't give in to tears.

Logan, her brother, her little bro, he wanted her opinion, it still counted, despite everything. No one else ever had, apart from her clients and employees. That was one reason she so enjoyed running her own business. She splashed her face with cold water and went back downstairs, sat down on the step again muttering something about the pub meal last night not agreeing with her.

She stretched her ears out sideways, pulling a face, something they did as children when the other one wanted to share a problem.

Logan laughed. 'Christ. What were we like? Sometimes Mum and Dad would let us stay up to watch *Strictly Come Dancing*. We'd kid ourselves we could do the lifts and insist they marked us out of ten.'

'We'd see who could burp the fastest and loudest by drinking a fizzy drink the quickest.'

They both eyed their Cokes and knocked the drinks back. Wait for it, wait for it. Tilda won.

She wiped her mouth, neither of them knowing where to look. 'You sure I'm grown up enough to offer advice?' she asked.

'It's about my future. I always wished I'd studied English. I grew to love reading and, at high school, loved writing essays. Gran was so passionate about words, it must have rubbed off on me. Being with Patsy has made me realise... I think my true calling might be to be a sports journalist.' He waited and squirmed next to her. 'Say something. Like I'm an idiot, right, for dreaming I could ever do that? I'd need to get my A levels first, then do a degree...'

'February, two thousand and... six, that was it, the Winter Olympics in Italy, you holding a carrot, with black paper wrapped around it and a fancy dress clown's nose on top, you used it as a microphone. You wanted to be one of the commentators, said it looked like a cool job travelling the world and you always loved the luge and skiing events. You even learnt how to say hello and goodbye in Italian. One Saturday night we begged Mum for pizza for tea, to make it authentic. You stood by the television, chatting as the events happened.'

'Mum got fed up in the end, said she couldn't hear the proper commentary. I felt like such a fool until you said I was brilliant and that the guy on the TV was boring. We went up to my room and you enacted Olympic events, telling me to commentate.'

'I did those ski jumps off your bed until Mum shouted up at us to stop making such a racket.' Tilda shrugged. 'Reckon you had your true calling back then.'

Logan had stood up now, eyes bright like they used to be when they were little, having secret midnight feasts and watching bats swoop outside, from the window. He reached into his pocket and pulled out a notebook. 'I found this in the loft too.' He handed it over.

They went into the lounge and sat on the sofa. The notebook was the size of a postcard, browned and curled at the corners. She flicked it open. A scrapbook? It contained wrappers of the favourite sweets the two of them would share, like strawberry pencils and Dolly Mixtures. Tickets too, to cinema screenings: *Cars, Happy Feet, Transformers.* Logan always did hoard 'memories' as he called them. There was also the page of one of the stories they wrote about themselves, taking it in turns to write each line. This one was about the two of them fighting with gold swords, slaying a dragon in the local woods. The Queen gave them both a medal and enough money so that they could live in their own castle, with servants and dogs, with pizza parties and a swimming pool.

'I made it when you left for boarding school, was going to send it so you didn't get homesick... but then you never replied to my letters. I remember having this sleepover at a friend's not long after I made it. His sister had just started high school too. She looked down her nose at us, said primary school was for babies. I wondered if that's what you thought of me, now that you were all independent, so I kept the scrapbook for myself.'

Tilda couldn't meet his gaze.

'Keep it if you want,' he said.

She flicked through it again. Eventually she closed it and ran her hand over the cover and blinked away the pain, before lifting her head. 'This studying... do you need to? Your name's quite well known, right? Couldn't you get into commentating on the back of that?'

Logan clenched his hands together. 'I've already been offered a gig, commentating on matches on a local radio station but... I want to do this properly, Tilda, and dig deep, get to the bottom of the issues that interest me, like the current debates over trans participation in sport, mental health provisions, how the sports world can support climate change initiatives...'

Wow. Her little brother *had* grown up. Sport was so much more to him now than how fast a luge could go or how far a skier could jump.

'Why not combine both opportunities?' she said. 'That commentating job could help you fund university. Yes, life will be busy, but we're still young, right? Now is the time to make the most of every twenty-four hours. Like I said, I'll help out with Riley, especially now that Milo is on board to help run the company.'

Logan's face lit up. 'I knew you'd help me work it out. You always were dead practical. That's the perfect solution. If I take that radio job, I'll be building up experience as well for my CV; I'll be keeping my name out there.' Laughter floated through from the kitchen. Logan tilted his head. 'You trust Milo, right? Riley thinks he's ace, she's usually pretty accurate when it comes to people and doesn't hold back if there's something about them she doesn't like.' He gave a wry smile.

'I do. We've both been to a rock bottom. Both pulled ourselves up. It's hard to explain, Logan, but having both got sober there's this unspoken connection, an... understanding between us. I've never had it with anyone else.'

'Wit woo, as Riley would say.'

Her cheeks burnt. 'It's not like that. Milo's nothing but a... a colleague. In any case, he's going on a date with one of my employees.'

Logan eyed her curiously and then sat back. 'Be careful, Tilda. The success I found showed me just how many leeches are out there. I don't like to keep going on about it and it's not about not trusting your opinion... it's about not wanting to see you hurt.'

He still cared? After all this time? Of course he did. Like Tilda had about him, keeping up with his career. The more they talked, the clearer things became, as if their conversation was like a stain remover, taking away the hurt and misunderstandings, to reveal the truth that had always been there... that it took more than ten years apart to break that sibling bond.

'This rock bottom...' he continued, 'what happened exactly, for you to turn things around, if you don't mind me asking?'

Tilda sat back too. Their elbows touched. It felt... right. 'One winter morning, very early, I was on my way to a cleaning job, in Market Street. It was still dark. To be honest, I was still a bit drunk from the night before. I was in a world of my own, that's the way I liked it, but I didn't see the first tram of the day coming. I walked onto the tramlines, I almost got... Fortunately, someone grabbed my arm and pulled me out the way, just in time. I stuttered my thanks; he could have got killed. I wanted to say more but he simply said anyone else would have done the same, before disappearing.'

'Modest and a hero? A rare thing these days.'

'The papers got wind of it and called him the "Streetcar Saviour". They set up a campaign to find him. He'd run off limping, having hurt himself in the fall we suffered after he pulled me off the lines... It was during the pandemic and the month Captain Tom died. Local papers needed another hero, a story to lift Manchester's spirits.'

'Was he ever found?'

'No. I didn't help the journalists much... I got the impression this man didn't want any attention and... I understood. Also, I didn't tell them he had a scar down the side of his hand... it was the only distinguishing feature and the press would have made a big thing of it.'

The door burst open and Riley stood clapping her hands. 'Lunch is served. Milo told me to say that. He says it's posh, like what the king's cooks would say.' She gave a little bow.

Tilda and Logan stood up. He caught her arm by the door. 'Please. Be careful of Milo. You only met him a few weeks ago. He's still a stranger in lots of ways.'

'Actually, that's not right, you see—'

Riley grabbed Tilda's hand. 'The food's getting cold, Auntie!'

She and Logan followed the little girl into the kitchen. Milo was on the phone, he laughed and said, 'See you Tuesday, Jazz.' Tilda pasted a bright smile on her face. It was good to see a couple getting together, where one of them wasn't a man called Yves who was really called Ian.

The kitchen table was covered with the food – the salad, rice, plates of burgers, sausages and chicken. Tilda would give some scraps to Dettol later. Only the bits that would get thrown out anyway. She wasn't going to turn into one of those people who doted on their pets. No siree. Rubber gloves hanging over the taps now, Milo handed out plates for them to fill, before going outside. He and Riley had set up the two deckchairs and two kitchen chairs on the patio. They could eat on their laps.

Logan couldn't stop staring at Milo's hand.

Riley passed Milo her plate and gave him an inquisitive look. 'Milo, what happened to your hand? Why has it got that mark down the side? I've been wanting to ask. We're friends, now, so it's okay, isn't it?'

'Riley! That's very rude,' said Logan and his cheeks flushed. 'Sorry mate. Not noticed it before.'

'It's okay,' said Milo.

Whilst he mumbled something about an accident when he was a boy, Logan raised one eyebrow at Tilda. She nodded.

Yes, Milo was the man who'd saved her, three years ago, the man who hadn't wanted thanks for pulling her off the tramlines. Tilda had been about to tell Logan how he'd risked his life for her and had wanted to tell him sooner, but felt she should still keep it secret, for Milo's sake. She'd recognised his face as soon as he'd shaved off his beard, and then studying his hands had confirmed her theory. With her hood, the scarf wrapped around her mouth, the darkness, Tilda had effectively been in disguise that dramatic morning, back in 2021, hiding herself from the cold and, as it turned out, Milo. And that was okay. He didn't need to know who she was. Milo hated compliments. His self-esteem was so low because of whatever had happened with his sister. It didn't matter that she recognised him as the Streetcar Saviour. He'd run away on that winter morning. It wasn't her place to bring back the memory.

Tilda was sensible, never took risks, and neither of those qualities had been compromised by her taking in a stranger off the streets – because Milo wasn't a stranger, not to Tilda. He'd saved her life and fate had called on her to do the same for him. Milo now had lodgings, a job and possibly a girlfriend in Jazz. Tilda had repaid the debt. It was time to back off. She had a brother and niece to focus on. What with growing the business, any romantic attachments would get in the way. The only friend she needed came from grapes, just one or two glasses, every night. Moderate drinking. Easy peasy.

Thoughts about a relapse, you couldn't get rid of them, not once they took hold, like the twistiest grapevines.

The four of them filled their plates and sat outside. After eating, Riley lifted the pair of barbecue tongs to play with the coals, stamping her foot when Logan told her to put it down. Instead of shouting like Mum would have, he explained that hot coals were dangerous for children *and* adults, that they weren't to be played with. Riley sulked for a while, but her mood soon blew away and she sat on her dad's lap. The last time Tilda and her brother had been close, *they* were the little ones being told off by a parent.

The ball of grief for the time they'd lost, grew and grew in her stomach. That was the thing with finding something dear that you'd lost, it reaffirmed its value. The scrapbook, the reason Logan had never sent it, cut through her like one of the gold swords in the little story they'd made up.

This afternoon had been so special. A family moment Tilda would never have considered possible a few weeks ago. Laughter. Good food in the sunshine. Genuine affection. But she still couldn't wait until the house was hers and she could go about soothing her sense of guilt. Dettol crept up to her deckchair and patted her foot with her paw. Discreetly Tilda handed down a small bit of chicken. The cat understood. A bit of what you fancied did you no harm at all.

24

FEBRUARY 2021

Tilda

Tilda walked out of Piccadilly Station and down the hill towards Market Street in Manchester city centre. She finished her chocolate bar and threw the wrapper on the ground, with just a tinge of guilt. However, it didn't land and instead wafted away, on the breeze, in the direction of the Village. It was 6.30 a.m. Several homeless people lay huddled in shop doorways, cocooned in grubby sleeping bags and coats, squashed cans and butt ends littering the ground by their sides. One man sat up, holding a conversation with a rubbish bin. Poor sod. Imagine letting yourself get into that state. Tilda went to walk past but something pulled her back. She delved into her coat pocket and found several coins. She tossed the money into the empty takeout cup by his torn rucksack. Car lights flashed as she pulled down her hood and tightened the scarf around her mouth. She adjusted her earbuds and turned up the playlist of throwback tracks, from her childhood. So what if, now and again, she wallowed in what could have been? Tilda avoided the eyes of commuters who headed up the hill to catch a train to their daily hamster wheel. One woman bumped into her as she hurried past.

Tilda span around, fists clenched. 'What's your problem?' she shouted.

The woman walked away, even quicker. Tilda rubbed her eyes, tired and dry from another night of drunken sleep, tears threatening. These days she didn't always recognise the Tilda reflected back in shop windows.

Flexible temp cleaning had been the perfect job for seven years, it kept her sane. She didn't have to talk to anyone and could do the work on automatic during an especially bad day when thoughts raced. Scrubbing and brushing made her feel alive, real. The imaginary voices, in the middle of the night, were getting worse, and at about three this morning she'd sat bolt upright, convinced a dog had jumped onto her bed. She licked her lips, throat parched, head throbbing, the usual first-thing words running through her head.

Today's the day. I'll stop drinking. Or cut down. Maybe just one glass, tonight. No, half a bottle. At twenty-five I'm officially an adult, now. New beginnings. Yeah, this is totally do-able.

Do-able until she'd done two cleaning shifts and hardly eaten. Consequently she would mis-read her body's pleas for care, and instead of sleep and nutritious food, give it a couple of bottles of cheap Chardonnay.

Tilda passed the huge bronze statue of Queen Victoria at Piccadilly Gardens. Apparently, that royal would drink whiskey mixed with red wine. On desperate days, Tilda didn't care what she knocked back. One night last week, in the early hours, as the shops were shut, she'd drunk half a bottle of mouthwash. She walked into Market Street as 'Doctor Pressure' came on her playlist. The dance routine she and Logan performed to was all she could see. Someone shouted at her. Whatever. It would only be some chugger or Jesus freak. The shouting got louder as she pictured Logan, arms stretched out, spinning around when the siren came on in their favourite song and... Tilda gasped. She was standing on the tramlines, a warning signal rang out, to the right, and the tram's lights were only a couple of metres away. She froze. Moving forwards or backwards, which would make for the quickest escape?

Did she even care?

An end might be a good thing. No one would miss her. Certainly not Logan or her mum. A sense of emptiness tugged at every fibre of her being as the world went into slow motion. Death couldn't be worse than the loneliness, the despair, the sense of not fitting in, all the things that alcohol had turned around into being everyone's else's fault, into no one else understanding. And maybe she'd be reunited with Dad.

Out of nowhere an arm grabbed hers, someone else was on the tracks, the tram's lights blinded her, they would both die. She couldn't allow that, that person was an innocent. As they yanked her away, she didn't resist. In fact Tilda pushed herself back from the tracks to help, so that she and... it was a man... got out of danger even more quickly, with barely seconds to spare. The tram passed, before grinding to a halt. She landed, thump, on top of a firm chest and long pair of legs. An earbud fell out. A figure got up and stood over her, tall, rubbing his leg. He held out his hand. The street lamp picked out a jagged scar.

Shaking, Tilda reached out her hand too, 'Doctor Pressure' still playing, and instinctively she intertwined her fingers with his, as the man hauled her up. It was the way she and Logan would always hold hands. Tilda pulled away as soon as she was upright. A small crowd had gathered.

'Thank you... thank you so much,' she said, realising, to her surprise, that she meant it.

Despite everything, Tilda was glad to be alive.

The man shook his head vigorously. 'Don't say thanks. I don't deserve it.' With that, he rushed away, limping as he went.

As people fussed over her and a policewoman turned up, Tilda stood, shaking from head to foot. She could have been killed. What would she have had to show for her life? She didn't have a nice home, hadn't learnt how to cook and lived off junk food and takeout; she hardly ever cleaned up her own place, and lurched from moment to moment with no routine. So much for being an adult; she'd bummed her way through her early twenties. Tilda wasn't that different from those people she'd called poor sods, curled up in their sleeping bags, talking to inanimate objects.

Tilda was cocooned too, in her drinking, in her solitary life. Was there a butterfly, in there, waiting to find enough self-respect, enough self-belief, to emerge? Sobbing, she knelt on the floor. The policewoman crouched down next to Tilda and put an arm around her shoulders.

'It's okay, love,' she said. 'You've had a shock. Let it out.'

Tilda did. She let out the truth she'd hidden from, that had grown in recent months – that her rock bottom had become so low, she hadn't cared whether she died or lived. The policewoman didn't judge. Didn't dismiss. Instead, she passed Tilda details of a treatment centre.

* * *

Milo

Whistling, Milo walked up Market Street. He'd spent a night in Manchester, testing out the nightclubs' latest vibes. He was heading to get an early train back home to crash out. A few hours' sleep and he'd be ready for his evening shift and to report back to Kofi, his manager at Shakers in Wilmslow. Milo had worked there for a year and loved the freedom his boss now gave him to use his initiative. Keeping a finger on the pulse of clubbing in the city centre had been his idea. Kofi was supportive – the lockdowns had hit nightclubs especially hard, and Shakers needed to do everything it could to get back on track and get punters out dancing again. Kofi often regaled staff with his stories about the infamous Hacienda club in Manchester, closed now but enjoying its heyday in the eighties and nineties. How he'd seen Madonna there, anecdotes about guns and gangsters, about how – when ecstasy came along – punters only wanted to drink water and bar takings suffered; how the place had brought house and techno music to the UK. Shakers had its own aspirations – to provide a classy night out where customers who otherwise wouldn't, could let their hair down. Milo drank the night away, lemonade after lemonade, in the city once a month and always had a keen eye for the new trends – lately, the growing popularity of mocktails and local craft beers.

He smiled at a passer-by. Sobriety filled him with joy, as long as he blocked out memories of his sister, Grace. It hit him sometimes... watching the younger punters moving to the beat, the laughter, the banter, the energy; three things Grace had in abundance, especially when she danced. Without booze he had no escape from the guilt. Milo turned up his collar. But things had turned around. He had people in his life now, in AA, who understood the self-hate, the self-pity. His flat above the club was... homely, with shelves of his beloved fantasy novels and DVDs, the cushions and throw he'd picked up from IKEA. A little hideaway. Kofi had let him redecorate, he'd chosen cream and Nordic Grey, the latter actually being a relaxing shade of blue. Plant pots completed the simple, calm vibe, so different from the chaos in his life, in his early twenties. Gratitude filled him every day, for his new family in AA, for the colleagues who respected him. He'd dated a few women, cooked them dinner with heart, and the sex, that intimate skin-on-skin contact was... comforting above all else. He only slept with women who made it clear they wanted no-strings-attached sex though. Because Milo was still scared of getting close. He didn't trust himself to be a worthy, caring man who wouldn't put a girl-friend in danger.

Milo squinted to his right as a tram approached. That figure, in a hood, didn't look as if they were going to stop for it. He shivered. It took him back to the tragedy surrounding his sister. He broke into a run, shouting at the top of his voice. People stared at him, having not seen the danger that woman was in. The tram, doing its best to stop, was seconds away from hitting her, she wasn't moving away from the tramlines. Milo lunged forwards as he went on the tracks and grabbed her arm, pulling her away with all his strength. She helped as well and fell on top of him. Quickly he jumped up, wincing with the pain from his leg that had twisted as he fell. He extended his arm and pulled the stranger to her feet; Milo had never seen such dark eyes. She'd intertwined her fingers with his.

Don't thank me. I don't deserve it. My sister lost her life because of me. I didn't save you. I don't do that. All I did was pull you out of the way. Anyone else would have.

Milo muttered some words to her, and as people gathered around, he ran away as fast as his injured leg would allow.

25

Four o'clock and Tilda had waved Riley away, as the little girl turned to give a thumbs up out of the back of Logan's car; a sensible, white SUV – not the low-slung racy sports number Tilda had imagined a professional footballer would drive. She hadn't had the heart to say no when her niece pulled out a pack of cards, after lunch, wanting the four of them to play Snap and Old Maid. Then Milo dug out a carton of ice cream he'd bought, along with sauce and sprinkles.

She loved how Milo had embraced Logan and Riley and helped Tilda welcome them. On her return to the kitchen she was met by the kettle boiling. Milo was finishing drying the dishes.

'Fancy a few laps of the park?' he asked, in a bright tone. 'I could do with walking off that fourth sausage.'

'No thanks. I've... had a bit of stomach-ache, since last night. If you don't mind, I just want to hole up on my own, in the lounge, until bed. I'll make myself a snack for tea. Why don't you go out by yourself?' she suggested, hopefully. 'I... I've put a pile of laundry in the lounge. I'm going to do some ironing whilst watching TV.'

'Or we could play Monopoly? I've got an old set in my room. Riley's got me in the mood for a board game.'

Tilda's fingernails dug into her palms. She was standing on the edge of her sobriety, keen to jump off, if only he'd get out the way.

'I want to be alone,' she snapped.

'Oh, right... of course.'

'Sorry, I... need some time to myself. It's nothing personal. Please. Go out for a couple of hours?'

Tilda hated herself, a more unfamiliar sentiment lately. She went up into her room and grabbed a big baggy jumper, slipped it over her head and attempted to hug away the guilt. It was no good. She still shivered, despite the warm season. Her home was now Milo's, she shouldn't make him feel like a visitor who had to go out if she asked him. Fifteen minutes later, she crept downstairs, as the side door, around the back, creaked shut. She hurried into the kitchen and reached back into one of the cupboards, pulling out the other screw-top wine bottle. She'd bought two as there was a special price offer for bulk buys, that was definitely the only reason. Tilda could have hidden it in her bedroom, could have drunk there, but that would have been admitting she was stepping back into the past and the days when she'd drink the day away, in bed, and not get up. Tilda's life was moving forwards not backwards. Therefore, the lounge it was. Civilised. Moderate. She pressed ice cubes into a mug and once in the lounge closed the door behind her.

Tilda dropped onto the sofa and placed the mug on the coffee table. She turned on the electric fire for the first time in weeks, despite it being the summer, needing a cosy hug from the room. She shivered again and then unscrewed the bottle and poured out the wine, right to the top of the mug and replaced the screw cap. She placed the wine bottle on the floor, down the side of the sofa, so that the remaining wine was out of her sight. The mug looked at Tilda, it was plain-coloured, sturdy, as if it didn't know anything about its contents that made people wobbly. Tilda reached out but then folded her arms tightly around herself and collapsed back against the upholstery, rocking to and fro.

Getting sober had been so difficult. She'd never forget her first conversation with the group therapy's facilitator.

'How do you feel about your first session?' he'd asked.

'The others won't like me,' she'd muttered. 'I've nothing to show for my life. No partner. No career. No home. I'm such a loser, and they will wonder why I'm even drinking. I haven't been in a violent relationship, haven't been in care, I'm not on drugs or out on the streets. They won't understand how hard it's been, simply being spurned by my brother and mum. They'll think it's a poor excuse, me with my private education and money from my gran, compared to the trauma they've no doubt gone through.'

'Dearie, dearie me,' he'd said, in a disdainful tone. 'You believe the world revolves around you. Newsflash – everyone in group will be focused on their own problems, certainly at the beginning, they won't be interested in yours. And wow, talk about an ego, believing you've got a crystal ball and can see into the future and read people's minds.'

No one had ever spoken to adult Tilda like that. She'd almost left on the spot. But she'd stuck it out, beaten those cravings, even though it had meant, at first, fighting the pull to get wasted, minute by minute. She'd walked in nature, done meditation, cooked healthily and read her beloved fantasy books that eventually, once again, became the escape they were when she was a child.

Tilda covered her face with her hands. The scrapbook came to her mind and the ticket to the movie *Happy Feet*; how she and Logan had pretended to be penguins when they got home. They'd tried to walk around with eggs in between their legs, like a penguin caring for its young, but they broke. Mum had been furious about the mess, blaming Tilda, the eldest, for not knowing better. She picked up the mug and raised it to her lips, just as the door opened.

Milo strode in. Took the mug.

'What the...?' Tilda spluttered.

He smelt its contents, went to the window, opened it and threw the wine outside.

'What the hell are you doing?' stuttered Tilda and she stood up, suddenly feeling way too hot.

'I could ask you the same question.'

Perspiration pricked across her body. 'That was an... an unusual cold tea I bought.'

'Tilda. Come on. It's me. I'm no idiot. That was white wine. I've seen this coming.'

'What rubbish. That's all in your head,' she said and moved left, blocking out the bottle around the corner.

Milo's eyes narrowed at her body movement and he swooped past her and picked up the Chardonnay bottle, tipping its contents out of the window as well. He put the empty bottle down on the TV unit and went over to Tilda. He placed a hand on her shoulder.

'It's okay,' he said gently.

Tears in her eyes, she shook him off angrily. He sat down on the sofa and held out his hand. She remained standing. 'How did you know? Been spying on me?'

'No. I didn't need to. Last Thursday when I got back from AA, and you wouldn't let me in, said you'd dropped a glass of hot chocolate and were worried about Dettol's paws getting cut by the glass, you looked... cagey and your eyes were red and swollen. I've lied enough in my life because of booze and it resonated. Then, when I finally came in the kitchen stank of air freshener. It reminded me of how I'd suck on mints if I was trying to camouflage my drinking. As for covering up the smell... why would you bother if it had been hot chocolate? That's a delicious aroma. Nah, it didn't add up, especially as I'd just come from a meeting with members sharing how they used to hide their problems – working late, or so they told loved ones, making up illnesses for when they couldn't drag themselves into the office. Like today, you saying you had a stomach-ache... it didn't stop you eating two burgers and ice cream.'

'That's all you've got?' she said tightly.

'No. Last night, in the pub, that supposed orange juice you grabbed and spilt down me – by the time we got home my shirt smelt of alcohol, vodka I reckon. And today you were almost rude to Logan, getting him to leave as soon as we'd finished cards, and towards me too. It's not like you.' He put up a hand. 'Not judging. I've done far worse, but behaviour that's out of the ordinary, out of character, that's a sign of danger for a recovering addict.'

'Bravo, Poirot,' she muttered.

'What's happened? Why now? Why when everything's coming

together? Logan's back in your life and with a niece who loves seeing you, and you've got big plans for Wright Cleaners...'

She turned and gazed out of the window.

'Let me help,' he said softly. 'Please, Tilda. You've been so good to me.'

Her eyes pricked. He had no right coming in here and taking her drink, this was her house.

'I'm sorry if I've embarrassed you. That wasn't my intention. I... I don't want to see you risk everything you've worked so hard for, that's all. I know what it's like to watch your life crumble around you.'

'It's a lot of stuff... Shane... Ian... I mean, Yves... but the thing that's cut deepest, it's... Logan.' Her voice cracked. 'I'm only recently realising how much I've let him down. I should have seen he was unhappy with the footballer life years ago. Instead, I wallowed in a sense of being hard done by.' Milo shook his head as she told him about the letters that had never been posted.

'Wow. That's quite a deception on your mother's part.' He gave a low whistle. 'You must both feel deeply frustrated about what... what could have been if she'd not interfered... I'm so sorry, Tilda. But he's back in your life now,' said Milo, with an edge that caught her by surprise. 'He's found his calling eventually, got a wonderful daughter along the way... You're being way too hard on yourself. Count your blessings. The two of you have a future together. It's certainly not worth having a relapse over.'

'I'm making a fuss over nothing?' she said, stung by his words. That's what Mum used to do, belittle her feelings. Tilda showed him the scrapbook.

'But at least you get to see him. Be grateful for that. You're so lucky. I'd do anything to see my sister again.'

'Contact her then,' said Tilda and jumped up. 'If we're dishing out no-nonsense, straight advice, which you clearly are, then I say be the first to reach out, Milo. You intervened and reached out on my behalf. Give me her number if you like and I'll get in touch with her.'

'It's not that easy...' he said. 'My situation is more complex.'

'Of *course* it is. No matter that my brother's been through hell, on his own, whilst I was too self-absorbed to see that.' She shook her head and stalked into the hall. Tilda pulled on trainers. 'I need some air. A pub will be open. At least a bar server isn't going to judge me.'

'Tilda. Don't do this. You've been incredibly strong in these last years, using the tools you used to get into recovery.'

'Tools you've ruined!' she snapped and her voice caught. 'Until you turned up, I had a way of living. That's gone to pot.'

'Tilda, eating the same meals every week, spending most of your leisure hours – as well as working ones – cleaning, living a life that is so solitary... that isn't recovery, not long-term, not for the rest of your life. It's a different kind of prison to addiction. You need to find a middle ground.'

'Says you who needs to contact his sister, but is too much of a coward.'

Milo called her back but mortified, angry, Tilda didn't listen. She ran to Crouchden Park, past the black spiked metal gates, and collapsed onto the bench by the pond. She should never have invited Milo into her life, sticking his nose in, spoiling that damn cat. The pair of them had brought nothing but chaos. A sob rose in her throat but she swallowed it back. Mindfully she studied her surroundings, the pond's reeds shimmying from side to side, a mallard's green head glossy under sun rays – nature, the great calibrator, checking in to see that Tilda was where she should be. She inhaled deeply, the smells of fresh grass and algae calming her. Bees buzzed, a frog croaked, birds chirped and trees rustled, the sun breathed warmth onto every leaf, nature providing the perfect summer soundtrack for a meditation. Tilda closed her eyes. Breathe in. Breathe out. A breeze brushed her nose. Her shoulders relaxed and she sank back into the bench.

An hour later she got to her feet, just wanting to go to bed. She walked down the road, towards her house. As she neared, her pace quickened. No. It couldn't be. Yes. It was. Tilda's hand flew to her mouth. Smoke was coming out of the front of her home.

26

Tilda reached her house and stumbled into the garden, almost falling over. She pressed her nose against the side door's window and couldn't see anyone in the utility room. Taking her key out of her pocket, Tilda hurried around to the front of the house, desperate to see where exactly the fire was based so she could put it out. She fumbled with the key. If Tilda had gone in through the back, she might not have been able to get into the lounge, it could have been cut off with flames. She pushed open the door and stood in the hallway. Wafts of smoke escaped from under the lounge door. The smell was acrid, like burning plastic, almost chemical. Crap. Tilda had left the electrical fire on and it hadn't been used since the colder weather, weeks ago now. Was there any way that could have caused the trouble?

'Milo! Dettol!' she shouted. He could be taking a nap in his room and maybe Dettol had joined him. A painful scream shot down the stairs. Tilda raced up and had to stop at the top and bend over, on the landing, a wave of nausea overwhelming her. This was all her fault. Another scream came from Milo's room. Had he been hurt and rushed upstairs away from the fire? She flung open his door.

Oh. Thank God. No one was there. He'd left his Judas Priest CD playing. That explained the shrieking. Under any other circumstances she'd have laughed.

Could they be in her bedroom? Tilda only locked it at night now. Heart racing, she hurtled into her room but she could only see the mess Riley had deemed 'ace'. Bathroom. That was it. No, wrong again. Tilda ran down the stairs, two at a time. The kitchen was empty, and when she'd checked the garden, they weren't in the utility room.

Crap. Crap. Crap. That meant only one thing.

She raced into the kitchen, soaked a tea towel and held it up to her mouth. She went back into the hallway and tentatively touched the lounge door's metal handle, yet it wasn't hot. She'd open the door ever so slowly at first, taking the risk that flames could leap out to suck up fresh oxygen. Shaking, she imagined the worst scene behind the door panelling. She flinched as sirens rang in the distance. A passer-by must have called the fire service. Thank goodness. She should have rung them herself. Nevertheless, every minute counted. Crap. Tilda didn't know how to do CPR. She thought back to that first night Milo had stayed over, in the lounge, ill, and how his feet hung off the end of the sofa; how he'd sworn when she woke him up, a confused Milo believing he was being mugged. A man of such tall stature, intelligent, funny, who'd been reduced to sleeping anywhere he could, who demonstrated oh so quickly that material belongings didn't dictate character.

The sirens becoming louder and louder, Tilda pushed the door open and narrowed her eyes. Oh. The smoke was hardly thick. She exhaled. The room was empty. Tilda peered around the corner of the door as the sirens stopped and an engine rumbled outside. The electric fire had been unplugged and the fire blanket from the kitchen, thrown over the pile of laundry next to it, Tilda closed the door again, and was about to search for the cat when a familiar voice let its way in, from outside. She'd left the front door ajar. It was Milo. She darted outside to see him talking to a couple of firefighters. Tilda raced out and threw the tea towel onto ground.

'Tilda? What were you doing in there?'

Unable to speak, she stood, trembling at the possibility of what could have been. 'I got back about ten minutes ago, saw smoke, and worried that you and Dettol must have been trapped inside... you weren't in the garden, so I came in the front.' She lunged forwards and hugged him tight, swiftly gathering herself and pulling back.

'Right... okay...' Milo stared at her. 'We were indoors but around the time you'd have got here, we went out the back, after I dialled 999.'

'We must have missed each other by seconds. What the hell happened?'

They moved to one side as the firefighters entered the house.

'I don't know. I'm sorry,' he said, cheeks flushed. 'I feel like I've caused a fuss. I rang the emergency services before realising I could put the fire out myself. I was in my bedroom and when the smoke alarm on the landing ceiling went off. I guess I panicked – about Dettol, about your lovely home being ruined. I called Dettol and she came running in from the kitchen. I shut the lounge door and took her outside.'

'You did the right thing. Is she okay?' *Please don't let Dettol be scared or hurt in any way.*

'I found the cat carrier in your shed. I also worried the sirens could have caused her to run into the road, so I left her sitting in that, by the side door.'

'Thank God.' Her words were barely audible.

Milo hesitated and then took her in his arms. 'Understandable you being upset at the prospect of missing my sparkling company...'

'Don't joke about it,' she said, but couldn't help a small smile. 'Sorry for being an idiot, earlier. I should never have mentioned your sister.'

'Glad you – at least – aren't still angry with me,' he said and pulled away. 'Dettol is furious I've locked her up.'

Tilda wanted to run to see the cat but needed to speak to the chief fire officer and tell him about leaving the electric fire on. Nervously she waited as the firefighters checked out the damage. Almost an hour later she could finally speed-walk around to the back where Milo sat by the cage, scrolling on his phone. He jumped to his feet and raised an eyebrow.

'Thankfully the damage really is minimal. The pile of laundry I'd put in there went up but not much else in the lounge is flammable. Thank goodness. The fire chief advises us to sleep elsewhere tonight and get an electrician in, first, thing, to check the wiring and the appliance. I've been intending to replace that fire. I got a new TV for the lounge first, when I moved in. A stupid priority, in retrospect.' Tilda crouched by the cage. 'Dettol, you... you are such a good girl.' Tilda poked her finger through a gap. Dettol studied her then licked it. The cat pushed her face forwards and Tilda ran her fingertip over the M on Dettol's forehead.

Matilda. Milo. Dettol's M. It was as if fate had brought the three of them together.

She stood upright again and took a deep breath. Time to get a grip and sort out this mess. Ringing the insurers would be a good start. She looked up at Milo and recalled when he'd first come back to her house, when the washing machine flooded, and how she'd been struck by how tall he was. Since she'd got to know him, Milo had filled his height, with an abundance of understanding and authenticity that shone out. 'Thanks Milo. I owe you one.' Her voice wavered. 'I'm glad you're okay. I've got used to the man who faked a bout of flu to get a bed for the night.'

He rubbed the back of his neck. 'Damn. There's me thinking my acting had been so convincing that Warner Bros would sign me up as the hero of their next fantasy series.'

'You've been a hero today,' she said, and her voice wavered.

'Just looking out for myself,' he said, and a muscle in his cheek twitched. 'After all, this is my place of work as well as my home.'

Tilda couldn't help giving a smile again.

'My dear, what happened, how can I help?' A woman pushed open the gate and hurried over, wearing a floral dress and luminous purple shoes. Her greying auburn hair was tied in a long plait that draped around one side and hung down the front. Carrying an empty tray, she walked in a lopsided manner and rubbed her hip when she came to a halt. 'Tilda, I'm Anushka from next door. We haven't had a proper chat since I introduced myself when you moved in, ooh... a long time ago. You're a busy young lady, aren't you?' Her eyes twinkled, yet concern etched her face.

'I'm so sorry, you must have been scared a big fire might be spreading to your property,' said Tilda, quickly explaining everything that had gone on.

'Too right, love my little home, memories littered everywhere that give me a sense that my late Rajesh is still around.' She swallowed. 'But furnishings can be replaced. I was more concerned about you and so glad no one is injured. I saw quickly that it was a minor incident. We all got off lightly.'

The word *we* made Tilda feel part of something. 'Thank you… Anushka. It's been a bit of a shock. This is Milo.'

The woman studied the two of them and her eyes crinkled.

'And Dettol.' Tilda pointed at the cage.

'Ah, my mistake, I've carried on calling her Dotty. A determined little thing, she used to come over to mine for a bit of peace and quiet; the previous owners had two small children. Nice enough family, so I was surprised they left their cat behind. The day before they'd asked if I'd have her, but I go on a lot of cruises with my friends, it wouldn't be fair.' Anushka bent down. 'I've always loved a tabby. She's such a pretty one at that, aren't you Dot… I mean Dettol.' Anushka straightened up. 'Both of you come around to mine when you're done and I'll brew up, again. I've already fed and watered those lads and lasses in uniform. A nice hot drink and some of my chocolate burfi, that'll sort you out.'

Oh. That was kind. Tilda nodded, surprised at herself for genuinely wanting to get to know a neighbour.

Anushka went over to the cat carrier again. 'Dettol visited even more when you first moved in, probably didn't like the redecorating I spied as I walked past the house. Cats can be funny about smells. A friend of mind has a ginger tom and you should see his face if I wear my citrus perfume. However, Dettol's visits have dropped off, especially in the last month. She used to like to sit behind my patio doors when the sun shone. I hope you don't mind but sometimes I gave her cat treats.'

'Tuna is a favourite treat of hers,' said Milo, eyes twinkling as Tilda blushed and ignored him.

'Why don't I let her out of this cage, in my house, if you've got to be out for the next twenty-four hours? I've missed her company. She must be getting her extra cuddles elsewhere now.' Anushka picked up the carrier and made her way to the gate. 'I'll get her favourite shoe box out. Pop over and say goodbye to her before you go, if you like?'

'What a star,' said Milo, as Anushka walked down the street.

Tilda's neighbour was kind, generous, hadn't been nosy, hadn't blamed or judged. Perhaps Tilda didn't need to keep problems to herself, any more. 'I'll ring Logan. Or maybe not. I don't want to worry him over such a small fire.'

Milo put a hand on her shoulder. 'Of course you should ring him. Logan's your family.'

He was right. Tilda's eyes filled again. The effects of that smoke must have lingered.

27

Tilda and Milo spent the night in a budget hotel. She insisted on paying and booked two rooms. Logan was away, visiting an old friend from his football academy days, and said he'd come straight back, and that they could stay at his place. But Tilda wouldn't hear of him changing his plans. Logan passed on the number of an electrician friend who would only charge mates' rates and would prioritise them tomorrow. He also insisted on taking the two of them out for a pub dinner the next day, early enough for Riley to join them, after school, and still be back for bedtime. They agreed to meet at the Windmill.

That night Tilda and Milo ate in a bar next to the hotel. She didn't talk much and left half of the basket of chips and fish goujons. Half-heartedly she joined in a discussion around the ideas for the business that had resulted from the team meal in the Windmill. This week Tilda would look into Connie's idea of helping with laundry for one elderly client and Milo would research pricing for Jazz's idea of moving-house deep cleans. Despite the spurts of excitement in her chest over the solid plans that were falling into place for expanding Wright Cleaners, how much worse the day's events could have been began to sink in. She'd fallen quiet around at Anushka's, and struggled to eat the Indian sweets and drink tea. Anushka had given her a sharp look and disappeared into the kitchen, coming back with a strong coffee. Anushka's place reminded Tilda of her gran's, the fascinating items Mum called clutter, such as well fingered books of all genres, ornamental souvenirs from holidays and years old programmes from theatre shows. Anushka had waved them off with Dettol in her arms, her house guest until Tilda and Milo moved back in tomorrow.

After coffee, her new favourite drink, Tilda said goodnight to Milo. He was in the room beside hers. She switched the television on and sat through a quiz show and documentary, none of the content registering. Finally, she turned off the lights, and lay down in bed, hot and sticky. She opened a window and threw off the sheets but an hour later she was still awake. Tilda sat up and hugged her knees. Without Milo, without Dettol, life would fade to grey again, like an old, silent movie, with no colour, with no sound. Oh, she could add her own soundtrack, with her playlists and telly, but those wouldn't match Dettol's range of meows: sassy when she was hungry, trilling when a bird dared come near the window. The fire had made her realise that she did... Tilda loved that cat. Her eyes pricked. It was long time since she'd used the L word about anything or anyone. The way Dettol curved her body around Tilda's legs whilst she opened a new can of food, how she washed herself meticulously after eating, the way she used her wily feline ways to get the affection she desired. Dettol was a go-getter, a survivor, and found pleasure in the simplest of things like a cotton reel rolling across the ground, a shiny chocolate wrapper, and as for boxes, whatever the size or shape, she turned them into a bed or hide-and-seek spot. Dettol was giving. Playful. Creative.

If Milo wasn't around, she'd miss his infectious laughter and his soft tone. The mug, that hidden wine bottle... he'd simply been worried about Tilda when he'd poured the contents away, she could see that now. He'd been protecting her from a very bad decision. Tilda wasn't used to people protecting her. She could do that very well herself, thank you. Tilda ran a finger across her knee, imagining what it must be like to have someone always in your corner. Perhaps she'd never needed a man to propose. Perhaps all she needed was a good friend, who didn't need to design clothes in Paris or call her countless endearing names.

The best thing she could say about Mum was that she'd always treated Dad really well. They were both passionate about UK politics, the Olympics and whether milk should go in tea before or after water; common interests that, looking back, Tilda could see fuelled their marriage. Dad had missed out on a promotion once. Tilda had heard them discussing it late one night, in the lounge. She'd spied through the crack in the door, as her mother put her arms around him. Her mum told Dad his time would come, that it was the company's loss, that together, if he wanted, they'd work out a new five-year plan for his career. It had starkly contrasted with how she'd push, push Logan, and her reaction when Tilda missed out on becoming head girl at primary school. Her mum had suggested Tilda put herself forward as a candidate and, back then, Tilda was happier, had friends, thought it could be fun. However, she was shy when it came to mingling with the teachers, when it came to public speaking. She was made deputy head girl instead and that suited Tilda perfectly. Thrilled, she'd rushed home to tell Logan and her mum. However, the first thing her mother said was, 'What went wrong?'

Last week a client had rung up to complain, said Wright Cleaners' staff 'cleaned things too thoroughly when a wipe over would do', so that they could charge more; the proof being that they did things previous cleaners had ignored. Milo was listening in and she almost laughed at the indignant faces he pulled. After the call, he'd slammed the unfounded complaints that had been voiced. A small thing, but it had meant so much to share the load with someone who actually understood – who trusted that her business did have integrity, that she and her employees rightly provided a service of high quality.

Tilda hugged her knees tighter. That wasn't all. In the last week or two, when his arm brushed against hers, every time they watched a movie together, or when they played with Dettol on the lounge carpet, the strangest sensation built inside her. She'd never experienced it before, certainly not sober. Tilda was a grown woman, practical, hardworking, sensible too, but this new feeling inside didn't belong to her, but instead to a more reckless Tilda, wild and impulsive. As it grew, little by little at first, it occupied an increasing part of her thoughts, warning her that one day soon it would explode unless...

To hell with being friends, she wanted to kiss Milo.

To wrap herself around that long frame and lose herself to him.

To give herself, completely, in a way she never had with any other person.

Tilda liked Milo.

One hundred per cent.

She lay down again. Pulled up a sheet, higher, higher, and over her face. The fire could have been fatal. Or Milo could have packed and left after her comments about his sister. What *had* happened with this Grace? Was it more than an estrangement? But neither of those things had happened. Was this a second chance to get... closer to him?

Having hardly slept, Tilda pushed this idea to the back of her mind when she got up the next day, wishing she was at home and could go on one of their morning runs, to clear her head. She dealt with the electrician and insurers, and when she moved back in, caught up on some urgent work phone calls and paperwork. However, the romantic notions about Milo sprang back to the fore, dancing in her mind, when they met Logan and Riley in the Windmill. Her senses felt heightened around him and she talked on automatic, telling her brother how the electrician concluded the fire had been caused by the actual appliance, that the rest of the house's wiring was thankfully in order. Logan offered to help redecorate the lounge and Riley insisted she would too. Tilda wasn't going to claim on the insurance; the damage was minimal, there was no point in paying the excess. She did her best to pay attention to her brother and niece, whilst imagining how it would feel to trail her finger across Milo's lips that twitched when he teased, wondering whether his mouth was as soft as the tone he so often used. Milo went up to the bar to get more drinks. An orange juice for Tilda. The cravings had passed. For now.

Riley was drawing pictures.

'How are you, sis?' said Logan, after his last forkful of curry. He wiped his mouth. 'You seem subdued.'

Sis. Tilda swallowed. She didn't mind any more. In fact, she liked it.

'Events like this make you re-evaluate your whole life, don't they? Riley got ill once, some random bug. My whole world turned upside down until the hospital said she was going to be okay. It was a big step towards me realising I didn't want to be a footballer any more, it's such an all-consuming career.'

'I'm just glad everyone is all right.' She fixed a smile on her face and ate the last slice of her pizza.

'Milo's a great guy, isn't he? I wouldn't have thought to put Dettol in a carrier in case she got spooked.' Logan fixed his gaze on her face. 'You two are good together. I can see that, now. I was wrong about him.'

She gave a bright smile. 'Yes. We work well as a team. He's very easy-going. Meticulous too. With him on board, Wright Cleaners could really go places.'

'No... I meant... I could see you... *together*.'

Riley giggled. 'Auntie, your cheeks are the same colour as that cherry on my ice cream.'

'It's not like that,' she said, quickly. 'In any case, he... he's going out on a date tomorrow with one of my employees, Jazz.'

Logan leant back in his chair and shook his head.

'What?' asked Tilda.

'The Tilda I used to know fought for what she wanted.'

'Now wait a minute, who's saying... It's a platonic relationship, nothing more, and—'

He held up his hand. 'Remember that cuddly unicorn you wanted? You must have been about eight. It came from a cartoon you were obsessed with. You saw it in a shop but Mum and Dad said you had too many toys already. You were in tears all the way home. It was unusual for you, I hardly ever recall you acting spoilt, or crying for that matter.'

'I've still got it somewhere,' she mumbled. 'The show was called *Rainbow Unicorns*. Dad would watch it with me, on a Saturday morning. The toy was my favourite character, Cloudblossom.'

'Cool name!' said Riley and thumped the table. 'Your mum and dad changed their minds?'

'No. I decided they were right, so the next weekend I went through my plushies, then dragged a deckchair out to the front of the house and sold them to friends cheaply. Dad gave me a big hug and said well done for thinking of a way out of my problem. Even Mum was impressed – no doubt it appealed to her business sense. At Dad's suggestion, they made up the difference and he took me back to the shop.'

'That was so typical of you,' said Logan. 'Turning around a bad situation. Like when you turned ten. Mum left it too late to book the roller-skating rink for your party, the weekend of your birthday. You suggested she took you and your best friends to the park instead, to roller skate there, and then to a McDonald's. She wasn't a park person, but you said it would be much cheaper than a party. That won her over. I could tell you were disappointed, but you were always so practical and, in some shape or form, determined to do what you wanted. It's why I've been... surprised since meeting up again, to find out that you hated boarding school but accepted it. Someone else might have run away or continually pestered their parents, term in, term out, to let them come home.' His face darkened. 'I wish I'd known what you were going through.'

Riley was drawing again. She stuck her tongue out as she concentrated, picking up an array of different coloured pencils.

'You and I had... had become estranged,' Tilda said, to Logan, in a lower voice. 'Mum clearly wanted me out of the way. As far as being happy went, pretty soon I didn't see much difference between school or home.'

'But there's nothing holding you back from getting with Milo. It's obvious he loves having you around.' Logan put his palms on the table. 'Go on, sis. Go for it!'

'Like I said, I don't...'

Milo appeared by the table. He put down the drinks. 'Anyone up for a game of snooker?'

Logan raised an eyebrow at Tilda. She glared back at him. Riley looked as if she was trying not to laugh as she carried on colouring in.

'Sure, mate, let's do it,' said Logan. The two men picked up their drinks. Milo headed off. Logan lunged and ruffled Tilda's hair, before grinning and following him. She'd hated her brother doing that when they were little!

Riley shook her finger in the air. 'Dad's right, Auntie. I've seen your goo-goo eyes.'

'What?'

'Dad makes them at Cameron.' Riley pretended to be sick. 'You make them at Milo. I've seen it. Goo-goo eyes, that's what I call them.' She made circles with her fingers and put them up to her face. 'Dad says you're a strong person, like my mum. I want to be like both of you when I grow up.'

Tilda filled with an emotion she didn't recognise – warm, nostalgic, life-affirming. The opposite of what made her want to be drunk.

'Boys are yuk. Johnny, in my class, puts worms in his mouth.' Riley shuddered. 'But if you like one...' She pushed over the picture she'd been drawing. 'Maybe Milo has got magic.' Carefully she picked up her drink, with both hands. 'He must have, cos your face goes all shiny when he's around, as if he's cast a spell.'

Tilda studied the four stick figures in the picture – a child with black curly hair, with a triangular body, in red, an ice cream in one hand. Next to her was a man, his top had flowers drawn on it. The figure next to him had a triangular body, so a woman, with black hair like the little girl, and a striped cat at her feet. She had big, big eyes and held hands with a tall man on her other side who... Tilda lifted up the picture. He had a horn on his forehead and a rainbow mane trailing down his back.

'Goo-goo eyes never lie,' whispered Riley.

28

Tilda stretched and closed her laptop. She'd only done the urgent work, having spent the day cleaning the lounge. Milo had taken up the slack and, after his AA meeting at lunchtime, had spent the afternoon liaising with an unusually disgruntled client. Jazz had left fifteen minutes early, from one house. After phoning her, Milo discovered she'd stayed thirty minutes late the week before. The client hadn't realised and apologised for doubting Wright Cleaners. Then there was the pensioner who wanted Connie to address him as 'sir' and couldn't understand why she didn't respond when he clicked his fingers. Tilda recalled him, now – seemingly polite and old-school. It was unusual for her to be fooled. She listened in to the call. Milo was good. Calm, polite, firm and quick to reassure Connie that if he did either of those things again, Wright Cleaners would let that particular client go.

Tilda glanced at the fridge, sad she hadn't been able to stick the picture to it, that Riley had given her in the pub last night, but there was no way Milo could see it. Logan had suggested they redecorate the lounge on Saturday. Despite the windows being left open today, the room still reeked of smoke. Tilda had wiped the blinds and run the curtains through the wash. She used a spray cleaner on the sofa and armchairs. Whilst Milo was out, Anushka had come around to survey the damage and drop off a box of homemade biscuits. She suggested leaving out bowls of vinegar, apparently that would help with the smell.

It was so long since Tilda had had someone older in her life, to guide her and give reassurance. Despite her busy day, despite the unfamiliarity of letting people into her home, Tilda asked Anushka to stay for coffee. Dettol had jumped onto Anushka's lap and she'd stroked her striped back whilst drinking and eating biscuits. They'd chatted about the fire, Anushka's cruises and her late husband.

'It's nice to have someone to cook for,' said Anushka as she stood on the doorstep to leave. 'My Rajesh would hoover up my baking. Has Milo got a sweet tooth?' she asked hopefully.

'Yes. He even adds extra sugar to hot chocolate!'

'How long have you two been dating?'

'Oh, we aren't... He works for me... well with me, kind of, you see... And lives here... well, he lodges... Not that he did at first... but now he pays me rent and...'

'You need to get your story straight, Missy. What exactly is Milo to you?' Anushka grinned at Tilda's indignant expression, winked and left.

Goo-goo eyes. Oh God. Did Anushka see them? Tilda ran upstairs into the bathroom. She pictured Milo in her head and then asked the mirror's opinion.

Holy shit. That was pathetic.

Unable to stop humming, despite the horror, Tilda went back downstairs, suddenly all out of hum when she remembered tonight. Milo was going out in half an hour for his date with Jazz. She sat in the kitchen, nursing a fizzy drink. She breathed in. Breathed out. No. She didn't want wine. Okay she did but she wouldn't go to the back of that cupboard in the kitchen and hunt out the bottle she'd bought and stashed there again. She wouldn't make the most of having the house to herself. The fire had given her perspective. It was as if, before Milo, her life had been like an instruction manual, using basic sentence structures and non-flowery language, but now had morphed into an actual story, with descriptive passages, with characters, with emotion.

Dettol slept on one of the kitchen chairs. She leant over and picked her up. Supporting the cat's back legs with one arm, like Milo did, Tilda stroked the soft fur.

'I do love you, Dettol,' she whispered. 'Sorry I gave you such a clinical name. Dotty is actually quite pretty. But we won't change it now. Dettol has grown on you.'

Dettol gave a small meow and burrowed her head into Tilda's shoulder. Tilda's breathing slowed and she closed her eyes, leaning her cheek into the stripes. Dettol relied on her, gave her a purpose apart from running the business. Oh, the cat had always been there, in the background, but now Tilda cared, that was the difference. She'd bought frozen coley fish squares and would cook one, tonight. Dettol deserved a more varied diet. Tilda had ordered a catnip toy online, along with a cat brush. Riley would be so excited. The heavy metal music upstairs came to a halt and solid, measured footsteps came down the stairs. Crisp shirt. Gelled chestnut hair. Chinos. Tilda tore her gaze away.

Milo came over and tickled Dettol's head. 'You okay, Tilda?' He sat down next to her. 'The lounge looks so much better, already. We'll lick it into shape this weekend. How about one night this week, after we shop for the wallpaper and paint, we go to an out-of-town store and look for a new electric fire?'

'Sounds like a plan. Thanks, Milo. Right. You'd better get off.'

'Keen to get rid of me?'

'No.' She could tell what he was thinking.

'I can't cancel tonight, otherwise I'd keep you company.'

'Milo. I don't need a babysitter! You have fun.' *Can't cancel.* Must really like her.

'We haven't talked about... what with the fire...' He cleared his throat. 'Thursday, Tilda. Come with me to AA. You don't have to give your name or talk, just sit and listen. You never have to go back again if it doesn't feel right.'

'I'm okay. Honestly. It was a blip. You don't need to worry.'

He bit his lip. 'Okay. But promise me if the old cravings come back, you'll tell me. No shame in it.'

He walked out of the side door, leaving Tilda feeling hopeless. How could she fight for a man who was interested in someone else? Jazz's name alone exuded glamour. And Tilda liked Jazz, she was a good worker, considerate too. She'd sent Tilda a follow-up email thanking her again for the lovely meal and added that working for Wright Cleaners was the best job she'd ever had. Gah. Tilda needed some unicorn magic to solve the conundrum.

She put Dettol back on one of the chairs, reached into her pocket and pulled out Riley's drawing. As she unfolded the paper she noticed, for the first time, writing on the other side. She turned it over and read the spidery list, each word written in a different colour.

> *How to get your younickorn*
> *Beach*
> *Dance*
> *Sinma*

Oh. The universe had been listening. But dating advice from a six-year-old? Had it come to this? She gave a sheepish smile. Well Shane had been a mistake, online dating was a minefield and Ian a major embarrassment. What had she got to lose? Tilda scanned the list again. Reading in between the colourful lines, and spelling mistakes... maybe Riley was actually saying Tilda needed to be more adventurous. She liked Jazz, wouldn't interfere or meddle, but there was no harm in Tilda bringing the fun factor into her and Milo's friendship.

Fun, like when Riley did her little dances, or Dettol played with string; like when Logan reminded her of their childhood japes and Anushka, next door, turned up with biscuits; like when Tilda met her employees for dinner and it turned into a night of good-humoured banter, and like when Milo mimicked unreasonable clients. In fact, so much of her time with him was filled with laughter, caused by his expressions when his chilli con carne turned out too hot, or indignant comments if he wasn't happy with the way a favourite fantasy series ended.

Tilda stood up and jigged from left to right, she spun and kicked a leg in the air, doing the moves Riley had taught her, dancing as if no one was watching apart from a slightly baffled cat she no longer saw as snooty. Fun was a new word in Tilda's life. A word she was growing to like.

She put music on and danced a little more. She picked up Dettol again and swayed with the cat in her arms. After that, she went online and ordered takeout, even though it wasn't the weekend, even though it wasn't a special occasion. Far too much arrived. So what? She and Milo could finish the noodles and lemon chicken, the spring rolls and crispy duck, tomorrow. She ran a deep bath and tipped in the remnants of an old bottle of bubble bath she found under a pile of clothes in her room. A glass of Coke in her hand, Tilda lay in the steaming water. Dettol strolled in, sat down and washed her face. Tilda hadn't shut the door as she was in on her own. This was new. Tilda always had made a point of locking the bathroom door, as well, but the bullying ghosts of boarding school weren't so vivid these days.

'A proper girls' night in, we're having,' she said.

Dettol meowed back.

Half an hour later, Tilda went downstairs, barefoot, in her dressing gown. She yawned and slumped into a kitchen chair, having put milk in the pan. Her phone buzzed. Milo! Perhaps he was on his way back, on the train. She'd wait for him to arrive, they could drink hot chocolate together. She could even suggest a late game of Monopoly. A warmth spread through her limbs, not due to the after-effects of the hot bath. She tapped on the text.

Oh.

Right.

Milo wouldn't be home until tomorrow morning.

He was spending the night with Jazz. He'd be back early, ready for work.

The phone fell out of Tilda's hands and Shane's sneering voice came into her head, laughing at the prospect of her having any romantic future. She looked down at her bare feet, smelt the bubble bath on her skin, her back ached slightly from some ambitious dance moves... what a fool she'd been. Tilda jumped as Dettol leapt onto her lap. Her eyes filled as amber, almond-shaped ones met hers. Dettol butted Tilda's chin with her wet nose. Half past eleven. It was time for bed. Fun was dangerous, it got you hurt. Whereas routine was the opposite. Tilda turned off the pan and poured the milk down the sink.

As she went to turn the kitchen light out, a meow floated in, from the utility room. Tilda paused and went in. Dettol ran up to her and lay down on her back, twisting from side to side, giving little meows.

Yes, routine was important, but girl pals were too, or so popular culture had always told Tilda. She picked the cat up and went upstairs for their very first sleepover. Once snuggled in bed, Dettol crept up to the pillow and fell asleep next to a restless Tilda, one paw gently resting on her human friend's shoulder.

29

Tilda woke up at seven the next morning. Dettol lifted her head as Tilda sat cross-legged on the floor and did ten minutes of meditation. She paused. There was no WhatsApp message to check. Was a fake, French love interest better than none? A cold shower, in the name of good health, brought Tilda back to her senses, shaking her head at the name Yves St Laurence, yet hoping that Ian's life was in a better place. She brushed her hair, and then changed into black trousers and a white shirt. Tilda applied her favourite scent, for a few seconds wrapped up in her gran's arms, a soft moment within the rigid routine. At seven thirty precisely she arrived in the kitchen and tipped cat food into a bowl. Twenty to eight and it was time for Tilda's breakfast: cereal flakes with fruit, five walnut halves, a small handful of raisins and two tablespoons of probiotic yogurt on top.

At eight o'clock sharp, after brushing her teeth and flossing, after rinsing out with mouthwash, Tilda settled down at the kitchen table with her laptop, sunshine streaming onto the table from the window. What a beautiful, blue-skyed sunny July day. The side door creaked and Dettol ran into the utility room. A deep voice said hello and Milo walked into the kitchen grinning, despite the bags under his eyes.

'Good time?' she asked, in a bright tone.

'Great, thanks,' he said. 'I texted last night in case you were worried. You see—'

Tilda held up her hand. 'You're a grown man. No need to explain. How is Jazz?'

'Fine. Really good. But it's not like...'

Oh God. How embarrassing. He was acting as if he knew about Tilda's... feelings for him and didn't want to hurt them.

She picked up the business phone. 'Better take this.' She headed into the utility room and talked into the dead line, ending the charade as soon as she stood outside. Tilda waited ten minutes, admiring a row of starlings on the building ahead, their jewel-like speckles glistening in the morning sunshine. When she strode back inside. Milo was at the table, in front of his laptop. This didn't need to be awkward. Logan and Riley might be disappointed but she wouldn't fight for a man who had taken things to the next level with another woman. That didn't mean she couldn't fight to keep a friendship that had come to mean so much. To throw it away because a romance wasn't reciprocated made no sense. However, she was grateful, for once, that the doorbell rang. She darted out of the kitchen and arrived a few minutes later carrying both a parcel and an envelope with a French stamp on it. The latter must have been from her mum, though it wasn't her birthday or Christmas. Tilda bit the insides of her cheeks. She went straight to the bin and chucked the envelope away. Milo caught her eye and gave her an understanding nod, in the way only a good friend could. She shook the parcel at him, before carefully undoing it.

'Wow. These certainly grab your attention.' She passed a bundle of flyers over to Milo. The colour palette was blue and yellow, a popular one with advertisers at the moment. They'd ordered them before the team meal at the Windmill last weekend, so hadn't incorporated any extra ideas, like the discount to new clients. But they'd brainstormed the ideas Milo originally mooted, and on the front services were listed, including carpet and upholstery cleaning. She and Milo had researched what local companies charged, and factored in the purchase of equipment. The list was next to a colourful photo of a basket of cleaning products. On the back was the pricing. They both agreed transparency was the best option, to avoid people being put off ringing if they were concerned about the costs. They'd only ordered a small batch of flyers, to test out what effect they had. If it was positive, the next batch would include the staff's other ideas like shed and garage clear-ups. Perhaps prices for window and gutter cleaning too. Callum had already emailed Tilda the phone number for his uncle who'd offered to talk to her about what exactly went into offering such services.

'These flyers were such a good idea of yours,' said Tilda. 'I want to rush out and deliver them straightaway.'

Milo beamed. 'Why don't we?'

Tilda ran her hand over the flyers 'Let's do it! Around Crouchden. This southern side. The more suburban estate – away from the train station – probably fits our target market.'

'We could race it – take on a certain number of streets each. The last back home has to...'

Make dinner? Wednesday was cottage pie. Nothing about that inspired Tilda. She'd grown to like Milo's spontaneous cooking.

'Go out to get our favourite takeaway coffees and cake later this afternoon to refuel,' Milo suggested.

'Deal.' They shook hands.

Milo's phone rang. He put it to his ear. 'Hi Jazz. Sure... Hold on...' He stood up. 'Back in a minute, Tilda.' He hurried upstairs, laughing as he went into his room. A door closed.

She sat down and held up a handful of flyers. Tilda had a lot to be grateful for. She took a photo of them and sent it to Logan. Immediately he replied with open mouth face emojis and they texted to and fro. Logan told her he had contacted the radio station and they'd already emailed him the contract for his commentating position.

Milo came downstairs, wearing his joggers and trainers. 'Good to go,' he said. 'You get changed and I'll select streets for each of us. I'll print us each out a map with them marked. I don't want to take my phone if I'm running. It's on charge anyway.'

Twenty minutes later, it was nine o'clock, they both stood in the back-yard, each holding a map as they did stretches, rucksacks on their back,

Dettol watching with curious eyes as she washed her face in the sun, having eaten more of the fish Tilda had steamed yesterday.

'Ready to be beaten?' she said. 'Four streets each. Give me your map – I need to check you haven't given me the longest route.'

He rolled his eyes in a comical manner and went to pass his over but she gently pushed his shoulder. 'If I trust you with running my business, guess I need to trust you with this. You're a twelve-stepper, right? You've done a moral inventory, been scrupulously honest about your shortcomings, made amends with the people you've hurt?'

'Since when did you know about that?'

'We were told about the Twelve Step Programme in treatment. Sounds gruelling.'

Milo stopped stretching. 'Yes. It is. Life-changing – and hard when you can't contact the person you want to say sorry to, above all others.'

'Your sister?'

His silence answered her question. Tilda wanted to ask more, but he'd seemed so happy before she brought the subject up. She ran out of the gate and left down the road.

'Hey!' he shouted after her. 'That's cheating!'

She stopped and turned around. 'No. It's called tactics. Get your money ready to buy me that coffee. Should see you back here around eleven.' Tilda laughed at his fake outraged face and began running again. Anushka was in her front window, watering a plant and waved. Tilda waved back as she sprinted past.

Four streets felt like eight as she had to run up and down a drive for every single house. Her knees ached and perspiration dripped. Tilda turned into the last street, berating herself for not having brought a water bottle in this weather. By now she was walking. It was almost two hours since she'd seen Milo. He could be at home already, showered and waiting. Tilda would never live that down. She finally arrived at the last house. An elderly man in a Panama hat sat in a plastic chair on his lawn, pruning a tall shrub. He stood up and rubbed his back, leaning on a stick.

'No junk mail, I get enough of that blasted stuff,' he said.

Tilda stopped. 'Oh, right. Yes, of course.' She smiled and went to leave.

'What is it you're selling, anyway? A funeral package? Details about a care home?'

Tilda spotted a stain down his jumper, the trousers that were creased all over. It reminded her of a pensioner who lived next door in her childhood. Dad used to mow her lawn. Tilda had been playing out once and the woman gave a loud tut. She'd come out holding her glasses in her hand to pick up some litter that had blown onto the drive. It wasn't until she'd put them back on to read a discarded leaflet, that she noticed she'd spilt her breakfast down her top. Tilda couldn't understand her upset. At eight years old spilt food was part of life.

'No, cleaning services,' Tilda replied. 'I have my own business. We do all the usual tasks indoors, plus carpet and upholstery cleaning. We're going to be adding extra services, such as helping with laundry and cleaning out sheds and garages.'

The man leant on his stick. 'Extortionate prices, I'm guessing.'

'No. It wouldn't pay, what with the cost-of-living crisis. I need to stay competitive.'

'My Annie could spot a rip-off a mile away. Right to the end when she died last Christmas. She could always pick out the true bargains in the January sales, clocking dishonest retailers that included goods at a higher price than normal.'

'I'm sorry for your loss,' said Tilda and she walked onto the lawn, picked up a stray branch he'd lopped off and put it in a bag by his side.

He rubbed his back again and his severe expression cracked. 'To be honest, I... I've let things slip since Christmas. Annie was younger than me. It's only now I realise how much she did, keeping the house in order, and the garden. If you don't mind me saying, you look as if you could do with a cold drink. Would you care to join me, I was about to have a lemonade? Then you could take me through your pricing. It's... been hard to admit that I do need a hand.'

But then Milo wouldn't definitely win the challenge. She met the old man's hopeful eyes. Tilda stretched out her and. 'Tilda Wright. Nice to meet you.'

Bony fingers clasped hers. 'Bob. Bob Marlow. Pleased to meet you, Tilda.' She followed him inside, helping him up the step.

One lemonade led to two with biscuits, albeit out-of-date according to the packet but she wouldn't worry about that. His house needed a refresh, although she could tell he'd done the best he could. Tilda had seen far worse states of cleanliness in some businesses that should have known better.

'I'd suggest a fairly deep clean for the first session and after that it will simply be a matter of a light clean, say, once a fortnight. You'd like help with laundry?'

'I never was the best at ironing. My luck was in when I married Annie, I'd been single for a long time and met her at a friend's retirement party. Apart from her wonderful, loving qualities' – he teared up – 'she always said she found housework therapeutic. The shed needs a damn good tidy too. I used to make model trains, back in the day.' His face brightened. 'They are stacked up in there. I... had an idea I might give it another go, my hands are nothing like as unsteady as my legs. If I had a bit of space in there...'

'I'd love to see your models. I wouldn't have the patience for a hobby like that.' Bob became more animated as he led the way, chatting about how much he enjoyed learning about the history of each train. The shed itself was sturdy and its wooden panels had been treated. The contents were a mess but the inside was dry and didn't smell of mould.

They headed back to the house. 'Thanks for the lemonade, I must get going, the office calls – well, my kitchen table and cat, that is.' Wobbling a little, Bob took her into the kitchen again before walking into the hallway. 'Why don't you have a think about the services of ours that interest you, and give me a ring in a couple of days? Is there anyone you can talk it over with?'

'I've talked it over with you, lass. That's enough.'

'Okay! Ring me when you have some dates in mind.'

Tilda ran home, re-energised, whistling as she put her key in the lock. Wringing his hands together, Milo appeared in the utility room, still in his running outfit.

'Where have you been for the last four hours?' he asked. 'Is everything all right? I thought you must have had an accident. It was stupid of us not to take phones and—'

'Milo. Slow down. I'm fine.' She told him about having to walk the last street, and then about Bob, as they went into the kitchen.

He rubbed the back of his neck, a habit of his. 'Sorry. Just worried. I knew you were unfit, but had no idea it was this bad...' He caught her eye and did his best to smile.

'You okay?' she asked.

A shy look crossed his face that made her want to kiss him more than ever. 'I've come to care about you, Tilda. You've done so much for me. It's new for me, looking out for another person. I've not allowed myself to get that close for so very long.'

Tilda's heart pounding, they sat down at the table. 'The fire made me realise I cared for you too,' she mumbled. Warmth spread up her arm and colour flushed into her cheeks. She didn't know what to say, or rather did, but couldn't find the courage.

I want you Milo. Want us to be together. It's like I've lived in a lonely castle these last years and somehow you've found a way to reach it, despite its moat and drawbridge, the gatehouse, despite its curtain wall and the lookout points. Despite every defence, you've found a way through.

She jumped as his phone rang and Milo took it out of his pocket. 'Jazz? Hi. Yes, I'm on for tonight.' He left the room, talking about meeting her at seven.

They'd had a moment, right? Her and Milo.

He came back downstairs, and opened the fridge. He pulled out a sandwich on a plate and passed it to her.

'Thanks.'

He gave a bow. 'Anything for my boss and landlady.' He opened his laptop. 'Read through this whilst you're eating. The blog has been empty for a while. I've collated ten ideas for posts, such as things to check when employing a cleaner, top five stain removal tips, we could do how-to videos for, say, cleaning the toilet properly, and do a frequently asked questions post about general household cleaning.' Milo picked up the business phone. 'Right, I've got a couple of potential new clients to ring back. I'm going to need that coffee and cake before long.'

His mouth twitched as he dialled the number, she knew he was laughing inside but didn't want to show it. Tilda kicked him gently under the table. He looked across and she pulled a face. His eyes crinkled.

She'd never had a friendship like this, where she felt completely safe, where she felt completely herself. And them having a moment or not, Tilda wasn't going to do anything silly to jeopardise it. She especially wasn't going to start drinking again.

30

Milo went out again at seven, casually smart, with a healthy glow. He'd filled out too after the recent weeks of eating properly. To her surprise, he'd made them both pasta before leaving, so he couldn't have been meeting Jazz for dinner again. They might be going to the cinema, or 'sinma' as Riley had put it. Tilda had just hung up after a chat with her niece. Riley was so excited to share news about a school trip she'd been on, to a hat museum. A little thing, but it meant so much that Riley couldn't wait to tell her aunt. The little things that had changed in recent weeks felt increasingly big.

Tilda stretched and washed up the dishes, still aching from her flyer delivery run earlier in the day. Bob Marlow had rung this afternoon, keen to crack on with the shed clear-out. Humming, she emptied the sink. She'd always dried the dishes straightaway but now left them to drain. She ran herself a glass of water and glanced down at the bin. Now that Tilda was the only one in the house, the unopened envelope called loudly. Why had her mum broken her usual routine of only sending her a birthday or festive card? What if it was something important about Logan? She gave an irritated sigh, flipped open the bin and retrieved the envelope, now smeared with pasta sauce. She took the letter out and sat at the kitchen table. Tilda drank the water, ignoring the voice in her head that said reading the letter would be easier if it were vodka instead. She took a deep breath and unfolded the sheet of paper. A cheque, folded in half, fell out.

Hello Matilda,

So, after all this time, I hear you've got back in touch with your brother. Logan told me you are keeping well. No doubt he passed on my perfectly reasonable explanation of why I held back those letters in the loft. What I did may feel unfair, but if you ever become a mother, you might understand the maternal drive to help your offspring achieve their potential.

He tells me you've settled for running a cleaning business, and in a less salubrious area like Crouchden. For some reason he's most impressed. That's why I'm writing urgently. I'm concerned you're trying to lead him astray, like when you were younger, telling him his mother didn't know best. Obviously, I know he was talking about quitting football before you came back on the scene, but that is nothing but a blip. Paul Scholes returned to the game six months after announcing his retirement. Messi only lasted two months retired, in 2016. But now it seems you are back in Logan's life, with your down-to-earth job and ways. The son I know would never quit the starlight for good. His current determination not to go back to the game must be down to you. Whoever heard of a professional footballer starting college at twenty-six, just when he's on the brink of moving up to even bigger and better things? How will I explain that to my friends? It's humiliating. All to work at some two-bit radio station. Those who can, do. Those who can't, teach. And those who can't even teach... do what? Logan is a doer – that was obvious to me from the moment he was born. He was walking at six months old! Like you, most of his peers took at least a year.

Why can't you be a more supportive sibling, like Princess Anne? You've always been jealous of your brother and never understood the concept of hard work. You let a private education slip between your fingers – fingers that have basically ended up cleaning other people's toilets.

Well, bravo. You've almost scuppered everything he's worked so hard for. I say 'almost'. He won't listen to me. But there's one last chance for you to do the right thing and back off. Tell your brother to go back to the club, to drop this ridiculous idea of going back to school. Likelihood is, anyway, he'll fall flat on his face. Study was never Logan's strong point.

I regret that relations between you and me are so poor, Matilda, but there comes a point when a parent has to stand back for their own sanity, and admit they can do no more. You made no effort to achieve good grades at the very expensive school I sent you to, nor an effort to mix with the other girls. Every child has teething problems at first, somewhere new, but you didn't even try to fit in. You said it was bully-ing, but then you also complained about the prestigious holiday camps I sent you to, wishing you could laze around at home instead. I didn't bring up a daughter to throw away such golden opportunities and leave school to set up on her own, in some crummy bedsit, without discussing it with me in advance. All of these things have been on you alone.

Logan isn't even talking to me now. He's a good man and doesn't deserve all this trouble and being let down by his sister.

I enclose a cheque. It should be enough for you to move away from Manchester and out of his life. If you can't act out of decency, do it for the money. No need to give me your new address.

Clarissa

The letter fell out of her hands and onto the table. Tilda could hardly breathe. She bent down, holding her head in her hands. Everything went black for a few moments. Scraping back her chair, she ran upstairs and was violently sick in the toilet. She flushed the chain and slumped on the bathroom floor, tears running down her cheeks.

Mum believed Tilda was such a lowlife that she could pay her off? She blamed Tilda for the decision Logan had taken, saying she'd let her brother down, echoing thoughts Tilda had had for different reasons, about herself? She stumbled down the stairs, slipping at one point. Tilda got back to her feet and headed straight for the kitchen cupboard where she'd hidden the wine. She reached to the back and pulled it out, grabbed a mug and headed into the smoke-damaged lounge. Blocking out the sun, by drawing the newly washed curtains closed, she sat in the dim light. Then Tilda unscrewed the bottle's cap and filled the mug right to the top. Wine spilt over the sides as she hurriedly lifted it to her mouth.

31

Tilda woke up with a dry throat and thumping headache. She switched off her alarm and turned over. Sunshine streamed through a crack in the curtain. Such expectant, cheerful weather made everything worse. Nothing could make Tilda get up today.

Mum genuinely believed she'd done everything to help her daughter reach her potential. She saw the school bullying as Tilda's fault for not fitting in. Mum truly believed Tilda would try to ruin Logan's life. Worst of all, the part of the letter that cut most deep, even worse than offering her money, was the way she'd signed off. *Clarissa.* Did that mean Tilda no longer had any parents? She shouldn't have cared, but a sob ripped through her chest and she burrowed her face in the covers, falling back into fitful sleep. Eventually, knocking woke her up. It was nine o'clock.

'Tilda? Everything okay? I've brought you a mug of tea.'

Crap. She dragged herself out of bed and trampled on several crisp and chocolate wrappers on the floor, along with used tissues, as she crossed her room. She caught sight of herself in the mirror as she headed for the door. What a mess. Tilda didn't care. Milo was interested in Jazz. She didn't have to do anything to impress. She unlocked the door and opened it just enough to take the mug.

'Sorry, Milo. I'm not well. Splitting headache.' She passed him the business phone. 'Would you mind going through the messages to check there's nothing urgent?'

'Sure...' he said, after a long pause. 'Let me make you something to eat.'

'I'll have a can of soup, or toast, later, but thanks. Leave the phone on the kitchen table when you go to your AA meeting. I'll probably be okay by this afternoon.'

'Do you want me to stay in?'

'No. I'm fine. Thanks for the tea.' Tilda closed the door firmly. She went back to bed and took a big gulp, then lay down again. Closed her eyes. Anger built at how little faith her mum had in Logan, how she doubted his decision to leave football and scorned his ability to get a degree. Scratching crept under the door, from the landing. Tilda got up again. Opened the door. Dettol charged in and jumped on the bed. Tilda clambered under the covers once more. The cat came right up to her head, settled down and kneaded the pillow with her paws, purring loudly. Tilda didn't react, still going over and over that letter, and how her mum wanted to pay Tilda off, as if she were some criminal.

A tiny nose battered hers and Dettol licked her wet cheek.

'You soppy so and so,' mumbled Tilda. She tickled Dettol under the chin, sniffed and sat up, not everyone classed her as the enemy. She leant down by the side of her bed and hoicked up the best pick-me-up... a pile of her favourite fantasy reads. She bent down further and reached for more, under the bed, then sifted through them, fond of the curled, brown pages and scruffy covers. *Eragon*, *The Lord of the Rings*, *Northern Lights*, *Dragon Keeper*, the Narnia and Harry Potter books, and... of course, *The Last Unicorn*. How could she have forgotten that beauty? A magical story where a unicorn, Lady Amalthea, goes on a quest to find out if she is truly the only one of her kind left.

Tilda always dreamt of one day meeting more Tildas – her own tribe who would understand her ways, who wouldn't think she was too much or too little, like other people did. Too quiet, too private, too tidy, not outgoing enough, not sexy enough, Shane threw that last one at her after saying she'd never find someone to marry. Perhaps those other Tildas didn't need to be human though. Dettol acted as if Tilda was everything she needed – a feeder, keeper, a tickler in all the right places.

A knock at the door again. Tilda glanced at her alarm clock. Twenty to twelve.

Milo's voice came through the door. 'Going to my meeting. Do you need anything before I leave? Another cup of tea? Do you want me to buy anything? Paracetamol?'

'No. I... I feel a bit better. Might have a shower. See you later.'

She waited until the side door, downstairs, banged shut, and then went to the bathroom. After a shower she pulled on a baggy T-shirt and loose jogging trousers, half-heartedly she ran a brush through her hair and fed Dettol. She pulled out a yogurt from the fridge, then sat down at the table with her personal phone. A notification came up from Messenger. She clicked into Logan's conversation. It was a photo of Riley. Tilda couldn't help smiling. Her niece had made a paper hat last night, inspired by her trip. It was tricorn shaped and covered in flowers, coming down past her eyes and ears.

Tilda brushed a finger over the image, ran the cold tap and knocked back a glass of juice, in that instant knowing what she had to do as a response to the letter from *Clarissa*. She left the half-eaten yogurt, hurriedly pulled on trainers and grabbed her keys. Dettol ran out ahead of her into the sunshine, and Tilda locked the side door behind her.

Running as fast as she could, Tilda reached the other side of Crouchden in twenty minutes. Perspiring, Tilda slowed as she turned into a busy street and passed a grocery shop. A burly member of staff stood in its doorway, eyeing every customer with suspicion. She continued down and turned left into Church Road. Crossing a graveyard, she came to the church, a greystone building.

This might be a bad idea. She went to leave but a woman who was about to close the church doors, caught sight of Tilda. She had pigtail cornrows and a ring through her nose.

'Coming in?' she called.

Tilda hesitated.

'At least have a glass of water, you look thirstier than the house plants I always manage to kill.'

Clenching her fists, Tilda went in. On a table to the right of closed swing doors, was a jug of water and glasses. The woman filled one for Tilda and handed it over.

'At half time we have hot drinks and biscuits, but I put this out as it's so warm today.' The woman went to the doors. 'There'll be seats at the back and you don't have to talk, or even give your name... You've not been here before, have you?'

Tilda shook her head. Stomach too knotted to finish the drink, she put it on the table and followed the woman in. No one showed any interest in her, they were too intent on listening to a man who sat in a chair at the front, facing everyone else. He wore a football T-shirt and was surrounded by semi-circles of chairs. She sat down quietly, three rows back, glad for the sense of invisibility.

'...So, that's my story and why I'm so very grateful to AA,' said the man. 'Right. Have we any newcomers today?'

A young man, to the right, put his hand up. Tilda bowed her head.

'Welcome,' said the man in the football T-shirt. 'Anyone else?'

Silence fell. It lasted a few moments. Tilda squirmed in her seat.

The man at the front started talking again. 'Okay, my advice to you is just to listen, at this stage. You may not relate to everything people have been through, but you might to the feelings. We are here to help.' He looked around. 'Right. Let's open up to the room.'

'My name's Georgie and I'm an alcoholic,' burst out an impatient voice from over on the left.

'Hi Georgie,' everyone else said in unison.

Tilda leant sideways and spotted a woman in her thirties, wearing a halter-neck top, with neatly coiffed bobbed hair.

'I went to a big family do last weekend. Wasn't looking forward to it. I've always been the black sheep. It's the first family event I've been to since I stopped drinking last year.' She smiled. 'I'm eight months and four days sober now.'

Faces smiled.

'I went prepared. Set my boundaries. If anyone talked down to me, I'd rehearsed my phrases, and told myself I'd be perfectly within my rights to leave.' Her voice wavered. 'I'm so grateful for AA. It helped me realise that

I was drinking to fit in – and that I didn't need to, I'm okay just being me.' She pulled out a tissue and wiped her nose. 'Mum started first. Asked me why I wasn't drinking. Told me I was "even less fun than usual" without a beer in me.'

Tilda sat very still, taking in every word.

'She asked me if I'd got a proper job yet, instead of poncing around with my art, even though I work hard in a gift shop to cover my bills and have been promoted to supervisor.' Georgie smiled. 'I did it, guys – resisted going into defence mode and spurting out that self-justification crap. I simply told her if she couldn't be supportive, then I'd rather not chat. I ate the meal sitting next to a cousin I've always got on with, and then left early. So... thank you AA. These rooms have given me the strength to stop drinking, yes – but also to demand the respect I deserve. That's huge.'

An elderly woman next to Georgie patted her arm. A man turned around and must have smiled, as Georgie reciprocated.

The room fell silent again. Then a cough. 'My name's Milo and I'm an alcoholic.'

'Hi Milo,' replied everyone.

Tilda turned to look down her row, way to the left. Milo caught her eye. His eyes widened. Cheeks warmer than the July sun, she gave a small smile. His expression didn't change for a moment and then he gave a smile back.

'The last few weeks have been hard, so hard, but also positive, in the end,' said Milo, to the room, his voice wavering. 'The strength of AA, these meetings – phone calls with my sponsor that had become less frequent, but still offered compassion when I made them – all of this helped me stay off the booze when things fell apart, when I ended up on the streets a few months ago... But my life turned around recently. And it was due to a single act of kindness shown towards me, which has affected my life in so many ways. A single act that, in importance, has grown and grown.'

Tilda's eyes pricked as he caught her eye, before speaking to the room once more.

'It's not been plain sailing though. I've been forced to think more about sibling relationships.' He exhaled. 'I've only ever spoken about this in detail to my sponsor... I guess I've hinted about it here, before, when I've shared, said an accident to do with my sister kick-started my addiction journey. But I'm ready, now, to share fully. I realise I'm never going to be completely well, that the shadow of a relapse will always lurk, unless I talk about it.' He swallowed. 'Grace was the best sister. Fun, caring, an animal lover, a dancer. Grace always shared her chocolate.'

Other members smiled.

'One weekend, Mum and Dad were away... my uncle babysat. He hadn't got kids of his own but we were ten and eight, not tiny. He'd babysit sometimes, order us pizza and we'd watch videos. That weekend he said we could go to the shop on our own, up the high street, get ourselves anything we wanted from the sweet shop and takeaway. He said I was in charge and it was my job to look after Grace. Turned out afterwards he'd arranged for his girlfriend to come over and wanted us out.' He paused. 'We were so excited. I felt grown up. We'd never been allowed to go up the high street on our own before. I held her hand tightly, there was lots of traffic. We bumped into a group of boys from school, older than me. I got talking, laughing with them. I didn't even notice that Grace had let go of my hand. A witness said afterwards, she'd seen a purse in the road. She ran to pick it up. Grace was always so helpful and probably hoped to find its owner. Brakes screeched. I saw Grace, frozen, staring at the front window of an approaching car. I ran straight to her but got there too late. The car clipped my hand in the process, that's how I got this scar...' He stared at the side of his hand. 'It's a constant reminder of how I let my sister down.' He gulped. 'Mum and Dad were in bits. They completely blamed my uncle, said I was a child and should never have been put in charge. But I couldn't forgive myself, couldn't bear to witness... to feel their grief. So, at sixteen, I left home. Never went back. I still have night-mares about the accident. But...' He wiped his eyes, 'the person I'm staying with, the one who showed kindness to me, has made me realise it's never too late to reconnect with someone you once loved very much. I'm going to get in touch with Mum and Dad again.' He sat up straighter. 'My share is full of gratitude too. There's no way I'd still be here without AA – or if I was, I'd be totally messed up.'

Oh, Milo. If only Tilda had known, somehow worked it out, even though he'd deliberately hidden the truth, that his sister had actually died. All Tilda wanted to do was put her arms around him. First, she had to sit through several more shares, taken aback each time by how she related to the feelings of desperation, hopelessness and self-disgust, of the day-to-day grind of staying sober during challenging times, whatever different means they all used, despite the varying journeys that had led them to booze. More than one story featured family problems, and took her back to her time in treatment when Tilda was told it was her reaction to a situation that was the main problem. A powerful realisation because it meant change was possible.

That's why she'd come today. It was her choice as to whether she let her mum's letter drag her down.

Tilda chose not to let it.

The man in the chair announced a fifteen-minute break for refreshments. Tilda stood up and went out into the nave of the church. Several members headed straight outside with cigarettes and vapes. Finally, Milo came through the swing doors. The woman with the cornrows punched his arm and gave the thumbs up. They chatted briefly then another member hugged him. Tilda headed over, stood on tiptoe and embraced him, tightly.

'Well done. That can't have been easy,' she said.

'Funnily enough, I feel... so much lighter. Relief set in as soon as I started talking.'

'I understand now why you got so annoyed with me, before the fire, when you poured my wine out of the window. I was talking about how I'd let Logan down for not being there. But he still had a life, had still achieved loads... now I understand why you told me I should count my blessings. Unlike Grace, my brother's still around.'

'I shouldn't have got angry, Tilda. I'm sorry. Mental suffering isn't something you can compare.'

They went over to the table and picked up cups of coffee.

'The girl with the red hair, in the photo, that frame in your rucksack... I thought it could be a daughter you had, but it's your sister, isn't it?'

He nodded.

'She looked lovely... and the spit of you. Didn't working in a nightclub act as a constant reminder – young people dancing night in, night out – remind you of her and what you feel she missed out on? I mean, if the TV talent show upset you so much...?'

'Perhaps going into that industry, in a warped way, was me punishing myself.' Milo shook his head. 'Without AA, I'd have gone insane.' His face brightened. 'I'm so proud of you, coming today. Dettol got into the lounge this morning, I went in and found that wine bottle, next to the full mug, the first one you poured by the looks of it. You got close, didn't you, but somehow didn't drink?'

'Very close,' she whispered. 'Instead, I sat up all night, in my room, eating rubbish, drinking coffee, crying.'

'I saw a letter – but I didn't read it. Was it to do with that?'

At that moment a bear of a man came over, even taller than Milo. He patted his back. 'Great share, mate. Way to go.'

Milo spotted someone and waved, and... *Jazz* came over? She gave Milo a thumbs up and then stopped when she saw Tilda.

'I had no idea...' said Jazz.

'Me neither, about you,' said Tilda.

'I was taken aback to see Milo at the Windmill. We've known each other through AA for a little while.'

Milo headed off to get biscuits.

'I understand now why you two got together,' said Tilda. 'Like-minded spirits and all that.'

'Got together?' Jazz frowned.

'Well... the date on Tuesday... Milo stayed over?' Tilda's ears felt hot.

Jazz's jaw dropped, then she laughed. 'Jeez, Tilda, no way! He's more like an older brother...' Her voice dropped to a whisper. 'A very annoying one at that.' She grinned. 'He's a good guy, though. Through a charity I work with in my spare time, I do talks about addiction and had some coming up, at a couple of youth clubs this week. The person I was doing it with on Tuesday – who was going to share their story as well – had to drop out, so Milo offered to step in. The all-nighter was because of a crisis – our stories sparked one kid to admit he had a drug problem. The parents came in to collect him, we helped talk everything through. It was gone midnight by the time we'd finished and we were exhausted. I lived nearby and offered Milo my sofa. Obviously, AA is anonymous, we don't tell outsiders about other members, so Milo wouldn't have been able to tell you how he knew me and why we were meeting up.'

Jazz and Milo weren't an item? That meant... Pleasure rushed through Tilda's body in a way not even the buzz from alcohol could.

Milo appeared with the packet of biscuits. 'Did I miss anything?' he said.

Jazz winked at Tilda. 'No. Nothing important. Right, I need the loo before the next half.' She dashed off.

The woman with the piercing came over and reached for a shortcake triangle. 'Staying for the second half?' she asked Tilda.

Tilda gazed around the room, feeling seen for who she truly was – one of them.

'Yes,' she said and helped herself to a biscuit.

32

Tilda and Milo sat out with lunch, in the garden. She sipped her Coke, Dettol at her feet, a few flakes of tuna left on the ground. They chatted about the unrelenting heat of July and the even hotter weather due for August. Eventually, small talk faded away, replaced with the hum of passing traffic.

'The letter was from Mum,' said Tilda abruptly.

Milo stopped eating. 'What did she want?'

It poured out – her mum's accusations, her view on Tilda's difficult past.

'But you were bullied at school,' he said and put his Coke on the ground. 'How could she not see that? Why wasn't her first instinct to protect you?'

'I have no idea. Gran said as much once, when Mum dropped me off for part of the summer holidays at the end of my first year. Mum said that to get on in life, women especially needed a backbone and that those girls had learnt to cope at boarding school and I needed to as well. I'd never seen Gran so angry.' She bit into her sandwich. 'You haven't heard the best of it yet.' Tilda told him about the cheque.

'*What*?' he said and got to his feet, knocking over his Coke.

Tilda grinned. She couldn't help it. But then, just as quickly, tears sprung into her eyes. 'Why couldn't she care as much as you do?'

Milo crouched by her side, slipped an arm around her. 'Don't torture yourself with the whys and what ifs. I've done that for years over my sister's accident. Why did it happen? Why is life so unfair? Why her? Why not me? What if that purse hadn't been there? I'm realising that not everything has an explanation or answer.' He wiped a finger under one of her eyes. 'What are you going to do with the money?'

'I don't know.' Should she tell Logan about the cheque, about everything their mother said? Tilda sniffed. 'With this recent letter, along with the ones Logan and I never received as children, they've reminded me of another one that became a game-changer.' She hesitated. 'Come upstairs for a minute.' Milo followed her inside. Tilda went up to her bedroom and paused outside the door. She rolled her lips together. 'Come in,' she mumbled. 'Be careful not to fall over. I need to clear the floor.'

'Only if you want me to. It's your personal space.'

'I... don't need the clutter everywhere any more. I want to display my books and reorganise my clothes. Riley is desperate to take me shopping for brighter colours.' They exchanged smiles. 'It's never going to be pristine, but I'm beginning to accept that's okay, I don't need to hide any untidiness. Life gets messy and I guess it's normal if my room – my house – reflects that sometimes.' She pointed to the bed. 'Take a seat.' She held her breath, studying his face for signs of disapproval at the toiletries and clothes on the duvet.

Instead, he simply made a space, sat down and beamed as he picked up her book. '*The Last Unicorn*? Man, I haven't read this since high school.' He flicked through whilst Tilda rummaged through her chest of drawers. About to give up, she rummaged again at the back of the top drawer. Her face lit up and she pulled out a creased letter.

Tilda sat on the bed, next to Milo and he put the book to one side. 'Did you ever write a letter to alcohol?' she asked.

'A what?'

'It's something we were advised to do, during treatment. A goodbye. Some people thanked alcohol for being a support but said they didn't need them any more. Others wrote as if alcohol were an old toxic friend and explained, in quite certain terms, why they never wanted them back. The whole idea seemed stupid, but, actually, it massively helped and made my resolutions more concrete.'

'What tone was yours?'

Tilda passed it over. 'Read it if you want. After a few weeks of not drinking, I could see how much alcohol had taken away from me. Alcohol was certainly never a true friend. It was two-faced, always telling me the next mouthful would make everything better.'

Milo sat silently and turned it over to read the second page. When he'd finished, she took it back. 'Listening to you today, talking about your sister... tell me if I'm overstepping Milo, and sorry if I am, but... I don't think you need to write a letter to alcohol.' Tilda had been worried when he first moved in, but day by day, she trusted more in his sobriety. 'The last few months have shown how strong your resolve is not to slip. It withstood you losing our home, your job. You got through it.'

'With the help and kindness of others.' He butted her gently, with his body, sideways.

Her breath hitched, just a little, at the physical contact that sent her pulse racing.

She turned to face him. 'You need to write a letter to your sister, instead. A goodbye letter to Grace, in the context of the accident.'

Milo's eyebrows raised. 'To Grace? But I wouldn't know where to start.'

'Tell her about your life now.'

'But—'

'What harm can it do? You took the first step, today, in the meeting. I'm so very, very sorry Milo, about what you've been through. She sounds like a wonderful little girl. I hope, deep down, now that time has passed, now that you are older, you see that your parents were right and that your uncle should never have let you two out on your own. You've already worked out, like you said to me, that not everything has an explanation. Perhaps it can stop now – you torturing yourself.'

'Write a letter to your sister.

'Stop running away, Milo.

'Finally face her.'

Tilda grabbed a notebook from her dressing table, scrabbled around and found a pen. She opened it up and tore out a fresh page, and gave it to Milo, on the bed, with the notebook to lean on. Tilda patted his shoulder.

'I'll go and rescue our sandwiches from the wasps,' she said and left.

Two hours later and Milo was still refining his letter. His sandwich remained on the bed, uneaten. Tilda worked downstairs, keeping them both supplied with cold drinks. She closed down her laptop as footsteps came down the stairs. He came into the kitchen and handed over a sheet of paper.

'Are you sure you want me to read it?' Tilda asked gently.

'Yes. You and Grace would have got on, you know?' He dragged his chair next to hers. She lay down the letter, on the table, between them and linked her arm with his. He squeezed it against his side.

Dearest Grace,

Hi. It's me, Milo. I miss you. Have, every day, these last twenty years. You'd be twenty-eight now, the same age as my friend, Tilda. Did you know, Julie appeared on a TV talent show? The two of you loved dancing so much. It drove me crazy when Girls Aloud songs would blast out of your bedroom and the two of you made the house vibrate with your moves.

I worked in a nightclub for a long time and would imagine you out dancing with mates, perhaps a boyfriend – or maybe a girlfriend. I'm so sorry, Gracie, that I couldn't save you. I should never have got talking to those older boys, but I was flattered they stopped, wanted to impress them. I've never admitted that to anyone before. My friend, Tilda, blames herself for letting her brother down and not spotting that he didn't really want to be a footballer. But, as an outsider, I can easily see that it wasn't her fault. She had no way of knowing, given the circumstances. And I've tried, lately, to be an outsider too, when it comes to my own life, looking back on the accident. Uncle Cal shouldn't have sent us off, on our own, like that. I was only ten. If those boys hadn't stopped or if that purse hadn't been in the road, none of this would have happened.

In other words, sometimes shit happens that we have no control over.

I'll never forget you lying in my arms, the colour draining out of your cheeks, me shaking you, begging you to stay awake. How, so typically, seconds before you passed, you, my little sister, gave me a toothy smile, tears in your eyes, and a little nod as if you'd guessed what was coming next. You were so brave and that ripped my heart into shreds.

I won't say I've lost you, because happy memories are still in my head, reminders of you day to day. When there's only one cookie left in the jar, I mentally fight you for it. Remember us each racing to grab it, Mum would roll her eyes and snap the cookie in half? Whenever I see a robin, it reminds me of how excited you got at Christmas; you always pointed out how the bird's red chest matched Santa's outfit. If I spot a trail of ants, I recall us marching up and down, pretending to be them; you said it must be great to spend your life with lots of friends, like that. One time we played out near a field, by our house, and a bunch of kids were trampling on a colony that had emerged from a soily area. You pushed the kids away and protected the rest of the ants until they found safety in the undergrowth.

All these signs, Gracie, tell me that you've not gone. Not completely.

You'll always be part of my life.

Never forgotten.

Love you.

Milo xxxx

Tears streamed down Milo's cheeks. Tilda cried too.

'It's beautiful,' she said.

'I need some fresh air,' he croaked.

Tilda took his hand and led him into the garden. The two of them stood in the sun, its rays drying their tears. Dettol had come out and was staring at a patch of ground, by one of the chairs. Tilda and Milo followed the cat's gaze.

Where Milo's drink had spilt, a line of ants marched up and down. He studied them for several seconds, before looking up, towards the sky. A smile crossed his face.

33

Tilda woke up and stretched. Milo had been quiet yesterday after writing his letter to Grace the afternoon before, happy to escape into the busyness of a working Friday as he lined up several interviews for the following week, as the two of them pressed ahead with their plans for expanding Wright Cleaners. They'd only take on one more person, right now, until they saw the results of the flyers, but so far things were positive. Enquiries from potential new clients were definitely up.

The noise from a road sweeper muffled the cooing of pigeons outside her window. She and Milo had agreed to get up early, even though it was a Saturday, spurning the jog that now often started their day, to get the lounge ready for redecorating.

Even though it was a Saturday. A few weeks ago, it had been normal for Tilda to get up with the sun whether she was working or not.

Logan and Riley would be here in a couple of hours to help. Tilda jumped out of bed and drew open the curtains, to be met by a sky as blue as the butterfly she'd spotted in the garden last night. She and Milo had sat out enjoying an iced drink after work, eating the mango cake Anushka had dropped off. She was off on a cruise next week and said she was simply repaying Tilda's kind offer to drive her to the airport.

The notebook Milo had borrowed caught her eye, on the dressing

table to her right. What a few months it had been. For the first time in...
forever, she imagined catching a plane and flying off to a relaxing, exotic
island, away from the hustle and bustle of Manchester. Except it wouldn't
be that tranquil, because the happy image that came into her mind also
featured Riley, swimming and waving in the sea, with Logan by her side,
floating on his back, sunbathing, and Milo drinking a mocktail, wearing a
Hawaiian shirt and sunglasses.

An idea came into her head.

Before Tilda could change her mind, she messaged Logan. He replied
immediately with a row of smiley faces and consequently turned up
before the time they'd originally agreed. Tilda and Milo were finishing
breakfast. Riley charged into the kitchen and petted Dettol before
standing in front of Tilda with her arms folded.

'Daddy said you've got a surprise but wouldn't tell me. What is it?' She
jigged up and down and clapped her hands.

Milo raised an eyebrow. 'I hope it includes me. I like surprises.'

Tilda winked at Logan. 'It does. I've changed my mind about redecorating today. We all deserve a little holiday. Your dad has packed your
costume and armbands, Riley, because we're going to Lytham beach!'

She squealed and ran around to where Tilda was sitting and threw
her arms around her neck. Tilda unpeeled her niece, laughing, not taking
for granted the affection that her life had been so lacking.

'Do I get to take my inflatable too?' asked Milo and he pulled a
comical face. Riley giggled.

'You must put your costume on, under your clothes, Riley, and then
we'll make up a picnic,' said Tilda. 'You are on bread buttering duty. We
have crisps and drinks, mango cake from Anushka next door, and I'm sure
there will be lots of ice cream to buy in Lytham.'

'Whoop!' Riley grabbed Tilda's hands and insisted she got up and
danced. Logan got out his phone, hesitated and then put on a track –
'Doctor Pressure'. He moved across the room, to where Tilda and Riley
stood.

'Remember?' he said to his sister, shyly.

'How could I ever forget?' She took his hand.

'Grace loved this song,' Milo said and his voice caught. 'Drove me crazy, her and Julie dancing to it, on repeat.'

'Who's Grace?' asked Riley, and she let go of her dad and aunt and went over to him.

'My... sister. She... had an accident a long time ago. I miss her a lot.'

Riley tilted her head. 'Then you and me should dance to it. She'd want that. It would make her laugh, us dancing to a song you hated and she loved.'

Milo's eyes glistened. 'Little one, you're absolutely right.'

'I'm not that little!' she protested as he got up. 'You're mega tall.'

Logan laughed. 'Sorry mate. She's got a point.'

Riley grabbed Milo's hands, swinging them from side to side, whilst Dettol stretched and lay on the floor, in a sunspot, away from the madness of the humans. Once everyone had cooled down, Tilda set to work with Riley making sandwiches. She and Milo slipped into their costumes too and packed towels. Being a parent, organised Logan had plenty of sun cream to go around. He offered to drive as well. Milo said he'd sit in the back with Riley. Tilda glanced at him, now and again, via the pull-down mirror on the passenger side. After finally talking about Grace, perhaps spending time with Riley brought back memories of his sister.

'I have good news about my new career plans,' said Logan, whilst Tilda wondered how to tell him about their mother's letter. He turned the car onto the motorway and a long stretch of road lay ahead. 'Despite my application being late, a Stockport college had room to give me a place to study the A levels I need. It will take two years. I'm going to down-size my house. With the money Gran left us and my football earnings, I bought a four-bed detached place. But I don't need that now. I've found a new-build near Reddish, a two-bed terrace, Riley will still have her own bedroom. I'll have the income from commentating and Tim – a friend of the guy who contacted me from the radio station – reckons he can get me another gig, doing write-ups of football matches in a newspaper local to him.' Logan shot Tilda a quick sideways look. 'I'm so excited! Whatever happens I finally feel as if I'm on the right track, in a way I never have been.'

'I know what you mean,' said Tilda. 'I'm so happy for you, Little Bro Lo.'

'Thank you, Big Sissy Sis.'

'You two are weird,' shouted a young voice from the back.

They reached Lytham in just over an hour, Tilda grateful for the car's aircon. Traffic was heavy and they had to drive around slowly for twenty minutes to nab a space in the carpark at St Anne's beach. They unpacked the car and set up camp not too far from the Victorian pier. When its mock-Tudor front came into view, Riley squealed and pulled at Milo's arm, dragging him through the crowds. Tilda and Logan caught up as the golden sands came into sight. Riley stood, shoes off, with her hands on her hips. She pointed out to sea.

'The water is so far away. We'd better run.'

Logan looked at Tilda. 'You thinking what I'm thinking?'

'That one time we came here with Mum and Dad. They hadn't checked the tide times and Mum was horrified that it would take thirty minutes to walk out to the sea. He chased her, making monster noises, to get her running. It's one of the few memories I have of her letting her hair down, of laughing loudly.'

'How about we have lunch and build sandcastles until the tide is due in, later this afternoon?' said Logan. 'We'll go on the pier, too, visit the amusements.'

It didn't take long for Riley to pull off the clothes covering her red swim-suit. She found it hard to keep still whilst Tilda applied sun cream to her skin. Tilda breathed in the cream's coconut smell, grateful for the distraction as Milo stripped down to his swimming shorts. She didn't want to get caught looking at him because of Riley's goo-goo eyes theory. As soon as Riley was done, Tilda unpacked the food, it was already twelve. Flicking away flies bored of washed-up seaweed, they sat cross-legged and ate cheese and tomato sandwiches. Silence fell as they watched the world walk past: elderly couples in long trousers and sunhats, groups of youngsters carrying volley balls and water guns, families with red-faced babies and cooler bags, and young couples, arms around each others' waists, stopping to kiss.

Everything felt quiet and loud at the same time, with the breeze and salty air. Tilda zoned out of life, away from work, away from her mum, and could simply *be* – until she focused again and life hit her straight back in the face: the cries of babies, loud banter of teens, dogs barking from the concrete promenade and seagulls screeching, the stomping feet of children running past, kicking up sand as they did. A birthmark caught her eye on Logan's back. It took her back to trips to the local pool. Dad would take them at weekends and the three of them would play floating mushrooms, hugging their knees, face in the water, bobbing up and down on the surface.

Riley fidgeted, suddenly demanding she needed to pee. Tilda offered to take her but Logan said he wanted to explore the pier anyway. In her black one-piece, Tilda stretched out her towel and leant back on her elbows.

'Have you told Logan about the letter?' asked Milo, screwing his empty crisp bag up into a ball.

'No. I will today. He needs to know how low my mum is capable of going. It's not because I want to spite her, it's more a case of protecting him from letting her persuade him to give up his dream. I'm not showing it to him, though. I don't want Logan to see what she said about him not being good at studying. It could knock his confidence before he's even got started.'

Milo lay down next to her. 'You're a good sister.'

She turned her head. 'Trying to be. Lots of time to make up for. I'm grateful for the opportunity.'

'I messaged Mum on her old email address, last night.'

Tilda sat upright. 'Milo... that's brilliant. What did she say?'

'No idea. Contact has been sporadic over the years. I've stopped replying and haven't got in touch for so long. She may not want to know me, now. She said in one of her last emails that Dad found it too painful to keep attempting to get in touch. I was drinking back then and blocked out the hurt I was causing. I daren't check my emails today. What if they are angry? What if it's too late and one of them is ill, or...?'

'There's only one way to find out.' Tilda turned to him. 'You survived a childhood trauma, an addiction, being beaten up on the streets... You're one of the strongest people I've come across, Milo Campbell. You can open an email.'

He sat up. Got out his phone. He took a deep breath. 'Maybe you're right.' Milo brought up the email icon and tapped in. 'They've replied,' he said, in a full voice. His finger hovered over the screen before he tapped again. He positioned the phone so that Tilda could read it as well.

Son, Dad and I are both so very happy that you've got in touch. So very happy. Dad is writing this with me. Both of us are crying. Yes, we want to see you. For so many years we've wished, hoped, this moment would come. We don't blame you for any of it – the accident, you moving away... What you went through, no child should ever have to endure.

The cleaning business sounds great. You always were tidy as a young lad and would even clean up the mess in Grace's room. Remember how you started charging her, a packet of sweets a week? We have a dog now, Benji, he's the naughtiest, loveliest terrier ever who doesn't understand the meaning of neatness.

Oh, Milo. We've missed you so very much. Please get back to us quickly. Let us know this is for real and set a date to meet. Wherever you want. We just want to hug you.

Lots of love, Mum and Dad xxxx

Milo's hands were shaking.

'Message them back, Milo. Don't keep them waiting a moment longer,' said Tilda in a hushed tone.

He got up. 'I'm going for a walk. Need to clear my head.' He went off, mobile close to his face. Tilda gazed out to the sea that was slowly making its way in, comparing the email from Milo's parents to the letter she'd got from Clarissa.

Clarissa. How had they got to this point? Was Dad looking down at his family, tears in his eyes? Losing him had changed Mum's life, it had hit her as hard as it had hit Tilda and Logan. The three of them had been inconsolable at his funeral. But that didn't excuse how Mum had contrived to keep Logan and Tilda apart as children, how she'd pushed out her daughter.

'Tilda! Tilda!' Riley walked over, very carefully. She held out the biggest chocolate éclair, almost as long as Riley's leg from her knee to her ankle. Lytham was famous for them.

'Wow. Thank you,' said Tilda. 'What are you guys going to eat?'

Logan grinned and fetched a knife from the hamper. 'We had to buy it as soon as we saw it, and come straight back. Riley couldn't wait to try it.' They cut it into four and wrapped up Milo's for later. Afterwards, Riley set about building a big sandcastle with a moat. She didn't want any help apart from looking for shells, later, to decorate it.

Tilda wiped her mouth, lying next to her brother, both of them keeping an eye on her niece. 'There's something I've wanted to tell you, Logan... a couple of days ago, I got a letter from Mum.' His expression darkened as she related most of what their mother said. He couldn't believe she'd attempted to bribe her own daughter. 'I've told you in case she tries to get into your head, saying journalism is a stupid idea, or tries to convince you that you've been swayed by my support.'

'I appreciate that, sis, but there's no chance of that. Something changed inside me, when I found the letters she'd hidden. I'm not making allowances for Mum any more. I've no longer any desire to please her. I've got Riley and Cameron. Also, Patsy and I get on and her parents are great... And I've got you again too, now. That's all the family I need.' He linked his arm through hers. No words were necessary and Tilda had never felt so at peace with the world.

'The cheque... my first instinct was to tear it up.'

'Seriously?' Logan shook his head. 'She can afford to lose that amount. Keep it.'

'You think? I did wonder... how about we put some away for Riley's future? And after everything that's happened with Milo, I'd like to do something to help the homeless. It's been eye-opening, learning from him what it's really like, out on the streets. All he needed was a safe place to stay, to get back on his feet.'

'And someone big-hearted and open-minded enough to give him a chance,' Logan said and gently pushed her shoulder.

Tilda blushed. 'He's business-minded, has great initiative, I'm sure between us we could come up with something. What do you think?'

He squeezed her arm. 'That sounds great – turning Mum's cruelty into kindness.'

When Milo returned, the sea had neared enough to go swimming. They packed up the bags and covered them with towels, before stashing them by a sand dune. Riley insisted on wearing her donut inflatable, around her waist, as she walked. Logan took her hand and they strolled up ahead. Tilda and Milo followed. She glanced up at him, sideways. It was time to reveal the truth.

'I've got something to tell you!' they both blurted out, at the same time.

Tilda grinned. 'You first.'

'Not likely,' Milo said and scooped her up before running towards the water. He reached the tide and waded in.

'Milo Campbell! Don't you dare throw me in! Put me down this instant!' she hollered.

He put her on her feet, laughing. The water already came up to her waist.

'Last one underwater speaks first,' she said and grinned before crouching down and disappearing under the water.

34

Tilda came up coughing. A mouthful of sea. She spat it out.

'Bad luck,' called Milo. 'Nothing quite beats the taste of briny weed.'

She swam over and trod water in front of him. Logan and Riley approached, him swirling her around in the giant yellow donut. Riley put circles up to her eyes and gave Tilda a pointed look. Tilda submerged herself again and when she came up Riley was giggling.

'Daddy, let's go over to that red and white ball.'

'It's a buoy.'

'Don't be silly, it's not human.'

Logan gave his sister and Milo a hard-done-by look, before leaving, dragging the donut behind him. Tilda swam to slightly shallower water so that she could stand. She ducked her shoulders under the water, to keep warm.

'Okay. Happy to speak up first,' she said to Milo. Under the water she took Milo's hands. 'You said at the AA meeting that a single act of kindness had helped you out... Me giving you a place to live, right?'

'Yes. It was kind... brave of you. I was a stranger.'

'But the thing is, you were the one to be kind to me first.'

'Helping with the washing machine flood?'

'Not just that. When you shaved off your beard, you see... I recognised you from three years ago. You were the man who pulled me off a tramline, early one morning.'

Milo's expression didn't change.

'It's you who deserves the thanks. That turned my life around, you made a difference, helped me realise I'd hit my rock bottom and that I needed to get into treatment. That's the real reason I took you in. You weren't actually a stranger to me.'

Milo pulled her closer. 'Tilda... the thing is... I recognised you too.'

'*What*?'

'Not at first but your dark eyes made you seem familiar, and then, when I'd been beaten up, you helped me to my feet by intertwining your fingers with mine to pull me up. It took me right back to how we held hands by the tramline – as did your perfume. I... I didn't think you'd remembered me.'

'How could I ever forget the man who saved my life?' She shook her head. 'All this time, you've known?'

'Yes, us men need reassurance too,' he said and smiled. 'I wouldn't move in with a total stranger either, but when our fingers linked like that, I felt a connection.' He brushed mussed up, dripping hair away from her face. 'I guess maybe there's no such thing as a single act of charity, of compassion, because... kindness breeds kindness.'

Tilda's mum had never understood that. Nor did most of the teachers at boarding school, or the other pupils. You didn't get the best from people by criticising, by instilling fear. The power of kindness was like a secret you didn't get to know about until it touched you. For a fleeting moment she pitied her mother.

'I didn't say anything, didn't want to remind you of that traumatic night,' he said, 'not when I realised that was what you were referring to when you talked about something big that had made you get into recovery.'

'You wouldn't accept my thanks at the time, so I'm thanking you now. You were my hero. You're a good person. The tram could have hit you.'

Milo pressed his lips together. 'I'm trying,' he said, eventually, 'trying to believe I'm not bad through and through. I feel so much better after writing that letter. It sank in yesterday how I have been running away from Grace and her memory, but I don't need to any more.'

'I'm so glad,' she murmured.

They stared into each other's eyes, neither pair quite so dark as before.

'Tilda!' called Riley's voice.

She turned to see Riley holding onto the buoy. The little girl took her hands off and made punches in the air, then jabbed her finger in Milo's direction.

'What *is* Riley doing?' asked Milo.

Telling me to fight for what I want. Tilda slipped her arms around his waist. 'Do you believe in magic?' she whispered.

'Of course. You've only got to look at the giant lizard family to know that the dragons that inspired those in our favourite reads, did really once exist.'

'Me too,' she said and stood on tiptoe. She cupped his cheek. 'Milo, you've changed my life as if you've cast a spell.'

You can do it. At the AA meeting, Georgie's share was about putting up boundaries. Sometimes, moving forwards in life might be about pulling down boundaries too. 'Come on a date with me,' she blurted out.

Those chestnut eyes widened, the pupils dilated, and he bent his head. 'There's no one I'd rather go on a date with, than you,' he whispered. As his lips touched hers, the water didn't feel so cold, the happy shouts of bathers faded into nothing. She didn't read much romance, apart from her gran's novels, but if Tilda did, she'd have had better words to describe her emotions. All she knew was that right at that moment, a life so broken that had begun to heal in recent weeks, finally became whole again. She felt like Bastian in *The NeverEnding Story*, like Bilbo satisfied at the end of his journey in *The Hobbit*, like Harry defeating Voldemort. Tilda felt as if she'd completed some quest.

The four of them swam back to the beach, Tilda and Milo side by side and Riley clinging on to her dad. As they reached the sand, they joined hands, Tilda and Riley in the middle, the dragon egg ring shining in the sunlight on Tilda's finger.

'How about a piggyback race?' said Logan. 'Sis, I'll take you. Milo, want to take a donut?'

Riley did a little dance and pulled off her inflatable. Milo gripped it under one arm. Tilda and Riley clambered onto the men's backs.

'Ready, steady...' said Tilda.

But Logan didn't wait and started running, chuckling as Riley shouted out with indignation. Almost at the sand dunes where they'd left their belongings, Milo turned his head and shot Tilda a glance, having caught up with just the little girl on his back.

He winked at her.

Tilda winked back.

Her brother roared with a final burst of energy as the finish line neared, but tripped over a patch of seaweed, and Big Sissy Sis and Little Bro Lo fell onto the sand together, laughing like children.

ACKNOWLEDGEMENTS

My twentieth book. Wow. It's been quite a journey since I first got published in 2013. I've worked with some amazing people, over the years, and couldn't ask for a better publisher than my current one, Boldwood Books. From the marketing team, to design, to editors at all levels, I send huge appreciation. A special mention goes to Isobel Akenhead. I highly value her enthusiasm, perceptiveness and humour – and Instagram stories! The whole Boldwood experience shouts collaboration and transparency, possibly the two qualities I value most from a publisher.

I'm also grateful to my brilliant agent, Clare Wallace from Darley Anderson Agency & Associates, for her continued guidance, support, and caring, efficient manner; for her belief in me; for not asking me to be anything other than what I am.

My family, as ever, have propped me up, during challenging bookish moments. Martin, Immy and Jay, I love you more than words can say – and that's coming from a writer!

Author friends, thank you for being there and giving me perspective when this rollercoaster of a career faces a dip. A particular mention goes to the Boldwood author Facebook group and my Manchester writing mates.

I must also mention The Friendly Book Community group on Facebook that cheerleads so many authors and provides endless banter and warm-hearted humour – as long as no one mentions brioche!

Bloggers, I'm continually bowled over by your generosity of spirit, giving up time to review books, often to a schedule. Enormous thanks.

My acknowledgements can never pass without mentioning the people all of this is for... you readers. Your interest in what I've got to say means so much. Thank you. Thank you. Thank you.

A Single Act of Kindness – the theme of this novel is in the title and I've dedicated this story to Jenny who works for Wigan libraries. I was due to do an event for one of the libraries there, in 2023 but had to email an apology explaining that health issues had unexpectedly worsened and I would have to pull out. I'd only met Jenny once but she emailed back telling me look after myself and said if I ever needed a 'neutral ear to listen', she was always there. Jenny gave me her phone number. I was so touched by this act of kindness and it's stayed with me since.

I'm lucky, I have a great support system and haven't needed to take Jenny up on this kind offer. But not everyone does. Kindness matters and that's what this book is about. In a world full of wow-factor aspirations such as owning that sports car, getting that high figure salary job, having thousands of followers on social media, BEING KIND needs to be up there too. Kindness can change someone's life. It can stay with someone forever. Even if it makes a difference to someone just for a moment, what could be more powerful than that? It costs nothing and we've all got it, in our hearts.

With much love.

Sam x

ABOUT THE AUTHOR

Samantha Tonge is the bestselling and award-winning author of multi-generational women's fiction. She lives in Manchester with her family.

Sign up to Samantha Tonge's mailing list for news, competitions and updates on future books.

Visit Samantha's website: http://samanthatonge.co.uk/

Follow Samantha on social media here:

 facebook.com/SamanthaTongeAuthor

X x.com/SamTongeWriter

 instagram.com/samanthatongeauthor

ALSO BY SAMANTHA TONGE

Boldwood

Boldwood Books is an award-winning fiction publishing company seeking out the best stories from around the world.

Find out more at www.boldwoodbooks.com

Join our reader community for brilliant books, competitions and offers!

Follow us
@BoldwoodBooks
@TheBoldBookClub

Sign up to our weekly deals newsletter

https://bit.ly/BoldwoodBNewsletter

Milton Keynes UK
Ingram Content Group UK Ltd.
UKHW041820110424
440865UK00002B/4